THE
GOOD WIFE

THE GOOD WIFE

JACQUI ROSE

MACMILLAN

First published 2025 by Macmillan
an imprint of Pan Macmillan
The Smithson, 6 Briset Street, London EC1M 5NR
EU representative: Macmillan Publishers Ireland Ltd, 1st Floor,
The Liffey Trust Centre, 117–126 Sheriff Street Upper,
Dublin 1, D01 YC43
Associated companies throughout the world
www.panmacmillan.com

ISBN 978-1-0350-3014-9

1 3 5 7 9 8 6 4 2

A CIP catalogue record for this book is available from the British Library.

Typeset in Plantin by Jouve (UK), Milton Keynes
Printed and bound by CPI Group (UK) Ltd, Croydon, CR0 4YY

Visit **www.panmacmillan.com** to read more about all our books
and to buy them. You will also find features, author interviews and
news of any author events, and you can sign up for e-newsletters
so that you're always first to hear about our new releases.

To Georgia and Marc. How proud I am of you both. X

'The Prince of Darkness is a gentleman.'

William Shakespeare, *King Lear*

1

NOTTINGHAM

Ava Barclay slowly began to come round from the deep sleep she'd been in. She groaned quietly, not wanting to open her eyes. Not wanting to move. Jesus, she felt like shit. She wasn't sure if it was her head that hurt more or her ankle. Though for the life of her, she couldn't remember what she'd done to it. Moreover, she couldn't remember most of what had happened last night.

She could vaguely recall getting ready to go out after work. Then she'd taken a taxi into the centre of town to the new bar on St James's Street, Nottingham. But from that point onwards everything became hazy. She had a faint memory of ordering her first glass of red wine, then somewhere during the evening the tequila shots had started, and perhaps a few whisky chasers had been involved as well?

Her thumping headache and the burning behind her eyes said there had been, and the rawness in her nostrils told her that she'd been snorting coke. This was confirmed by the wraps on the floor, next to the empty condom packet. Thank fuck they'd used precautions.

God, what had she been thinking? Well, she supposed that was the problem, wasn't it? She hadn't been thinking, otherwise she wouldn't be lying here, in this state. Fuck.

Angry with herself, she yawned and peeled open her eyes. She looked around the messy room and tried to think back to how she'd got here.

'So, sleeping beauty's finally awake?'

Ava stared up at Michael. Good-looking, muscular . . . butt naked, apart from his wide handsome smile. 'I thought you'd never wake up.' He grinned and massaged his penis, which immediately sprang to life. 'So what are we going to do with our morning?' His piercing blue eyes twinkled suggestively.

Checking her watch, Ava pushed herself up on her elbows and groaned again at her pounding headache. The sheets felt sweaty and, right now, she wasn't in the mood for anything apart from a strong black coffee. She certainly wasn't in the mood for chatting. 'I'm so sorry, I've got to get to work, Michael.'

He stared at her coldly. 'It's *Mark*. My name's *Mark*, not Michael.'

'Shit, sorry.' She smiled apologetically though she was angry with herself for getting herself into this situation . . . *again*. 'That's what I meant.'

'Yeah, I'm sure it was.' His voice dripped with a mixture of irritation and disappointment; she'd clearly bruised his ego.

She'd been certain his name was Michael. But like with everything to do with last night, she only had fragments of memories that she couldn't piece together. Not that she was sure she *wanted* to piece them together. One-night stands weren't ever her finest hour, but they seemed inevitably to follow on from an evening of drinking.

She screwed her eyes closed for a moment.

Humiliation washed over her.

She should know better. Christ, it wasn't like she was some horny teenager, was it? She'd be forty next month, yet here she was in a stranger's bedroom, with the hangover from hell, on a weekday, when all she'd wanted to do last night was get something to eat and a quick drink after a long, tough day at work.

Trying to ignore how shit she felt, Ava swung her legs over the edge of the bed. She winced and took a deep breath to swallow down the nausea which had suddenly hit her. Then she got herself unsteadily onto her feet, feeling the cool of the wooden floorboards before beginning to pick up her clothes, which were scattered across the bedroom floor. The room was basic, but clean enough. A tall grey wardrobe stood in the corner with a matching chest of drawers. A green comfy-looking chair piled with clothes was next to the PC by the window. None of which gave her any clues to what he did and where they'd met last night.

The sooner she left, the better. The morning after the night before was always awkward.

'Look, *Mark* . . .' She emphasized his name and met his eye as she quickly did up her skirt's zipper. 'Thank you for the evening, I really enjoyed it.' Tying her long, wavy brown hair into a ponytail, Ava attempted to give him her best smile. What harm did a little lie make? He wasn't to know she couldn't remember anything about it, and she really wasn't about hurting people. Or she tried not to.

Still completely naked, Mark stepped forward, taking Ava's face into his hands. He leaned down for a kiss. It was long and lingering, and did nothing for Ava. Impatiently she wondered how much longer he was going to draw it out.

Eventually, and much to her relief, he pulled away.

'So when am I going to see you again, princess?'

She cringed inwardly and, instead of maintaining eye contact, looked down at nothing in particular. 'I'm . . . I'm not sure, you know, there's a lot going on at work, and . . .' She trailed off.

He snorted with contempt. 'First you don't fucking remember my name, and now you're making excuses. You know, there's a name for women like you.'

'Really?' Now she stared directly at him as anger flashed through her. 'And what would that be, hey? Just because I spent the night with you, doesn't give you the right to judge me. From the little I remember, we were both in this together . . . Listen,' her tone softened, 'it's nothing personal. I just have a lot of things going on right now.'

Her phone rang in her bag.

'I . . . I'd better get that. It could be work.'

Grateful for the interruption, Ava grabbed her mobile out of her bag. She glanced down at the screen, letting out another quiet sigh.

Leaning over Ava's shoulder, Mark frowned. His handsome, chiselled face flashed with irritation again. 'Who's Tony?'

Ava shrugged apologetically, backing away towards the door. 'My husband . . . Tony's my husband.'

2

'God, Ava, you look like you've crawled out of a skip. You look well rough, babe.' Jude, Ava's secretary, looked up from her desk as Ava walked into her office.

'When I want your opinion, I'll ask for it, OK?' Ava snapped. Tossing her bag and coat onto the brown leather couch, she began to march down the hallway of her small but plush office, which was based in the centre of Nottingham.

A moment later, she stopped in her tracks and turned round. 'Sorry . . . Fuck, I'm sorry, I'm being a total bitch, ignore me . . . It was a long night . . . well, what I can remember of it.' She raised her eyebrows, but even that seemed to hurt her head.

Jude grinned, to which Ava smiled back.

She had a lot of time for Jude, who'd worked for her for the past few years. She'd liked her from the start, even though Jude had showed up for the interview in a pair of scruffy red baseball trainers, a pair of ripped jeans and an un-ironed shirt. She'd been loud and confident, despite having no work experience whatso-ever, but giving her the job had been one of the best decisions Ava had ever made. Apart from the fact Jude was loyal and a hard worker, she took Ava's all-night sessions as par for the course, and didn't judge – something that Ava appreciated. God knows, she judged herself enough without anyone else adding to the mix.

'You want me to get you a coffee, hun?'

'Would you? Right now, I would swap my house for one. My

5

head feels like I put it in a vice . . . Oh, which reminds me, if Tony calls, can you—'

'I'll tell him you're in a conference.'

Ava rested her butt on the edge of Jude's desk, which was in the main reception area of the office. Apart from her accountant, who came in once a week, and the building's cleaner, it was only Ava and Jude who worked out of the office. 'Am I that predictable?'

Jude gave a shrug. 'In a word . . .' She laughed without finishing off the sentence, but her expression quickly turned serious. 'Are you OK, though? I mean, *really* OK?'

For some reason Ava found herself battling back tears. She chewed on her lip, not trusting herself to answer without getting all emotional.

'Yeah, I'm good . . . It's probably a midlife crisis I'm going through . . . Another one!' It was Ava's turn to laugh but it sounded hollow, and they both knew it. She looked at Jude. 'You know, I promised myself I was going to stop this shit . . . Last night, I was going to prove to myself I could be normal.'

'Normal?' Jude pulled a face. 'Is there such thing as, *normal*? I don't think that even exists, babe. I once read a quote, it went something like *what's normal for the spider is chaos for the fly.*'

Ava touched Jude's hand. 'Thank you. Sometimes I don't know what I'd do without you.' Then, wanting to steer the conversation away from the chaos of her personal life, Ava grabbed the diary on the desk and began flicking through her appointments.

'Thank God, I've got nothing in the diary this afternoon – that means I can go home for a long soak and try to turn myself into the good wife, before Tony gets back from London.'

She winked at Jude, and made her way through a wooden door with a brass nameplate screwed into the middle of it: DR AVA BARCLAY. PSYCHOLOGIST.

'Jesus, who let you in here?' Ava jumped as she stared at the man sitting in the corner of her large, plush office. She went to open the door again to call Jude.

'Don't do that . . . I just want a word with you, that's all.'

'If you want to see me, you go through the normal channels. Make an appointment.'

'I didn't think we needed the formalities. Cos, like I say, I just wanted to see you, that's all.'

Ava stared at the shaven-headed man. Piercing green eyes. If she were to guess, she'd say he was in his late fifties, maybe sixty at a push. Going by appearances, he kept himself in good shape. Dressed well, head to toe: expensive black shirt and jeans; Nike trainers that wouldn't look out of place on her godson – a sign he was trying to hold on to his youth? No doubt he thought he was a God's gift to women, too. He'd probably been married and divorced a couple of times, and was currently bedhopping his way through any woman—

Ava stopped herself from analysing him any further. It was a bad habit she had; a pitfall of the job she was in. Certainly, her profiling wasn't always accurate. Far from it. Not these days anyway.

Her clients' body language often gave her a more accurate insight than anything they actually told her during their sessions. Her skill at seeing through the persona they tried to present with their words and behaviour and the way they dressed, and turning the spotlight on the real issues troubling them, was one of the things that had drawn her to become a psychologist in the first place. But over the years, she'd become jaded. She'd fallen into the trap of stereotyping. Partly because of her own personal experiences, but mainly due to the barrage of deception and double-damaged lives she was exposed to on a daily basis.

God, could she be more of a hypocrite?

Here she was, playing the part of the good doctor, the good wife, when behind the mask she drank too much, dabbled with too much coke, and trawled bars for meaningless sex with strangers she'd never see again.

She'd never turn the spotlight onto herself, of course. It was enough to tell herself this was simply who she was, and who she had always been. That was as deep as she was going to get with herself. Even when, as part of her training to be a psychologist, she had to undergo therapy, she'd stuck to the script, telling them what they'd wanted to hear: happy childhood, happy life. She'd told herself it wasn't a big deal. After all, she'd never met a psychologist who wasn't messed up; it seemed to be part of the remit for the job.

She brought her attention back to the man in front of her. The way he was staring at her sent a cold chill running down her spine. Oh God, she hoped he wasn't someone she'd picked up in a bar who'd decided to pay her a visit. That was the last thing she needed. She tried to make a point of steering the conversation away from who she was, and often she didn't give her real name, but on nights when she got stuck into the booze and coke, fuck knows what she let slip.

'Do I know you? I mean, have you and I . . .' She stopped short of elaborating; the thought that he might be one of her past pickups made her mouth go dry.

'Have you and I what?' He tilted his head, looking like he was trying to work out what she was getting at, and Ava decided that he was either a really good actor, or he wasn't one of her one-night stands. Thank God. But then, who was he?

Massaging her temples, Ava winced again at her headache.

'Look, whatever is you want, I'd appreciate it if you left my office. You can't just walk in here.' It was all she could do to keep her voice even.

He gave her a half smile. 'Looks like that's exactly what I've done, sweetheart . . . Maybe you should have a word with your secretary – you never know who might walk in off the street.'

'Look, just go. Otherwise, I'll have to call the police.' She was used to dealing with strange people in her job, but that didn't mean it got any easier. Over the years she'd been attacked by clients, although that had been mainly in prisons or hospitals for the criminally insane. It was one of the reasons she'd gone into private practice: she'd wanted an easier life.

'There's no need for that, I just want to get to know you, that's all. No crime in that.'

'Hey hun, I've made it with a triple shot. If that doesn't . . .' Jude cheerfully barged into the office, but she trailed off at the sight of the visitor, giving a puzzled look to Ava. 'Everything all right?'

'Everything's fine, darlin', I was just going.' The man winked at Jude as he spoke. He made his way towards the door, stopping in front of Ava. 'This has been nice . . . we must do it again, Ava.'

Then he slammed the office door behind him.

Ava turned to Jude. 'Why did you let him in?'

'I didn't. He must have slipped in when I went to the bathroom. Who the fuck was he?' Wide-eyed, Jude took a sip of the coffee she'd made for Ava.

For a moment Ava could only stare back at her, unformed thoughts racing through her mind. 'No idea. And I'm not sure I want to know . . .'

3

'Ava . . . hey . . . Ava, I'm home.'

Hearing her husband's voice coming from downstairs, Ava groaned inwardly. The guilt she felt whirled in her but she'd learned to push it away, like she'd learned to push away most of her emotions. It had been a hell of a fucking day. Her clients had, to say the least, tested every fibre of her patience. Three OCD sufferers, one habitual gambler, and a court-ordered client – a domestic abuser – who, by the sounds of him, hadn't stopped raising his fist or boot to his wife since the moment he'd said, *I do*.

Ava had hoped the glass of red wine and steaming-hot bubble bath would have gone some way to helping her relax. Her hangover was still lingering in the background when she got home, and all she'd wanted to do was lie in the bath and soak off the day. But now she had to smile, pretend all was well and, if she was lucky, get away with nothing more than a welcome-home blow job.

By now, she should be an expert on faking it. But lately she'd reached the point where her life seemed to be in freefall, and she couldn't lift a finger to stop it.

Ava took a gulp of the red wine, drew in a deep breath and painted on her smile. 'I'm up here,' she shouted, hoping she'd managed to inject a tone of enthusiasm. 'In the bath.'

She listened to the footsteps coming up the stairs and braced herself.

A moment later, a head appeared round the door.

'That looks good . . . mind if I join you?' Tony grinned. His cheeky boy-next-door looks lit up.

Yeah, she minded. She minded a lot, in fact. She wanted to be left in peace. Was that really such a bad thing? Was it wrong not to want to play the little wife role? Ava only just managed to stop herself laughing out loud. Who was she kidding? When exactly had she played the doting, faithful wife? Not even on her wedding day. While Tony was being congratulated and strutting around proudly, she had been screwing some random guest in the lady's bathroom of the expensive hotel Tony had insisted on. He'd wanted everything perfect for her and she hadn't been able to give him perfect in return. But how could he expect perfect when she was so damaged inside? Once again, Ava decided not to bother asking herself the question: what the fuck was wrong with her?

'Of course, you can,' she purred. Not that Tony was the least bit interested in her answer. He'd already started unbuttoning his shirt and her heart sank at the sight of the bulge in his trousers.

'I didn't expect you to be back so soon.' She held the disappointment from her voice.

Tony's brown eyes sparkled. Standing naked, he took Ava's glass, filled it with wine and took a swig. 'There's only so much coding talk I can take.'

This time Ava's smile was genuine. 'Oh please, who are you trying to kid? I know you, and you'd be happy to spend every waking hour talking algorithms and batch files.'

He winked at her. 'Now that's my idea of dirty talking.' He leaned forward and gave her a long, lingering kiss. He pulled away, but kept his face inches away from hers. 'Go on, say something else, it turns me on . . . say, JavaScript.'

They both burst out laughing, and he grinned widely. 'I love you, Ava.'

Say it back, she needed to say it back. '. . . I love you too.'

He stroked her face. She could smell his aftershave, mixed with the faintest smell of cigarettes. 'I know I've said it before, but I'll never stop saying it, because you need to hear it . . . I feel like the luckiest guy to call you Mrs Barclay.'

'It's *Dr* Barclay to you.' She grinned back.

'I'm being serious . . . It's going to be a whole ten years next week, *ten years*, since we got married.'

Fuck! She'd forgotten about that. 'Yeah, I know.' She sounded convincing.

'And in the whole of that time, I've never regretted being with you, I've never wanted anyone else, never thought about anyone else. It's always been you, Avie, I hope you know that, and I hope you know that I mean it.'

Oh God, she knew he meant it.

One-hundred-per-fucking-cent, Tony meant it. It wasn't one of those bullshit lines that guys liked to spout to get her into bed. This was *real*, and she guessed this was what love was supposed to be like. This was the thing that stopped her walking out on Tony.

Christ, she might be a lot of things but, ironically, she wasn't someone who went around intentionally hurting people. She cared for him. And she didn't want to cause him any kind of pain. She'd seen enough clients whose lives had been turned upside down by the simple human affliction of a broken heart.

And the things she did? Well, he wouldn't ever find out about them. Therefore, what he didn't know, wouldn't hurt him . . . It only hurt her.

Tony stepped into the bath, getting in behind her. Once again, Ava had to brace herself, working hard not to object. She shivered as he pulled her into him.

'Are you OK?'

As he began to caress her breasts, Ava was glad she had her

back to him: it was all she could do to fight back the tears. It must be the booze, she told herself. Hangovers always made her feel emotional.

'Yeah, I'm good,' she whispered, not trusting that her voice wouldn't break. 'And Tony . . . it's good to have you home.'

'It's good to *be* home.'

The water was growing tepid, but Ava could feel his erection. She only hoped he wasn't going to draw it out. She needed her bed and a decent night's sleep.

His arms wrapped around her. Lifting her slightly to ease her gently down on his penis, Tony entered her, groaning her name loudly as his breathing became quicker.

He began to thrust deeper and deeper, splashing the water over the marble floor tiles.

Ava suddenly felt Tony freeze. He pulled out of her, pushing her forward.

'Did you hear that noise?'

Ava scrambled around in the bath to stare at him. 'I didn't hear anything.'

Tony put his finger to his mouth. 'Sshhhh, I'm sure I heard breaking glass.'

Without waiting for an answer, he got out of the bath and grabbed one of the grey bathrobes from the back of the door. Ava leapt out after him and grabbed his arm.

'If you think you really heard something,' she whispered, 'maybe we should call the police.' She reached for her mobile, which she'd left on the antique bathroom cabinet.

Tony shook his head. 'No, wait – it might be nothing.'

'Yeah, and it might be something.' For some reason, Ava's thoughts turned to the guy who'd showed up in her office unannounced that morning. Over the years she'd dealt with the worst specimens of human life, and part of her was always waiting for a disgruntled client or one who had profound mental health issues to turn up at her door. One of her colleagues had been stabbed last year – a stark reminder of the precarious nature of her profession.

Tony gave her a quick kiss on the forehead. 'I'll be fine. Besides, I don't reckon my colleagues will be too impressed if I call them out just because I heard a noise.'

Ava's stare moved across his face. 'Who cares what they think. If someone's broken in, you—'

'—I didn't say anyone had broken in.' He gave her a crooked smile. 'All I'm saying is, I heard a noise. I think it's worth checking it out. Nothing more, nothing less . . . Don't look so worried.'

'You do know you don't have to play the hero for the guys at work.' Ava shook her head. Just before they'd got married, Tony had left a high-paying job at a cybersecurity tech firm based in Cardiff to become a digital forensics analyst with the police. It had certainly ruffled a few feathers in her family, to say the least.

His fringe fell over his forehead as he leaned into her, and Ava noticed the slight bags under his eyes. He worked hard, but she'd never been certain Tony was cut out for the job he was in. He was brilliant at the technical side of things, but the harrowing crimes he was exposed to, often involving children and vulnerable adults, had taken its toll on him.

She'd tried on more than one occasion to persuade him to go back to his previous job; those were the only times he'd ever got annoyed with her. 'I'm not one of your clients' – that was the line he'd use to cut her off. It would have been so much easier if he had been; then she could have brought into the open what she believed was the real reason he wouldn't give up policework. It was because of her. He didn't want to look like he couldn't hack it; he thought that would make him a failure in her eyes. But he couldn't be further from the truth. Ava wasn't looking for a tough guy. That was one of the reasons she chose Tony. He was the opposite of everything she was used to.

'I'm not playing anything or trying to be anything – I'm just going to see what the noise is, that's all. The wind was getting up earlier; maybe one of those ornaments you bought for the garden has smashed.'

'Then I'll come with you.' Ava grabbed her robe and tied it tightly around her waist. Not bothering to wait for Tony to object, she opened the door and crept along the landing, pausing at the top of the stairs.

'Has anyone ever told you that you're paranoid, Ava?'

She glimpsed over her shoulder, keeping her voice low as she replied, 'I'd rather be paranoid than have anything happen to you.'

Tony grabbed her, pulling her back. 'Well, in case there is a bogyman down there, I'll go first.' He moved past her, walking down the stairs into the large hallway.

'I'll check the kitchen.'

Ava nodded, aware her heart was racing far more than it should for someone who was trying to convince herself that Tony was right and it would turn out to be nothing.

'Wait . . . this is stupid, let's just call the police,' she hissed.

Tony gave her a withering stare. Ignoring her concerns, he opened the kitchen door and switched on the light. 'Like I thought, nothing.'

'Let's check the sitting room,' Ava insisted.

They went from room to room, and eventually Tony turned to give her a peck on the forehead. 'There you go: all fine.' He paused at the sound of the wind outside whistling around the house. 'I bet tomorrow you'll find something broken in the garden. But for now, we're all safe and cosy, so why don't we go back upstairs and finish what we started?'

He reached for her, but she stepped away. 'Give me a minute . . . I'll get another bottle of wine.'

'Well, don't be too long.'

She gave him a tight smile. 'OK.'

Taking a deep breath, Ava closed her eyes for a moment. Then she opened them and walked slowly into the kitchen. She certainly needed some more wine to get her through the night. Picking up strangers was so much easier than this. *Fuck.*

Despairing at herself, Ava reached for the fridge door, just as a hand slammed over her mouth . . .

4

Instinctively, Ava tried to bite down on the hand that was covering her mouth, but whoever it was just tightened their grip. Unable to twist her head to see who it was, she quickly brought her foot up and kicked backwards as hard as she could.

The hand dropped away from her mouth.

'*Oh fuck . . . fuck!*'

At the sound of the voice, Ava spun round. 'What the hell are you doing here? What the fuck do you think you're doing?'

'Well, that's a nice way to greet your old man, ain't it?' Billy Fields stared at his daughter, who stared back icily.

'Maybe if my old man wasn't such a prick, things might be different.'

He grinned at her, turning on the charm. 'I didn't want to give you a fright.'

'And how did that work out? You scared the crap out of me.'

He shrugged and kept his voice down. 'I didn't want Tony knowing I'm here. He's never very pleased to see me.' He winked.

'Well, that makes two of us then, doesn't it.' Ava folded her arms.

She knew a lot of women thought of her father as a catch. Handsome. Old school in the way he treated women. Protective. A wide boy from East London who'd done well for himself. Not that she knew fully what her father did.

When she was younger, she'd asked time and time again, but he'd fobbed her off with bullshit, refusing to give her a straight answer. It had made her feel disconnected from him. While all her friends had dads they talked about, dads who dropped them off at school, who showed up on sports day, her father had been something of an enigma. When she wasn't at school she was usually looked after by random nannies she'd never met before, who would show up explaining that her father was away on *business*, whatever that was. At the time, it had really bothered her. Now, she didn't give a shit what he did, or where he went, just as long as he stayed the hell away from her.

'So, I take it breaking and entering is your latest occupation?' She turned her back on him to grab a glass from the cupboard, then reached into the fridge for the bottle of white wine.

'Maybe if you answered my calls, Ava, then I wouldn't have to go to such extreme measures to see my little girl.'

She filled the glass and took a swig. 'Oh please, I'm not one of your conquests – that crap doesn't work on me.'

He sat down at the custom-made table in the grey and pink kitchen that Ava had designed last year. In actual fact, the whole of the house had been given a makeover, as it had been every couple of years since they'd moved in. It was all part of the facade, she supposed. Make everything look perfect. But as she knew only too well, all that glitters certainly isn't gold.

'You're not going to offer me a drink then?'

'Don't push your luck!' Ava gazed towards the kitchen door. 'You're not staying . . . Like you say, I don't want Tony knowing you're here.'

Billy ran his fingers through his thick salt-and-pepper-coloured hair and shrugged his expensive leather jacket onto his shoulders. 'Tony, not into playing happy families?'

'Not after you beat him up – funny that,' she snapped.

'He needs to man up and stop acting the pussy. So, he got a few slaps. I had harder from me nan when I was a kid.'

Ava fought hard to stop her irritation getting the better of her. 'What do you want anyway?'

'Has it ever occurred to you, maybe I just want to talk to my daughter?'

Mustering up as much scorn as she could, Ava replied, 'Yeah, it occurred to me. Then I remembered who you are . . . Now what the fuck do you want, *Dad*?'

'God, you can be hard! Come on, Avie, how long are you going to keep this up? Don't you ever get tired of being angry with me? Give us a break, eh. Fuck me, is this what they taught you when you did your psychology degree? How to hold a fucking grudge.'

Ava could see the hurt in her father's eyes, but she'd fallen for it too many times. She was a grown woman, for God's sake, and she wasn't going to be played by him *ever* again. 'Leave my job out of it. This isn't about anyone else, but you.'

'*Ava . . . Ava, you OK?*' Tony called down the stairs.

Billy nodded towards the door. His intense blue eyes dazzled as he grinned. 'You're keeping Loverboy waiting.'

Ava shoved her father in his chest, and he burst out laughing. 'That's it, get out of my house.'

'OK, OK I'm going.' Billy put his hands in the air in fake surrender, then strode confidently to the back door. But instead of opening it, he turned to face her, his smile fading. 'There was something actually . . .'

'Oh, here we go – how did I know?' Ava folded her arms.

'Don't be like that, darlin'. I came to see you first and foremost. I miss having you in my life – I've told you that enough times.'

'Let's not go over this again. Just tell me what you want, Dad.'

Billy Fields shrugged. 'Fine, have it your way, doll, but you know where I am if you ever need me.'

Ava sighed loudly. 'As you were saying . . .'

'OK, I just wondered if you'd had any . . .' Billy searched for his words, '. . . I dunno, fucked-up stuff happening lately.'

'What is that supposed to mean? What kind of *fucked-up stuff*?'

Billy stayed silent for a moment, and Ava could see a hundred thoughts rushing through his head. 'Ignore me, Avie, it don't matter. Like I say, I came to see you . . . but do me a favour, babe – be safe, yeah?'

An hour later, Ava lay in bed in the master bedroom, listening to the autumn rain lash against the window as she curled up in Tony's arms. Every time she saw her dad, he always messed with her head. It was part of the reason why she kept away. That and other things, of course. But she knew him, and she knew that he was keeping something from her. She couldn't even begin to guess what he'd been about to say, but she also knew there was no point calling to ask him. If he didn't want to tell her, nothing she said would change his mind.

'Ava?' Tony's voice broke through the darkness, interrupting her thoughts.

'I didn't know you were awake.'

'I can't get to sleep.'

'Things on your mind?' Ava's voice was quiet and caring. She wriggled round to face him.

'Yeah, you could say that . . . I was wondering why you had a love bite on your neck, which I didn't give you . . .'

5

Sitting in the conservatory that they'd converted into a dining room, Ava bit into her slice of buttered toast and stared out into the garden. A couple of birds were splashing in the small water fountain Tony had installed when he'd been going through a DIY phase, wanting to find a hobby that might help him relax. He'd soon discovered it had the opposite effect, leaving him frustrated by his lack of skill.

She took a hurried gulp of tea and checked the time. Her first client wasn't due until eight thirty, but she was in a hurry to get going. Anything rather than face the inevitable questioning from Tony.

'So, aren't we going to talk about this? Were you really going to sneak off without saying a word?'

Fuck. Too late.

Tony was standing in the doorway.

She could do without what was about to happen. Grabbing her breakfast plate and cup, she got up from the table. 'Firstly, I'm not sneaking off anywhere, I'm going to work – I have a client. Secondly, like I told you last night, it is *not* a love bite.'

'Yeah, but that's all you did say before you got up and went into the spare room.'

Tony didn't look like he'd slept at all, whereas she'd slept like the dead. Once again, Ava refused to ask herself what was wrong with her.

'I went into the guest room because I didn't want this . . . I

21

didn't want to argue. For God's sake, Tony, how old do you think I am? Even discussing this accusation makes me feel like a thirteen-year-old . . . I'm sorry, but I've got to go, I'm going to be late.' Ava moved to leave, but he blocked her way.

'Tell me what you've been doing. Tell me the truth.'

Ava stared at him. He looked dishevelled in a creased navy tracksuit, a far cry from his usual immaculate appearance. She'd been so stupid to get herself in this position, and she was angry with herself . . . and ashamed. She would never have allowed anyone to mark her neck if she hadn't been so pissed or fucked up on coke. But then, she would never have been sleeping with anyone other than Tony, if she wasn't so messed up.

'You're serious, aren't you? You really think this is a love bite?' If there was one thing she'd learned from her clients, it was how to gaslight.

'I don't think, I know . . . Avie, *please* . . .'

'No – stop. This is crazy talk. I have done nothing wrong. Now excuse me, I have to go.' She tried to pass him again, but he grabbed her, dragging down the grey cashmere turtleneck she was wearing.

'Don't treat me like a fucking fool, Avie.' He growled at her, his face red.

Ava met his glare. She'd never seen him this angry, although of course she realized it was from hurt. She slapped his hand away. 'The only fool around here, Tony, is you . . . I didn't even realize it was there, but the only possible person who could've given it me, is you. You obviously gave it me before you went away, and I didn't notice it there.'

Tony's shoulders slumped, he looked away. 'But . . .'

'But what, Tony? Go on, tell me. Tell me how you are so sure you didn't do this.'

'I would've remembered.'

'*Really?* Are you telling me you make a bloody mental list of all the things you do to me when you're fucking me, is that what you're saying?'

'No, of course I'm not saying that.'

She pointed at him. Hating how good she was at bullshitting him. 'No, exactly. Yet you think it's OK to go around accusing me of sleeping with other people? Do you know how hurtful that is? Last night, we were talking about our ten-year anniversary. Now you're accusing me of getting a fucking hickey . . . What has got into you?'

Tony fell silent for a moment then turned to look at Ava.

'OK, I'm sorry. I got it wrong.'

'Too right, you got it wrong.'

'It's just, when I saw it—'

'What? You thought you'd show me how much you trusted me, was that it?' Ava's voice dripped with scorn, and it passed through her mind how often she'd warned clients that it was possible to start believing in your own lies. And right now, that was how it was for her. Instead of being full of utter remorse, a sense of righteous outrage was rising inside her, even though she knew it was ridiculous.

'I'm an idiot, OK . . .' He closed his eyes.

Finally, guilt washed over her. 'No, no, you're not, Tony . . . I'm sorry. I could've reacted better.'

He looked at her. 'I do trust you, and . . . I'm sorry. That was nothing but jealousy talking. The thought of you with someone else made me . . .' He trailed off, then shrugged. 'It made me want to kill someone . . .'

6

Ava sat in her office and stared out of the window overlooking the car park. Her mind was racing, and she couldn't concentrate. She'd got to work in time for her first client: Paul, a man in his early forties with serious anger issues, who'd been coming to see her for over a year and had barely made any progress. Despite her efforts to focus, her mind had wandered off. Fortunately, Paul had been oblivious to her distracted state, keeping up a steady monologue for the full fifty minutes until the low chime of her timer had indicated the end of their session.

She'd got Jude to cancel the rest of the morning's appointments – something she would never do ordinarily. Actually, she couldn't remember the last time she'd done such a thing. Usually she was mindful that her clients were desperate and the weekly session in her office was something they clung to as if it were the only thing keeping them going. Cancelling could be the difference between someone keeping their head above water and drowning. But right now, she knew she wasn't going to be of help to anyone.

Grabbing her coat from the back of the chair, Ava hurried out into reception. 'Jude, I'm off, and I doubt I'll be back later. Can you manage here on your own?'

Jude took a gulp from her tin of Coke, which had gone flat. 'Yeah, of course, you get off . . . And Ava, I hope I'm not over-stepping the mark, but have you thought about taking some time off? I only say that because you haven't really been yourself lately. I'm worried about you.'

Ava stared at Jude. She was, of course, touched by her concern, but taking time out from her practice wasn't something she'd consider. She liked being busy, she liked not having to think. 'Thanks, Jude, but I'm sure by tomorrow I'll be back to my old self. All I need is a leisurely day, followed by a night in front of the telly – that's the best therapy.'

Jude raised her eyebrows. 'Is that what you tell your clients? Are you sure that's what the British Psychological Society recommends?'

Ava grabbed a biscuit from the open packet of chocolate digestives. She grinned. Jude always had a way of making her feel better. 'That's exactly what they say. Didn't you know, an all-night binge of a trashy box set is the official treatment for all kinds of disorders.' She bit into the biscuit. 'I'll see you tomorrow. And when you've finished organizing the new client files, why don't you take the rest of the day off yourself?'

Jude gave her a sideways gaze. 'Paid?'

Ava walked to the lift. 'Go on then, you've twisted my arm.'

'Double time, for having to work on my own?'

As she stepped into the small lift, Ava roared with laughter. 'Don't push it!'

As she drove, Ava couldn't help but think of her father. Why did she always let him get under her skin? She was tired of her dad getting into her head. But it was always the same. He had a way of making her house of cards come tumbling down.

'*Fuck!*' She banged on the leather steering wheel of her Audi 4x4, and suddenly did a left turn at the traffic lights, putting her foot down on the accelerator before she changed her mind.

It had been years since she'd been to her father's house. Not for want of an invitation – every couple of months, he'd call, telling her he'd cook her favourite if she dropped by. She didn't even know she had a favourite. Besides, she'd drawn a line in the sand with him . . . although it never seemed to prevent him creeping into her thoughts.

She took a right turn into Arlington Avenue and followed the signs for the A road that would take her to the village of Woodborough. Made up of picturesque properties, attractive public houses and a historic church, surrounded by wide-open spaces, it was widely regarded as one of the most sought-after locations in Nottingham. None of it held any attraction for Ava as she drove north-east.

Maybe it was because of what had happened with Tony, but she was going to have it out with her dad once and for all. That was what she told her clients, wasn't it? Face the problems head on. Well, for once she was going to take a bit of her own advice.

And with that, Ava switched the radio on and watched the speedometer hit eighty.

It was another hour though before Ava finally got to Woodborough. There'd been a diversion, and then she'd got stuck behind a tractor carrying bales of hay, which couldn't have gone slower if it'd tried.

During the journey, she'd smoked five cigarettes from the packet Tony left in her car the last time she'd given him a lift. Not that she was a sober smoker – usually she only had a cigarette when she was pissed – but she'd needed to do something to pass the time and distract her from wanting to turn back.

Sighing, Ava slowed as she drove along Main Street, passing the Nag's Head. Within moments she'd slammed on the brake, almost causing a grey Mini to plunge into the back of her.

Waving an apology, Ava quickly parked up and looked in the

rear-view mirror. Even though it was beginning to rain, she had a clear view of her father standing outside the pub, talking animatedly. That in itself wasn't unusual: it was the fact her dad was having an intense discussion with the guy who'd barged into her office yesterday.

She watched for a couple more moments, sliding down in her seat when her father looked over. Not that he knew her car – or at least Ava didn't think he did – and the blacked-out windows at the back would go some way to stopping him from seeing her.

Her phone buzzed, and she saw it was Tony, but immediately silenced the call; she'd speak to him later. When she looked back in the rear-view mirror, her father and the other man had started walking away from her.

Everything inside her said to turn round and drive home, but when had she ever followed the rules? Besides, she needed to know what was going on.

She gave it a couple of seconds, then grabbed her jacket and got out of the car. Cautiously, she began to follow them, keeping well back so they wouldn't spot her. That would take some explaining.

At the junction, they turned left up Shelt Hill, crossing the road to where a rusty white van was parked. Once again, she held back as her dad and the man he was in deep conversation with made their way into the Galleywood, a modern-looking bar with a gaudy neon sign outside.

Part of her was tempted to follow them inside; standing in the cold and rain wasn't her idea of fun. Still, she'd been in worse situations. Pulling up her coat collar, she let out a sigh. Something told her that she was in for a long wait.

7

An hour and a half later, the only thought in Ava's mind, apart from the fact she was soaking wet, was that she was bursting for a wee. She'd even tried to distract herself by texting Tony. It had turned into a long exchange of texts which had been surprisingly enjoyable. Even if, as usual, it was filled with untruths – at least on her side.

She'd told Tony she hadn't been feeling great, so she'd cancelled clients and had gone to the central library to do some research. He'd been nothing but supportive, even suggesting he would try to finish work early to cook her dinner and give her some TLC. She'd declined and thanked him, at the same time wishing he'd get angry, impatient, be less supportive: that way it would be easier for her. As it stood, the more he behaved like a doting husband, the more apologetic he was about this morning, the more she despised herself. It made her feel as though she wasn't good enough for him. Which, of course, she wasn't.

Ava had never been one for self-pity – far from it – but that constant sense of failure sat in her chest like a lead balloon. The only time she didn't feel it was when she was half-cut. It was amazing how a few vodka tonics could take away her despair.

Out of the corner of her eye, she caught a glimpse of a motor-cyclist. Absent-mindedly she turned her attention to the rainwater spraying off his back tyre while letting her thoughts wander between Tony and her father.

'Have you been following me?'

Ava jumped and let out a screech.

She whirled around to see her dad standing behind her. Her stare darted around, trying to work out where he'd come from. As if he could read her thoughts, Billy grinned.

'There's a back entrance to the bar. It takes you round to the other side.' He tilted his head and drew on the cigarette he was smoking. 'This is getting a habit, ain't it?'

'What is?' Ava snapped.

'Making you jump. But if you will sneak around.' He winked at her.

Humiliation rushed through Ava. Cold and wet as she was, she could feel her cheeks burning.

'I wasn't sneaking around or . . . or following you.' Even she didn't think it sounded convincing.

'No, of course you weren't.' Billy wiped the drips of rain from his face and laughed, not unkindly. 'Come on, Avie, it's like when you were a little girl and you used to follow me into my study and pretend you weren't there.'

'Oh, piss off, Dad. I'm not five years old anymore,' she mumbled. Unable to look at him, she stared at nothing particular up the road.

'No, sorry, of course you're not. It just always made me laugh . . .' He took another deep draw on his cigarette. 'Look, Avie, you're soaking wet – why don't you come back to mine and get dry? You'll catch your death out here, babe.'

Her head shot round to him. 'In case it hasn't escaped your notice, we're in the twenty-first century and I have a car parked down the road with a perfectly good heater.'

Billy licked his lips, something he always did when he was irritated. Regardless, he attempted a smile. 'OK then, we'll stand out here like a couple of drowned fucking rats. Whatever you want, babe. Now, are you going to tell me what you're doing here? Not that I'm complaining – it's good to see you.' His broad shoulders shrugged. 'I didn't think I would after last night.' He held her in his stare, his handsome face giving out nothing but warmth.

'It's OK, you know,' Billy added.

'What's OK?' Ava pulled a face, still trying to push down her humiliation at being caught.

'You coming here, then being worried how it might look. It's hard to swallow your pride sometimes. Fucking hell, doll, me of all people should know that. But I'm pleased you did. Like I said to you yesterday, I miss having you in my life.'

Ava blinked away the raindrops on her lashes. 'You really are something else.'

Billy's smile instantly dropped. 'What you on about?'

'You. You really think I've come here for a cosy lunch? With *you*?' She shook her head. 'Swallow my pride? You're a joke!'

Hurt immediately registered on Billy's face. 'Then what are you here for?' His voice was gruff and hard.

Ava stepped back under the tree she was standing by, hoping to get some cover from the rain, which was beginning to get heavier. 'I actually came here to have it out with you. Yeah, that's right, because I'm sick of you thinking you can just show up and mess with my life.' She dug her nails into her palms to stop herself from crying.

Billy looked and sounded puzzled. 'Am I missing something here? I came to see you, that's all. Nothing more, nothing less, just like I always try to do. Fucking hell, Avie, wanting a quick coffee with my little girl is hardly messing with your life.' He raised his eyebrows. 'You need to stop looking at things so deeply. If you really want to know what's messing with your head, it's all that psychology shit. Things can be just as they seem, you know.'

This was like a red rag to a bull for Ava. 'Oh, you mean like you? Like you're just as you seem?' It wasn't lost on her how much of a hypocrite she sounded.

Billy pulled up his jacket collar. 'Turn it in, Avie. What is it with you? You're always looking for a fight with me. You were the one who came here today. If I'm that bad, why don't you get in your *heated* car, and go back to your life.' He rubbed his face wearily.

She glared at him. 'You'd like that, wouldn't you? Stop me asking the awkward questions, stop me calling you out.' Her voice cracked as it rose in volume. 'Well not this time, *Dad*. For a start, you can begin by telling me who that guy was you were talking to.'

Billy stared back at his daughter. 'Avie, this is stupid, we're drenched – and you might not be worried about catching your death, but I fucking am. I'm freezing my nuts off here. Come on, please, let's go home and we can order a pizza delivery, then we'll have a proper chat and you can tell me what's *really* going on. Is it Tony? Work? Babe, you can tell me anything. I don't mind being your punchbag, if that's what you need.'

Ava covered her face with her hands for a moment. 'Oh my God, can you hear yourself? You are so frustrating. If this is how you were with Mum, no wonder she left when I was little.' Though the truth was, she couldn't remember her mum. She only knew what her dad had told her and, like everything to do with him, to garner the truth she had to look between the lines.

The problem was, he was so good at bullshitting. Like father, like daughter, she supposed. She wasn't proud of who she was. There was no excuse for her actions, she knew that, but at the same time she couldn't look at herself closely; it was too painful.

Pushing that thought away, she dropped her hands again and met her dad's icy gaze. 'You know, Dad, there's nothing wrong with Tony, or with work. It's *you*. The problem's you, and it always has been . . . Now I'll ask you again: who was he? And don't try to lie. I meet better liars than you every day.'

'Ava, I swear I don't know who you're talking about darlin'.' He threw his soggy cigarette down.

'The man I saw you talking to outside the Nags Head earlier. Who the hell was he?'

Billy shrugged again. 'You've got me there, doll. I don't have a clue who you're on about.'

'Don't lie to me!' Ava yelled, letting out her pent-up emotions and causing a passer-by walking their dog to glimpse across. 'Don't you fucking dare lie to me.'

As she continued to shriek at him, once again, the irony of the situation wasn't lost on Ava. Wasn't this what she did to Tony? Maybe she deserved a taste of her own medicine. 'I saw you, Dad. I saw you with my own eyes talking to him outside the pub, then you walked to that bar, over there, *together.*'

She watched her father clench his jaw, then he nodded. 'First off, you need to calm down, girl. You'll do yourself a mischief getting that worked up . . .' He was so cool and laid back, it was all Ava could do to stop herself from screaming. 'Now you come to mention it, Avie, yeah, of course, I know who you're talking about now. I'm getting old, the old grey cells ain't what they used to be.' He smiled, but it certainly didn't hit his eyes. 'That fella was looking for the bar. Some woman had sent him the wrong way, and as I was meeting a mate there, I said he could walk with me. That was it. When we got inside, he went one way, I went another. Then I came out the back way, saw you. Happy now?'

Ava laughed bitterly. 'God, Dad, I see where I get my crap from. They say the apple doesn't fall far from the tree. Now, if I'd been born yesterday, or if that man you say asked you for directions hadn't been at my *workplace* yesterday, I might believe your little story.'

Billy blanched. 'He did what?'

'Yeah, you heard me. This random stranger you claim to have just bumped into came to my office. So are you going to tell me who he is? Because strange men barging into my place of work makes me somewhat uneasy.'

Ava watched her father trying to compose himself. 'Nah, you must have got it wrong, doll.'

'No. That was the same guy. I wouldn't forget his face.' A thought suddenly came to her. She didn't know why she hadn't thought of it before. 'Oh my God, that's why you came to the house yesterday, wasn't it? You wanted to know if any *fucked up stuff* had happened. That's what you meant, wasn't it? You were talking about him.'

'No, no, I wasn't. Like I say, the geezer just wanted to know—'

'—where the bar was. Yeah, you told me.' She cut in with words which couldn't have been more loaded with hostility. 'I'm warning you, if you have put me or Tony in danger, I swear—'

'No.' It was Billy's turn to interrupt. 'No, I would never do that.'

'Wouldn't you? Really? Why don't I believe that?' She stepped closer to her father.

He grabbed her shoulders gently and his stare moved across her face as the rain continued to fall. 'I would give my life for you, doll. You hear me? Whoever came into your office had nothing to do with me. I wouldn't do that to you. Are you listening to me, Ava?'

Ava shook off his hands and started to back away from him, unable to stop her tears. 'I am so done with you,' she said, jabbing a finger at him. 'Do you understand me? And when I think about it, I don't know you, do I? I know nothing about you, not really.'

'Oh, come on, Avie, stop exaggerating.' Billy sounded tired. 'You know everything there is to know.'

'No . . . no, I don't.'

'Avie, you need to go home, darlin'. I don't want to fight with you . . . Just go home to Tony and calm down, go and be the good wife.' He stared at her, frustration and anger crossing on her face.

'You are unbelievable!' Ava looked away in disgust. 'You know something: what I don't have, I can't miss.' She turned to stare him in the eye. 'So, from this day on, I haven't got a father. You are dead to me.'

And with the sound of her dad calling after her, Ava began to run, not knowing, not caring where she was going.

8

Ava had lost count of how many whiskies she'd had. She'd also lost count of how many times her phone had rung. She'd ignored it, not even bothering to see who it was, and instead she'd ordered herself another drink. Chasing away her demons with alcohol in the small, busy pub on the other side of the village.

'I think you've had enough, babe, don't you?'

Ava looked around and in her hazy, drunken state, she saw her dad – somewhat in double vision – standing by the side of the bar she was propped up against.

'Leave me alone.' She struggled to stop her eyes rolling.

'I don't think your husband would appreciate that, do you? So, this is what's going to happen. You're going to come home with me and sleep it off. Then I'll drive you back, or you can call a cab, but I ain't leaving you here in this mess.'

He walked over to her, and although Ava attempted to put up a fight as her father put his arm around her waist to hold her up, it was fruitless. The next moment, she found herself being gently helped outside.

'I've got the car parked across the road – you think you can walk there, or do you want me to carry you, babe?'

'I'd rather crawl.' Her voice was slurred, and she was semi-aware of her dad's laughter.

'I'm worried about you, Avie,' her dad said as he opened the door for her and buckled her into his brand-new Range Rover.

'What would you have done if I wasn't able to find you? Anyone could have taken advantage of you in that state.'

She tried to focus on him fully. 'Then it's a shame you came along when you did, isn't it?'

The journey to the private road off Roe Hill where her father lived was a blur for Ava. She was only partly aware of passing the small row of shops and post office as they drove through the pretty streets, with her father's voice fading in and out as she dozed.

'. . . *Ava?* Ava, did you hear me? We're here.'

Ava opened her eyes, and promptly vomited in the footwell.

'Well, I guess it's better out than in, hey, darlin'. It's just a shame it had to be out in me Rangie.'

She felt her father rubbing her back as she bent over again, emptying the last contents of her stomach.

She sat up and wiped her mouth, turning her head slightly to the side to face her father. 'You're enjoying this, aren't you?' she slurred.

'What do you take me for, Avie? Fucking hell, why would I be enjoying seeing my daughter completely out of her nut on a rainy afternoon?' He let out a sigh that filled the car. 'I hate that we're like this. How did it ever happen? . . . Now come on, let's get you cleaned up – the smell is making me want to vomit.'

Perhaps it was the cold air, but by the time Ava had got out of the car and walked across her father's gravel driveway, she felt drunker than she had earlier on.

Billy lived in a sprawling house which he had lovingly renovated, with each room done out in the height of luxury.

With her father's help, she stumbled inside, and was vaguely aware of him taking her shoes off before leading her into the huge bathroom.

'Get that top off you, it's got sick on it . . . Here, put my dressing gown on.' He grabbed it from the side and passed it to his daughter.

'Black silk?' Even in her stupor, Ava was able to muster up scorn.

'What can I say? I'm a man of expensive, some might say, cheesy taste.' He chuckled. 'Now put it on, girl.'

She did as she was told, with some difficulty, as the room seemed to be spinning around. Then she felt her face being splashed with cold water.

'Jesus, that's freezing,' she slurred.

'Yeah, well, like you say, darlin', you ain't going to catch your death. Come on, babe, you can lie down in the guest room. Hopefully, by the time you wake up, you'll feel better, and we can have a proper chat.'

He led her through to the plush guest room, decorated in creams and golds, and gently steered her to the king-size bed by the tall window which looked out over the manicured garden.

Ava lay on top of the covers, her head sinking into the pillows.

Her dad took a soft cashmere blanket from the foot of the bed and laid it over her. 'I hate to see you in this state, Avie, but you know, it feels like this is the closest we've been for a long time.' He stroked her head, and Ava felt too tired to put up any kind of argument. 'Maybe you should throw up in my car more often . . . Right, I'll leave you to sleep, darlin'. I'm next door if you need anything, OK . . . And Avie, I know what you think of me, but that has never stopped me loving you. Never. I've always loved you, darlin', and I always will, more than anything, I'm just sorry that you don't know that.'

9

By the time Ava peeled open her eyes, it had gone dark. She had no clue if it was late, or just the late autumn, early winter evenings drawing in. Her mouth was so dry, it felt like it was made out of sandpaper. What the hell had she been thinking? She groaned. This was the story of her life. Worse still, she'd shown her vulnerability to her father. And unlike most times when she got drunk, she could remember everything. No doubt that was to do with the fact, on this occasion, she hadn't consumed as much alcohol as normal. As she lay there reliving her humiliation, Ava wished she'd had the foresight to drink more.

Moving her body slightly, Ava suddenly felt the bedsheets underneath her. They were wet. Oh my God, she hoped she hadn't wet herself. That was all she needed to cap off her humiliation.

Shuffling to the side of the bed, Ava reached over to switch on the lamp she could make out in the moonlight which was shining through the window.

She clicked it on, and the room illuminated in a warm, soft glow. Sitting up, she breathed in, thankful she wasn't feeling nauseous anymore, although her head was pounding as it usually did when she'd been drinking spirits.

She looked down at the wet patch, hoping that it would dry soon, without her father noticing.

Her heart jumped into her throat.

It was blood. She looked down at herself, checking out her body to see if it was coming from her.

What the . . .

The scream Ava let out stopped her next thoughts as she saw her father lying on the floor next to the bed with blood oozing from a deep wound on the side of his head.

'Dad . . . Oh God, Dad?' Ava dropped to her knees by his side. '*Dad*, it's me, Ava. Dad, please wake up . . . Oh Christ, Dad?'

She put her head to his face.

She couldn't feel or hear him breathing. Hurriedly she tried to take his pulse. Nothing.

'Dad? Dad?'

Her phone. Where was her phone? She needed to call someone. But a cold chill ran through her as the silence of the huge sprawling house seemed to close in on her. Her father must have tried to wake her, and that's why his blood was on the bed. He'd come to her, wanting her help, while she was asleep in a drunken stupor. Fuck. Fear and shame filled her, and she looked down once again at her father before hurrying towards the door. Whoever had done this to him had meant business.

Ava raced through the house, trying to find a landline. She needed to call an ambulance as fast as possible – that's if it wasn't already too late. The amount of blood he was losing, time was of the essence.

'Come on . . . come on, where are you?' She spoke out loud as she charged through different rooms, but she couldn't see a phone. Desperate, and about to run outside to bang on a neighbour's door, Ava suddenly spotted her mobile lying on the hallway table.

She grabbed it, pressing the emergency call button.

'*Fire, police or ambulance?*'

'Ambulance, I need an ambulance . . . but you need to

hurry – it's my dad, he's been attacked, and he's losing a lot of blood. It's a head injury, and I can't feel a pulse. Please, hurry.'

Ava proceeded to give the address, and as she put the phone down, a noise from the lounge distracted her. But before she had time to turn round, she felt a sharp blow to the back of her neck. The next minute, Ava Barclay blacked out . . .

10

'What I don't understand is why you were at Billy's in the first place.' Tony stared at Ava as she sat in the hospital bed in the single room waiting to be seen by yet another doctor. She'd regained consciousness in the ambulance, but they'd insisted on her being checked out. That was four hours ago.

'You told me you were doing some research,' Tony continued, and Ava noticed how strained he appeared. She didn't blame him, she blamed herself.

'Tony, my head is thumping, do we have to do this now?' Ava asked quietly, although she couldn't be 100 per cent certain that part of it wasn't down to the hangover.

He frowned and rubbed his chin. 'Sorry, you don't need me asking questions right now.'

Ava reached out and touched his hand. 'It's fine . . . Look, it was a spur-of-the-moment decision. He'd been in my head for a while, and I wanted to have it out with him. To tell him all the things I hadn't said. It sounds stupid.' She shrugged.

'No, of course it doesn't, but I wish you'd talked to me if you were going through stuff. You know you can tell me anything. Yeah, there's issues between me and your dad, but that doesn't mean you can't come to me.' He bowed his head. 'When they called me, I thought . . .' He blew out his cheeks, and Ava could see him reining in his emotions. '. . . I really thought something had happened to you . . . You know . . .' He trailed off.

Ava leaned forward and kissed him on his cheek. 'I know.'

At that moment, the nurse, a tall bespectacled man, walked into the side room Ava was in.

'Any word about my dad?' she asked, unable to stand the waiting.

'He's still in surgery, but I promise we'll let you know as soon as he's out. In the meantime, you need to get some rest . . . We've told the police they'll have to wait until the consultant has seen you before they can speak to you.'

'No, I'll speak to them now, get it over and done with.' Ava was adamant.

The nurse looked unsure. 'You've had a nasty bang to your head, you really need to rest.'

'*Please*, I want to talk to them. The sooner they catch whoever did this, the better.'

'So, you went to see your father at what time?'

Ava looked over at Tony. 'Er . . . I'm not sure.'

The detective, tall, thin, with a balding head, frowned. He held the pen he was using in the air. 'So let me get this straight, Dr Barclay. You went to see your father, Billy Fields, but you have no idea what time?'

'I'm sorry, everything is a blur,' she lied. Right now, she didn't have any other option. There was no way she wanted Tony to know that she'd fed him, as usual, a whole heap of bullshit. Besides, at this stage, it wouldn't make any difference to the investigation.

'Then tell me what you can remember.'

Ava picked up on the slight impatience in the detective's tone.

'Not much . . . I wasn't feeling well, so I decided to cut short my working day. I went to the research library—'

'And you have people who can verify that?'

Ava bristled.

'I can,' Tony chipped in. 'You texted me from there.'

Ava gave Tony a grateful smile. 'Yeah, that's right.'

'I was talking to Dr Barclay.' The detective was brusque. He spoke again to Ava. 'Witnesses who saw you there? Other people who can confirm your story?'

She shrugged, attempting to be casual. 'I guess. Honestly, I don't know . . . Anyway, does it really make any difference who saw me there and who didn't?'

He held her gaze. 'I'm just trying to establish timelines.'

'Yeah, OK, but I still don't see why that matters. You know I was at my dad's house. That's not in question.'

'Dr Barclay, is there a particular reason why you seem to have a problem with me asking you about your timings? You seem agitated.'

'Well, wouldn't you fucking be . . .' Ava stopped and took a deep breath to compose herself. She gripped the cool white sheets of the hospital bed. 'I'm sorry, I shouldn't have snapped, but yes, I'm agitated: my father's been attacked, and I don't know if he's going to get through the surgery, not to mention I was knocked unconscious.'

'I understand that, Dr Barclay. But all I'm trying to do here is establish the facts, and at this point, nothing is ruled out.'

The way the detective said it made Ava pause. 'Hold on, you don't think *I* had anything to do with this, do you?'

'Of course he's not saying that, are you, *officer*?' Tony frowned and stood up to return the glass he'd been drinking from to the small sink in the corner of the whitewashed room. 'She's already told you where she was and what she was doing.'

'Sir, I would appreciate it if only Dr Barclay answered the questions.' The detective turned back to Ava. 'All lines of enquiry at this point are open. Nothing has been ruled out as yet.'

Ava nodded. 'I understand, Detective . . .'

'Brown. Detective Brown.' He stared at her coldly.

'Well, Detective Brown, I'm hardly going to knock myself out, am I?'

He let out a contemptuous laugh. 'There are lots of things that people do when they're desperate, especially in an attempted murder investigation.'

Ava's blood ran cold. Hearing the detective say it out loud made it feel only too real. It also made her think she'd been stupid to try lying in the first place. She should've just told him the truth. Instead, she was spinning a web of lies which, if found out, would only make her look suspicious.

'Actually, there is something,' she said. 'There was this man. He was waiting for me in my office yesterday morning. He'd sneaked past my assistant and—'

'—you didn't tell me this.' Tony walked over to Ava and sat on her bed.

'I'm telling you now.' She turned her attention back to Brown. 'At the time, yeah, it was a little weird. But, as you can imagine, I have lots of, what you might call, *strange* characters coming to my place of work.'

Brown tapped his pen on his notepad. 'And how is this related to your father?'

'When I went to see my dad, I saw him talking to the same guy who'd been in my office. I asked him about it, but he refused to say who he was.'

'I thought you said you couldn't remember.'

Ava gave him a cold stare. She didn't like the spotlight being shone on her. It made her, to say the least, uncomfortable. 'This part I can,' she snapped. 'I remember it very clearly. As I say, Dad refused to tell me who he was, and we had an argument.'

'So, you and your father argued?'

Fuck, why had she said that? 'Not so much an argument,' she

backtracked. 'More a disagreement . . . It was frustrating. He said he didn't know who the man was and, well, I didn't believe him.'

'Do you always argue with him?'

Thoughts raced through Ava's mind. Every single time she spoke to him, every single time they tried to have any kind of conversation, they ended up in a fight. It had been like that as far back as she could remember. 'No. No, we don't.' From the corner of her eye, she saw Tony stare at her. 'In fact, I'd say we had a great relationship, officer. The best . . .'

With Tony and Detective Brown gone, Ava began to take stock of everything that had happened. She'd told the police everything she could about the man who'd been with her father. They'd said they'd speak to Jude, and in the meantime, forensics were scouring her dad's house.

It occurred to Ava that her dad wouldn't appreciate her talking to the police, nor would he appreciate them being in his house. He liked to sort things out himself, that much she did know. As far back as she could remember, he had never once contacted the police over anything.

Even when his car had been stolen, a brand-new Mercedes, paid for in cash, he'd not picked up the phone to them. She'd never really given it much thought. But it didn't make sense. It was one thing him hating the police for whatever reason, but not reporting his stolen car . . . or, that's right, she remembered now: his house and neighbouring houses were broken into years ago, and he'd refused to involve the police then, pretending he hadn't had a break-in, when in fact he had.

None of it made sense. But she'd given up trying to work anything out about his life a long time ago.

The door to the room opened and a young nurse, small and blonde, who Ava hadn't seen before, popped her head in. 'I thought you'd like to know your father's out of surgery. He's not out of danger yet, but he's a fighter.'

Ava nodded and found herself unexpectedly bursting into tears. 'He is.' Her voice was barely audible. 'Can I see him?'

'I'm afraid not. Not yet, anyway. The surgeon's put him in an induced coma to give his brain a rest.'

'OK, thank you. I appreciate you letting me know.'

As the nurse disappeared again, Ava was overwhelmed by the sense she'd come close to losing something that could never be replaced. She wrapped her arms around her knees and silently wept for her father.

11

'Dr Barclay, I must advise against discharging yourself. I'd actually go as far to say it's downright stupid . . .' The next morning, a grim-faced, grey-haired doctor, who looked like he'd been on duty all night, stood watching Ava pack the small bag that Tony had brought her late last night.

He'd driven home without complaint to get some wash things and a change of clothes for her. Although he hadn't had much choice, given that the police had taken away her bloodstained clothes. A matter of routine. A voluntary procedure, they'd told her. Ava found it ridiculous that they could suspect her of being involved in any way, though she knew she hadn't helped herself by lying to them.

'I'll be all right.'

'No, you *think* you'll be all right. With head injuries it's always advisable to keep a patient under observation for at least forty-eight hours.'

'I realize that, but I'm happy to take responsibility for whatever happens . . . Thank you.'

The doctor, clearly realizing he wasn't going to get anywhere with Ava, shoved the discharge papers into her hand. 'Well, I'm not happy about it, Dr Barclay. You of all people should know better.' He turned abruptly, storming out of the ward without another word.

A few minutes later, after handing the signed papers to the nurse in charge, Ava walked down the long corridor pretending to herself she didn't feel dizzy and trying not to gag at the strong smell of bleach.

She waited for the lift but, impatient, quickly gave up and instead climbed slowly up the three flights of stairs to the Intensive Care Ward.

Finding herself directly outside the ICU unit, Ava took a deep breath. She didn't know why she was suddenly filled with anxiety, nor why her hand was shaking as she pressed the buzzer.

'Hello?' A male voice answered.

'Hi, my name's Dr Barclay. I was told by the nurse on the ward I was on that you were expecting me. She called up earlier to ask if it was all right for me to see my dad, Billy Fields . . .' Ava spoke quietly into the intercom.

'Of course.' The reply came straight away, and the white double doors of the ICU unit clicked open.

The moment she walked in, she felt her phone buzzing.

It was Tony.

'Hey, Tony, can I call you later.' She nodded to the nurse, keeping her voice low. 'I've just walked into intensive care, I wanted to see Dad.'

'Yeah, sure. Is everything OK? I mean, with him.'

'Well, there's been no change since yesterday, which I suppose is a good thing . . . Listen, I'd better go.'

'OK, sure, I'll see you later, around 2 p.m. I've arranged for some time off, so I—'

'You didn't need to.' Ava was quick to interrupt. 'I discharged myself already. And before you say anything, this is my decision . . . I'll call you soon.'

'Ava—'

She clicked the phone off. She knew what was coming: a lecture on how she'd been hasty discharging herself. Right now, she wasn't in any mood to hear it.

'Sorry about that.' She smiled at the male nurse, who smiled cheerily back.

'I'll show you where your father is. But I warn you, it'll probably look a bit overwhelming because of all the equipment around him. So, try not to worry.'

Without offering a reply, Ava followed him down the corridor.

'He's over there in bay five.' The nurse pointed, and Ava noticed the nicotine stains on his fingers.

'Thank you . . . Actually, do you know how long they're going to keep him in an induced coma?'

'I don't, but the doctor should be around soon, so you can ask him . . . I'll leave you to it.' He smiled again, and wandered off in the other direction, leaving Ava to make her way to her father's bedside.

The bed was surrounded by the kind of machines and monitors she'd seen so many times on television. Tubes and multicoloured electric wires hung between the equipment and the plain white wall.

Her father's face looked swollen and bruised as he lay with his eyes shut. The only movement, aside from the various numbers moving across the monitor screens, was the flow of blood down the tubes her father was attached to.

For a moment, Ava could only stare, trying to take in how different her father looked. She'd always seen him as a strong, powerful man. Stubborn and opinionated. Set in his ways. Untouched by whatever life threw at him. Seeing him now, she thought he looked broken . . . vulnerable.

Shit. It was hard to look at him like this; maybe it was because of how dizzy she was, but she felt sick to her stomach.

'Dad?'

Tentatively, she approached him, touching his hand gently.

'Hey, Dad, it's me . . . I don't know if you can hear me, but . . .' Ava paused. She didn't actually know what to say. What was she supposed to talk about to a man she barely knew, whose life was hanging in the balance?

'Dad.' She tried again, although this time she closed her eyes as she spoke. 'I know our relationship has been off for some time – well, a really long time – and God knows it will take some fixing, but . . . look, what I'm trying to say is, no matter what's happened, I never wanted this. And once you've woken up' – she swallowed hard, removing the possibility from her mind that he wouldn't wake up – 'we'll talk. Properly talk, and we'll get this shit sorted out once and for all.' She breathed in hard and exhaled, opening her eyes at the same time.

Her thoughts were interrupted by her phone ringing once more. She pulled her mobile out of her pocket and rolled her eyes when she saw it was Tony *yet again*. She ignored it, but after he'd phoned several more times, she eventually answered. She knew she shouldn't be annoyed – Tony was just showing he cared, she should be grateful – it was so hard for her to accept him being loving towards her. It always was. It sounded like an excuse, but she'd never been able to accept it, not from Tony or from any of the men she'd been in a relationship with. If she allowed herself to understand why she slept around as she did, behaving as she did, it was because she was desperate to feel something.

'Tony, I told you that I was seeing my dad, I'll—'

'I know, I'm not checking up or anything like that, and I'm sorry to interrupt, but can you talk?'

Instinctively she stepped away from her dad. 'Yeah, sure, what's going on? Are you all right?' Ava frowned.

'I'm fine, but . . . I thought you'd want to know, one of my colleagues came to give me a heads-up. This is strictly between us, Avie.'

'Tony, now you're really worrying me.'

She heard him take a deep breath.

'Ava, there is no Billy Fields.'

Ava blinked. 'What are you talking about? Tony, what the hell are you on about?'

His voice became softer. 'There's no record of a Billy Fields anywhere. They've done every single check they could . . . I'm sorry.'

Ava's eyes darted around the ward, fixing on one of the nurses preparing medication for another patient. 'Tony, you're not making sense.' She still didn't understand. But she was aware she sounded panicked.

'Avie, what I'm saying is, whoever you think your dad is, he's *not* . . .' There was a long pause. '. . . Unless you knew that already?'

'Are you being serious?' Ava began to shake. Her voice catching with emotion, she continued, 'You . . . you have just dropped the biggest bombshell in my life, and now you're asking if I already knew that my father, *my father*, isn't who I thought he was? . . . I can't do this.'

She turned off her phone then walked across to her father's bedside. She stared at him, unable to grasp the thoughts rushing through her head. 'Dad, Dad . . . I've just had the weirdest fucking conversation with Tony . . .' She took a second to stare down at her father lying in a coma. She wasn't certain whether, at this moment, she hated him or loved him. 'He said your name isn't Billy Fields . . . Is that true, Dad? Because, if it is, if that's not your name . . . who the hell are you?'

12

For once, Ava didn't take her frustration straight to the nearest bar. She had other things on her mind as she looked over her shoulder, checking that no one was around. With the rain pouring down, she ran towards her father's house, taking the gravel path along the side of it, which was shielded from view by a row of manicured shrubs.

Ava stopped and checked again, searching the darkness until she was certain no one was watching. Then she reached into her bag and took out the small spanner she'd bought on the way over, after the cab had dropped her off in the high street.

Silently, she counted down from three, then she smashed the kitchen window with the spanner, wincing at the sound of shattering glass. She'd had no idea it'd be that loud. As quickly as she could, she tapped the rest of the glass from the frame then clambered inside.

Where to start?

She supposed the kitchen was as good a place as any. Switching on the lights, she made her way across to the drawers of the expensive, handmade units. She started opening them, stopping occasionally to make sure she was alone. Finding nothing out of the ordinary, she began to check the cupboards, hoping to come across something that would answer the questions filling her head.

Fifteen minutes later, Ava made her way to the room across the hallway. An expensive pool table took centre stage, bookshelves and paintings lined the walls. Again, she started to search, but there was little of interest, and nothing to tell her why her father had been lying to her all these years. Nothing to explain why everything she'd ever known was just a big fat lie.

Having looked as carefully as she could downstairs, she decided to check the rooms on the next floor. The first door she walked through took her into her father's study. The shelves were crammed with books Ava was certain her father had never read. Glass cupboards full of expensive boxes of cigars and solid silver goblets. Her father had always enjoyed collecting antiques, even if they were garish.

Her gaze moved round. '*What are you hiding, Dad?*' She spoke out loud, then as she had done downstairs, Ava sped through the drawers, skim-reading his letters. Everything was addressed to Billy Fields.

A thought came to her. Maybe the police had made a mistake. It was possible, wasn't it? From everything she'd found in the house, it was looking more and more that way. Why the hell had she straight away opted to believe what Tony had told her? She shook her head. God, she was so keen to prove her dad was a bad guy, wasn't she?

There was an edge of relief that this whole thing, him being someone else, might turn out to be bullshit. At the same time, Ava acknowledged that, deep down, there was a small part of her that had *wanted* to believe this could be a possibility. Because that way, she'd be justified in how she'd treated him all these years. It would absolve her of the guilt she was feeling.

She let out a long sigh and rubbed her forehead. She was a mess. It wasn't helping that she felt so bloody rough. It crossed her mind that maybe she should've listened to the doctor's advice: what she wouldn't give to be lying in bed right now.

Remembering where the bathroom was, Ava went to wash her face, hoping it would go some way to making her feel better. It didn't. She held on to the sink to get her balance, but the nausea and giddiness kept getting worse. Thinking she might faint, Ava sat down on the toilet.

She bent forward, taking long, slow breaths. She should probably call Tony to come and get her, or at least order a cab. She sat up gingerly, then tilted her head, staring at the walk-in shower in the corner. That was strange. Slowly and unsteadily, she got to her feet and shuffled over to where her gaze had landed.

She crouched down, directly underneath the shower head, and touched a couple of the tiles on the bottom row. Were they slightly larger than the others? Or was it the way they sat, not quite flush to the wall? Knowing how meticulous her father was when it came to clothes, cars and interiors, it struck her as odd that he would have allowed a builder to get away with this.

Frowning, she tapped the wall. The two tiles sounded different to the others. She continued to stare, trying to work out what she was thinking, until a twinge in her knees reminded her she couldn't stand here all night.

She reached into her back pocket and pulled out the spanner. With as much force as she could, she smashed the metal against the tiles, once, twice, three times, until they cracked and broke away from the wall, falling to the shower floor in a shower of fragments. Where the tiles had been was a hole.

Ava put her hand inside and tentatively felt around. Immediately her fingers touched something. She pulled it out.

A padded envelope.

She opened it, and her heart raced as she tipped out the contents: a passport. She flicked through the pages to the photo. There was a photo of her dad, but with a different name: Jonathan Sanders. Oh my God, was that who he really was? Was this her father's real name?

Her hands shook and she took a deep breath as a wave of

emotion rose up inside her. For a moment, Ava thought she was going to have a panic attack, but she swallowed and dug her nails into the palm of her hand to keep herself focused.

She looked inside the envelope again. There were two, three . . . four passports. Checking them hurriedly, Ava realized they *all* belonged to her dad. 'Oh shit.' Like the first one, they were all under different names. So, who was he? Who the hell was her dad? Jonathan Sanders? David Harding? Philip Richardson? Roger Bradey? Jackson Abbott? Or maybe he was none of them.

Ava fought back her tears and pulled out the remaining contents of the envelope: a legal document. She unfolded it.

House deeds.

She scanned the document. It was dated a few years ago. The address was in London, but then she stared in horror as she saw who the owner of the house was. It was her. And there was her signature, although she knew she'd never signed for any house. What the hell was going on? What was her father up to?

Putting her hand back into the hole in the wall, Ava rooted around again. There was something else, right at the back, and she swiftly pulled it out. She blinked. 'Oh please, no.' And very slowly she started to unwrap the small hessian package, willing it *not* to be what she thought it was.

'Oh fuck.'

She stared at the gun in her hand, but eventually she snapped herself out of her trance, wrapped it up again and placed it carefully in the envelope along with the passports.

Taking the envelope with her, Ava got up and headed down the stairs.

Right now, her father couldn't tell her who he was, which left it up to her. One way or another, she was going to find out *exactly* who the man lying in a coma in a hospital bed really was.

13

'Avie, you can go to a conference anytime. Avie, listen to me, this is silly.' Back at the house they shared, Tony walked around the bed, watching Ava throwing her clothes into her small suitcase. 'You only got out of hospital yesterday, and both of us know you should've stayed where you were . . . Avie.'

Grabbing a couple of pairs of jeans from her walk-in wardrobe, along with a white linen shirt and jumper, Ava gazed at him warmly. 'I want to get away, focus on work. I think it will be good for me.'

Tony shrugged. 'And how do you make that one out? Avie, no offence, but you look a bit rough.' He smiled sheepishly.

She grinned. 'No offence taken. And look, I'm not pretending that I feel great, but sitting around here worrying about Dad, isn't going to help me.' She hadn't told Tony what she'd found in her dad's house. She hadn't even told him she'd gone to the house, let alone that she needed to go back there to meet the workmen she'd called out to replace the broken kitchen door.

'I was half hoping I could look after you.'

She crossed to the bed where Tony was sitting and sat down next to him, taking his hand. 'Thank you, but I'd rather throw myself into work. The conference is in Brighton, so it's perfect. It's at the Blenheim Hotel. And I reckon a week away, by the sea, is just what I need.'

She held his stare.

'Are you sure it's the right thing to do? I mean, it all seems a bit sudden . . . I didn't even know there was a conference – or did I forget you telling me about it?' He looked sheepish.

'No, I didn't bother mentioning it because, at the time, I wasn't planning on going. But now it seems like a good idea. I can't even start to get my head around what you told me yesterday, and being here, at home, will only make things worse. It'll give me too much time to think.'

'Should I have kept my mouth shut?' Tony sounded upset, but it was for Ava, not for himself.

Ava shook her head. 'No. No, I'm glad you told me.' She was adamant. 'I would've hated it if you'd kept that from me. Secrets are never good.' God, she was a hypocrite.

'As long as you're sure. The whole thing is really shitty for you, Avie, but if I find out anything more, I'll let you know. I promise. But it stays between us. Even if, I mean . . . *when* your dad wakes up, you can't say anything to him.'

'Scout's honour.'

He winked. The strain on his face gave way to a smile. 'When were you *ever* a girl scout? Somehow, I can't imagine it.'

'Actually, you'd—'

A loud knock on the front door interrupted Ava.

Tony got up and crossed to the window. 'It's the police.' He glanced over his shoulder to Ava. 'It's that detective who questioned you in the hospital. Did he say he was going to speak to you again?'

Ava shook her head. She stood up, shoving the rest of the things into her suitcase. 'I need you to do something for me . . . Will you?' She spoke quickly as she clicked her bag closed.

'Yeah, sure.'

'Tell them I'm not here.'

'What?' Tony looked and sounded confused.

'Just tell the police I'm not here.'

'You want me to lie to them?'

'Oh, for God's sake, just do it, *please* . . . Tell them . . . tell them, I've had to go away to a work conference.'

There was another knock, only this time louder.

'Avie, what's going on?'

She grabbed her suitcase and handbag and started heading towards the bedroom door. 'I'll go out the back.'

'Wait.' He grabbed her arm. 'Ava, you need to tell me what the fuck is happening. Why don't you want to talk to them? For a therapist, you never fucking talk.'

She wriggled out of his grip. She didn't want a row. 'I don't want to be late for the conference. And you saw what they were like yesterday – they'll be here for ages, because they have this bee in their bonnet that I have something to do with it.'

Tony clenched his jaw. He stared at her for a while. 'And do you?'

'Don't ask me that.' She gave him a hostile stare back.

'That's not an answer. If you want me to lie to the police for you, then I need to know exactly what I'm dealing with.'

'I've just told you: I don't want to be late.'

'Avie, just because I don't kick up a fuss, because I let things go, that doesn't mean you can treat me like I'm stupid. So I'll ask you again: do you know more than you're letting on?'

Ava shook her head. 'It's crazy to ask me that. I'm your wife, Tony, not some would-be murderer.'

'Are you? Are you my wife? Sometimes I wonder.'

'What's that supposed to mean?' she snapped. 'Go on, what's that supposed to mean?' Anger surged through her.

Without warning, Tony punched the wall. 'You know what it's supposed to mean. If we're married, then we're not supposed to have secrets between us, are we?'

'We haven't.'

'Really? Then tell me what you're hiding.'

She moved past him. 'I'm not hiding anything. Now are you going to do what I ask, or not?'

Tony laughed bitterly. 'It seems you're not giving me much choice.'

Ava stopped at the top of the stairs. The hammering on the door started up again. 'Thank you, and I'm sorry.'

'Just go, if you're going,' he snapped.

'I'll call you.'

Tony blew on his fist, which was now red and raised from thumping the wall. 'Don't bother.'

Deciding it was probably better not to answer him, Ava slipped through the kitchen and out of the back door, heading for her car, pushing away the inevitable guilt. They'd make it up later and she'd show Tony that she appreciated him. But right now, he was the last of her worries.

14

Tony didn't want to start thinking how pissed off he was with Ava. She was testing his patience, to say the least. OK, she was worried about her dad, and this shit about him hiding his identity hadn't helped. But hadn't she been dealing with shit from her dad all the years he'd known her?

He wasn't being unsympathetic. It was the truth. Ava's relationship with her father had always been tense; at times it had been non-existent. That wasn't anything new. What was new was the way she'd been with him lately, and that preceded her dad's latest mess.

Ava had always been a good wife, although she had a tendency to be edgy, combative even. That was one of the things that had attracted him to her in the first place – aside from her looks, of course. But edgy and feisty seemed to have given way to distant and unpredictable of late.

What the fuck did she think she was doing, getting him to lie to the police for her? The way she had run out of the house had made her seem . . . well, it had made her seem like she was hiding something. And that pretty much described the state of their marriage at the moment.

'You look like I feel, mate . . . Fucking hell, that was some session.'

Sitting in the open-plan office, Tony looked up to see one of his colleagues, Joe Kingsley, a seasoned officer, leaning on his desk. Joe was stockily built and rugged; even so, Tony doubted that anyone would take him for a copper.

He grinned at Joe. He had a lot of time for him. The guy was old school, no nonsense, and said it how it was. 'You saying I look shit?' He laughed. 'Because I don't think I look half as bad as you do.'

'Yeah, but I've got an excuse. I was out on a bender last night. Fifteen pints, several whisky chasers . . . So what's your excuse?' Joe grabbed for the opened packet of chocolate biscuits and stuffed one in his mouth. He took a noisy swig of his coffee.

Staring at the computer screen, Tony winced at the image in front of him. He'd been working on a case which involved online paedophile gangs who'd been swapping photos and film footage across the globe.

It was his job to examine and investigate all the memory sticks and digital equipment the team had confiscated on their raids, as well as trying to retrieve deleted data. That was the easiest part. It was having to spend hours studying images of abused kids that got to him. He'd been in this job for just over ten years now, and he'd never got used to it. Something told him he never would.

Grateful for a distraction from the photos he'd been uploading, Tony switched off his computer and gave his full attention to Joe. He yawned. 'I'm all right, mate. Just a bit tired, that's all. What with Ava's dad and Ava being jumped on like that, you could say I've had better weeks.' He shrugged.

Wiping his mouth, Joe nodded. 'Yeah, that's pretty fucked up. How's Ava doing?'

Tony often chatted to Joe, but like a lot of the blokes around the station, he hardly ever opened up about the deeper stuff. The most he or anyone else would ever say was that their missus was giving them grief, or that they'd had to spend a few nights on someone's couch because of trouble at home. That kind of trouble seemed to come with the job; his colleagues had all been there at some point.

'You know Ava,' he said. 'Always the good wife.'

'Tell her she needs to give my missus a few hints, she needs them.'

Tony gave Joe a tight smile. 'She's shaken up. But Ava being Ava, she's just thrown herself back into work . . .' He trailed off, wary of adding anything that might prompt further questions.

There followed a silence between the two men. Eventually, Joe, looking like he didn't quite know how to fill the awkward moment, took another gulp of coffee and said, 'That's good . . . that's good, mate.' Then he lowered his voice, although the office was quiet today. Usually it would be buzzing with analysts and officers. 'Listen, I've got a bit of information I thought you might be interested in . . .' He scanned around before continuing. 'They're opening an investigation. Into Billy Fields.'

Tony sounded surprised. 'They already did . . . I mean, he might be the worst father-in-law of all time, but even he needs due process.'

'I'm not talking about the investigation into the attack that landed him in hospital. This is separate – and it's going to be hush-hush, because there isn't much evidence, just a few flags raised and coppers' gut instincts. And when you've had twenty-odd years on the force like I have, you learn to trust your gut. That and modern-day forensics.' He roared with laughter, causing the others in the open-plan office to look across.

'So, what are they thinking?'

Joe pulled a face. 'Money laundering, drugs . . . the usual. You fancy getting something from the canteen?'

Tony stood up, grabbed his jacket, and began to follow Joe, who continued to talk quietly as he led the way down the corridor.

'It might turn out to be a waste of time, but they want to know if he's involved in anything, and if so, what. It's not every day someone breaks into a residence like that, crammed with valuables, attacks the owner – Billy, or whatever his name is – and leaves without taking anything. So the question is, why. Who has he pissed off? And, from what I understand, whoever did this meant business. Your father-in-law is lucky to be alive. Have you any idea—' Joe came to a stop. 'Sorry, mate, I shouldn't have asked you that. I know he's family.'

Tony shook his head. 'Believe me, there's no love lost between Billy and me. Or between him and Ava. From what she's told me about his parenting skills, they left a lot to be desired. And I told you about that run-in I had with him, just before I got married. I'm being straight with you when I say I've never seen anything that raises any flags.'

'Yeah, well, you know how these things go, they'll probably call on you anyway. It's possible they won't turn up anything, but it all smells a bit sus.'

'I agree,' said Tony, stopping to look him in the eye. 'And Joe, I appreciate you letting me know.'

'*Mr Barclay . . .*'

Tony heard his name being called. He whirled around and let out an audible groan.

'Detective Brown, what can I do for you?'

Joe nodded to Tony. 'I'll go ahead. Those chips are calling me.' He disappeared into the canteen.

'We really need to see your wife.'

Brown stood inches away from Tony, who didn't like his attitude and matched it with a steely coldness. 'I already told you, she's at a conference.'

'Yes, you did, but I was wondering if you'd remembered where she was having that conference? Seems odd that a husband wouldn't know, don't you think?'

'Slipped my mind, that's all.' Tony tried to sound as casual as possible.

Brown nodded. 'You wouldn't be telling us tales, would you, Mr Barclay? You see, we've tried calling her, but she doesn't seem to be picking up her phone. Perhaps she doesn't want to. So, my advice is, if you do speak to your wife, tell her we want to talk to her.' He turned to go, but stopped, and winked. 'You can also tell her, if we don't hear from her, we'll have no choice but to put out a warrant for her arrest.'

15

'For fuck's sake!' Tony grumbled to himself as he sat in traffic, waiting for the temporary lights to change. He could think of a thousand things he'd rather be doing, but having had no luck getting through to Ava, he'd had no choice but to jump in the car and take the long drive from Nottingham to Brighton. And now, after a nightmare motorway drive, due in part to the heavy rain, he'd been stuck on the outskirts of Brighton for the past half hour.

He'd contemplated not making the journey at all, but Brown had acted like a dog with a bit between his bloody teeth, and he didn't want to risk the bastard delivering on his threat to issue an arrest warrant. No doubt he'd have the Brighton police go into the conference mob-handed and embarrass Ava in front of her colleagues.

She'd worked too hard for a jumped-up prick like Brown to come and destroy it all; he knew only too well how much repu-tation mattered in a job like hers. So, yeah, he was pissed off with her, but he wasn't about to let that get in the way of doing what was right. Besides, he didn't enjoy arguing with her, and the thought of seeing her outweighed his anger.

He sighed and finished the last of the tea he'd bought from McDonald's, which was now cold, and was relieved to see the traffic finally beginning to move.

Following the satnav instructions, he took a left. The hotel was five minutes away. He wasn't sure how long he was planning to stay. He was down to work tomorrow, but the idea of spending a couple of days on the coast with Ava was tempting. As she had said herself, it would do her good, and Tony had a feeling it would do them *both* good. He was sure if he spoke to his super, he could get time off. Plus, their anniversary was coming up in the next few days, so this would be perfect.

With a renewed excitement at the prospect of being able to relax with his wife, something they hadn't done for so long, Tony pulled up outside the hotel. He turned off the engine and grabbed the flowers from the passenger seat. It was a cheesy gesture, but it was better than showing up with nothing. Unable to hide his smile at the prospect of seeing her, Tony hopped out of his car with a big grin on his face . . .

'I'm sorry, sir, but we can't give out information like that.' The hotel receptionist, an elderly woman with a heavy-set face, stared at Tony. 'We never give out guest information.'

Tony shook his head. They were going around in circles. 'I understand that, but if you could just call up to Dr Barclay's room, then I'm sure she would come down. Surely that's not against the rules. I'm not asking for a room number, only for you to send her a message from me.'

'I'm sorry, I can't do that.'

He gritted his teeth, trying to keep a lid on his growing irritation. 'But I know she's staying here. She's here for the conference . . . Look, it's really important, I wouldn't ask you to do this otherwise.'

The receptionist's gaze shifted to the flowers Tony was holding. 'I'm sorry.' She folded her arms.

'OK, fine . . .' He went into his pocket and pulled out his wallet, getting out his warrant card. He slammed it on the wooden reception desk. 'Call Dr Barclay, and let her know I'm here, *now*.'

The receptionist's face darkened. 'I already told you, I *can't* do that.'

Tony pushed the warrant card towards her. 'That says you haven't got a choice.'

She smirked at him. 'But since your *wife* isn't actually staying here, I cannot be expected to call her.' She pushed the card back to him.

He frowned. 'I think you must have made a mistake.'

'There's no mistake on my part.' She held Tony's stare.

'But she's here for the conference. She told me.'

The receptionist gave an exaggerated sigh. 'I can't help what she told you, sir.' She stared at the hotel's computer screen. 'From what I can see, she hasn't actually registered for the conference.' She looked up at him. 'I'd suggest calling your wife if you need more information.'

Without another word, Tony marched out of the hotel and into the pouring rain. He made a dash for the car, jumping into the driver's seat. Grabbing his mobile from his jacket, he pressed speed-dial.

It went straight to voicemail.

'Ava, it's me. Call me when you get this, because I have just one question for you . . . where the *fuck* are you?'

16

Ava sat in the back of the cab, her head resting on the window. She was exhausted and her headache was worse than ever. She'd taken a couple of tablets on the train, but it hadn't done anything to shift it, so she'd downed a couple of miniature whiskies. They'd taken the edge off for a while, but now it was back with a vengeance.

'Down here for long, love?' The cab driver looked at her with his watery eyes.

'I'm not sure.' She pulled back her long brown hair and tied it up in a bun.

'Lady of leisure.' He laughed.

'Something like that.' She didn't want to be rude, but the last thing she wanted was to discuss her business with a stranger. Although, part of her evasiveness was down to her having no idea what she was going to do next. She'd rushed down here without a plan. And now she was here, the enormity of the situation was beginning to hit her.

She turned her head to watch the streets of London passing by. She'd told Jude the same story she'd given Tony: she needed to get away for a few days. She'd go to the conference, maybe take some time off.

'Do you want to get out here, love? There's roadworks ahead, but it's down to you. Meard Street is only a few minutes' walk . . . *Oi, watch where you're going!*' The cabbie shouted after a bike which had sped in front, causing him to brake hard.

'Yeah, no problem, whatever you think.'

He pulled over and Ava was only half listening to the driver grumbling about cyclists as she grabbed her bags and handed him twenty-five pounds.

'Keep the change,' she called over her shoulder as she set off in the direction of the house she apparently owned, weaving through Wardour Street before turning into Dean Street.

God, it'd been years since she'd been in London, and only once had she ever been to Soho. The mix of buildings, restaurants and coffee shops among the tall Georgian houses, gave it a contemporary, edgy feel. Ava took a deep breath, enjoying the sensation of blending into the crowd. For the first time in a long time, she felt a sense of freedom, room to breathe, and it dawned on her that when she'd last been here it had been as a single woman, not someone's wife.

Crossing over the road, she frowned as a tall, slim man barged past her.

'Look where you're fucking going, darlin',' he snapped, before disappearing into a cafe on the corner of Meard Street.

Ava didn't bother calling him out on his rudeness, concentrating instead on where she was going. She slowed as she looked for the house number, and halfway down she came to a stop, staring up at the four-storey building.

It looked vast. There was something imposing about the black door with a lion knocker on it. She craned her neck to peer up at the windows, their wooden blinds drawn and revealing nothing. The black railings which ran around the basement stairs were highly polished. The potted trees standing either side of the bottom step were immaculately kept. It was clear that either someone was living here in her father's absence, or he had someone looking after the place for him.

She felt a rush of anger. If he hadn't been attacked, she would *never* have known about this place. It would have remained one more secret in his life.

Pulling out the keys she'd taken from her father's drawer, she tried them one by one in the lock. None of them seemed to fit. *'Shit . . . Shit.'*

In frustration, she kicked the bottom of the door, and a chill ran through her as it opened slowly. She stared at the lock, and it was then she saw that it had been prised open.

The voice screaming in her head told Ava to turn around and walk away, but as usual, she found herself doing the opposite.

Leaving the door open for a quick escape, she placed her suit-case and bag down and stepped into the hallway. Heart racing, she fumbled in the darkness for the light switch.

Crystal chandeliers blinked to life, illuminating the interior.

She stood rooted to the spot, surveying her surroundings . . .

Even to the untrained eye, it was clear no expense had been spared – which came as no surprise to her. Her father liked to be surrounded by lovely things, and the hallway with its hand-painted gold wallpaper and framed art was right up his street. But when did he live here? Had he always? Was this a bolthole to escape to? Did he live here with someone? Was that the secret? Did he think she would have been jealous if she'd known he had a significant other in his life? . . . There were so many questions without answers. Part of her wanted to run back to Nottingham, to Tony, and pretend this was nothing but a bad dream.

That would be the easy way out, but it wouldn't give her peace or closure. So much of her life revolved around shutting things out, and she knew only too well the harm that caused.

She looked to the room on her right. It was a vast lounge; velvet cushions adorned leather Chesterfield sofas, and a grand fireplace dominated the far wall. Suddenly Ava frowned. She found the light switch and stared at the floor. It was strewn with letters and papers. The drawers on the highly polished Chinese cupboard had been ransacked. There was no way her father would have left the place in this state. No way at all.

Her heart still thumping, Ava hurried down the hallway and popped her head into the other room. It was the same story. Every drawer had been pulled open and her father's things had been thrown everywhere.

Someone had been here, and she certainly didn't want to bump into whoever it was. Backing away, Ava moved towards the front door. Her gut told her that this was very much connected with the break-in at her father's place in Nottingham.

Grabbing her bag, but leaving her suitcase in the hall, she pulled the broken front door closed behind her, and hurried out into the street. She was going to book into an Airbnb or a hotel; she wouldn't feel safe staying here, not now. She'd just have to come back in the morning when it was light and have a look around then.

Once again, she ignored that voice in her head, telling her the only thing she was going to find was a whole heap of trouble.

Walking slowly up Meard Street, Ava looked at her phone and saw that there were five voicemails. From Tony, no doubt. She'd deal with him later; right now she needed a drink.

There was a light drizzle as Ava made her way through the bustling streets of Soho. The restaurants and bars were packed, and music drifted out into the streets. As she wandered further, she thought again about listening to Tony's voicemails but just couldn't face it. She decided to send him a quick text instead . . .

Hey babe, hope all's OK. The conference is as boring as I thought it would be! But being away and by the sea is exactly what I needed.

I'm going to have an early night, so I'll call you in the morning. Love you xxx.

She pressed send, then continued to walk, heading for Old Compton Street. She was looking forward to a long drink, her head was racing, and she didn't know what to think anymore. She'd thought she'd been lost before, but that was nothing compared to now.

Seeing a bar on the corner, Ava headed towards it. She'd grab some food later and organize a hotel, as well as call the hospital to see how her dad was doing, but for now all she wanted to do was forget. God, how many times had she said that? She was becoming a cliché even to herself.

The moment she entered the bar, the smell of alcohol hit her. She let the hubbub of chatter and music wash over her as she took in the neon lighting which gave the place an eighties vibe. Leather and silver chairs were placed around the tables, and at the end of the room, over by the roped-off area, was a small dance floor.

'What can I get you, darlin'?' The barman, tall and probably in his early twenties, winked at her as he grabbed some empty glasses from the counter.

'I'll have a double vodka, neat with ice, and a bottle of your best red.'

He nodded, and gave her a handsome grin, showing off his sparkling white teeth. 'How many glasses do you want with it?'

'Just the one.' Ava shouted over the music.

He raised his eyebrows. 'You're going for it tonight.'

'I ordered vodka and wine, not an opinion,' she snapped, feeling humiliated. She didn't need someone booze-shaming her right now, especially a barman.

Putting his hands up in mock surrender, the barman busied

himself pouring her vodka and adding ice. He slammed the drinks on a tray and Ava paid for them, not meeting his eye. She wasn't proud of the way she'd treated him, and she knew she was too defensive when it came to her drinking.

'Thank you,' she muttered, and took the drinks across to the far corner, where she sat down and knocked the vodka back.

She tried to keep her mind on the moment, and concentrated on enjoying the atmosphere of the bar as she sipped her wine and watched people come and go, feeling the warmth of the alcohol take over her body and mind.

The minutes passed by, and with each glass of wine, she felt less on edge. Maybe it wasn't so bad after all. Deciding one more bottle of wine wouldn't hurt, she swayed unsteadily across to the bar, oblivious to the person watching her from the shadows.

17

Ava opened her eyes with some difficulty. God, her head was thumping. And she found herself staring up at the ceiling, trying to work out where she was. As usual she had no idea. She was in a bed, that much was obvious. How she'd got here was anyone's guess. She didn't have any recollection. She didn't even know what time it was.

Trying to adjust her eyes to the dark, Ava screamed when she saw someone sitting in the corner. She couldn't make out who it was, and she scrabbled to sit up, groaning inwardly when she realized she was only wearing her shirt and pants. She didn't even have to ask what had taken place; it was apparent.

'Hi . . . sorry about that, I'm not usually given to screaming in the morning.' She tried to sound chirpy. 'You gave me a fright . . .' But she trailed off, suddenly uneasy. This didn't feel like the usual pickup. Whoever it was hadn't said anything yet, and they continued to sit in the darkness in silence.

Ava could hear them breathing, and she tried again to engage them in conversation. 'So, I . . . I assume we had a good time last night . . . I know I did.' It sounded pathetic, and she knew it, but she also knew that she wasn't comfortable with the way this was going.

She looked across to the door on the other side of the room, and wondered if she should make a run for it. No, that was crazy. She'd hardly get further than the chest of drawers, especially given the way she was feeling. Her best option would be to keep calm and let this play out. If the guy was some weirdo, the last thing she wanted was to spook him and make matters worse.

'Anyway, I probably need to be getting off soon. But thank you for last night.' She spoke in a voice which she often used in her clinic with clients, trying to come across as unruffled. 'I have a lot on today, but I tell you what – why don't you give me your number and maybe we can hook up another time?' Now she was talking too much, but the silence was unnerving, given the situation she found herself in.

'I'd like that.' The voice came from the darkness.

Ava felt a prickle of sweat and tried to put it down to the excess alcohol she'd drunk rather than the fear she could feel creeping in.

'Yeah, me too.' Her voice sounded slightly too high. 'We had a good time, didn't we?'

'The best.' He sounded gruff, and he certainly wasn't giving anything away in his demeanour. 'I haven't had such a good time as far back as I can remember . . . You were wild, babe,' he added.

Hearing him speak about her like that made her heart sink. She wanted to jump in the shower and stay there until she'd scrubbed herself clean. When would she ever learn? 'Anyway, like I say, I've got to get off.' Ava looked around for her jeans, but she couldn't see them.

'Surely not yet, babe. Can't you stay a while longer? I was hoping we could have a repeat performance of last night.'

He stood, and walked across to the curtains, opening them up. It was only then that Ava, her heart racing, got a look at him.

'Oh my God.' She backed away. 'What the fuck are you doing here?'

'That's not very nice, darlin', especially not after last night.' He winked at her and grinned. 'Like you said, we had a great time, didn't we?'

Ava shook her head furiously. She was angry now. 'You think this is a joke . . .' She took another step away from him. 'What did you do to me?' Her voice teetered on the brink.

'And it's good to see you again too.' He chuckled. 'My name's Ben, by the way.'

'I don't care who the fuck you are, but you've got some serious problems.' She stared at the man who'd barged into her office the other day.

'*I've* got problems! Well, maybe you're right, maybe I have, but I don't think I'm the only one here who has, do you?'

'Go to hell . . . How dare you take advantage of me. *How dare you.*' She screamed at him.

'Me?' He smiled again, his manner still cool and collected. 'I think it was the other way round. I'd say it was you who took advantage of me. I was an innocent man until last night. You have opened my eyes to things that I didn't know were even possible, darlin'.' He whistled loudly then burst into laughter.

Ava spun away from him, humiliated and ashamed. 'I don't know what you're playing at, but you're not right in the head.' She struggled to get out the words. The next moment, she felt his hand on her shoulder.

'Get off me.' She shrugged him off and, furious, although more with herself, she turned round to face him, battling back her tears.

'Hey, come on, darlin', calm down . . . I was only having a laugh . . . If it makes you feel better, nothing happened.'

Ava blinked rapidly. 'What?' Her voice was a whisper.

He tilted his head. 'Nothing happened. You know, between you and me. I was only winding you up. It was a bad joke.'

Without warning, Ava slapped him hard across the face. 'You bastard.'

He touched his cheek, and for a moment Ava thought he was going to retaliate, but he nodded. 'OK, I deserved that. I'm sorry, I shouldn't have said what I did, I was out of order.'

The warmth in his words surprised Ava, and she stared at him. Unperturbed, he smiled at her. He was undoubtedly very handsome, but like her father, he knew it. There was an arrogance about him. And maybe she should've been, but for some reason, perhaps to do with her job or her hangover, she didn't actually feel afraid of him. However, that didn't stop Ava noting how strange his behaviour was.

'Look, I know you probably want me to go, but let me try to explain. I'm not here to do you any harm, I swear. Just give me a minute – hear me out, that's all I'm asking. Then if you want me to go, I will.'

She stared at him. 'OK, fine, but you can start by telling me who the hell you are. What do you want from me?'

'You could say I'm a mate of your dad's. What I told you when I came to see you in the office was true, I did just want to talk to you. Seriously.'

He held a smile while Ava tried to process everything. 'Do you know how weird that sounds? And . . . and you being here, it's fucked up. You do get that?' she asked, wondering if he really did. So many of her clients had no concept that their behaviour didn't fit with social norms or was downright wrong.

He nodded. 'I won't argue with that. I shouldn't have come to the office, but I had time to kill, and I was in the area . . . Not my finest hour, babe. I can see how it must look, and me being here now. I guess, if I was in your shoes, I'd think I was a bit of a weirdo too. But when I saw what was happening last night in the bar, I couldn't—'

'Then why act so strangely?' Ava interrupted, wondering if he'd followed her. She didn't want to talk to him about last night.

'And how come, when I asked my dad about you, he said he didn't know you and you were only asking for directions.' She tried to read his body language but he was too controlled, giving little away.

Ben shrugged. 'What can I say?'

'You can start by telling me the truth.' Her tone was hard.

Ava watched him walk to the side of the bed. He stooped to pick something up – her jeans. 'Here . . .' He threw them across to her. She caught them, and inwardly shuddered. She didn't even want to try to think how she'd ended up with him in this bedroom, wherever the hell this bedroom was.

'I am telling the truth,' he went on. 'Me and your dad are friends.'

'So why didn't he admit that?'

Ben shrugged. 'You know what he's like, he doesn't give up information easily, even to old mates and family.'

Ava thought she could detect a hint of bitterness in his tone, but she didn't say anything. She pulled on her jeans, not knowing what to think. She wanted to believe that he was who he said he was; rather that than feel she was stranded in a room with someone completely unbalanced.

She stared over his shoulder, looking around the opulent bedroom. There was a huge chandelier hanging down from the ceiling, the wallpaper was gold and silver, a plush cream velvet couch lined one side of the room and paintings hung from the walls. 'Anyway, where've you brought me?'

Ben looked at her strangely, his piercing eyes quizzical. 'You don't know where you are?'

Once again there was something about the way he said it that made Ava think she should know exactly where she was. Not wanting to admit anything to him, she snapped, 'Of course, I do . . . what I meant to say is . . .' she searched for words, but couldn't find any '. . . is . . . Look, this is crazy. Why have you been following me anyway? That's not normal.' She let out a long sigh; she could do with either the hair of the dog, or a nice strong coffee. 'You know I told the police about you? They'll probably want to speak to you.'

'What happened to your dad wasn't anything to do with me. You must know that.' He reached for his jacket, which was hanging on the back of the chair, and pulled out a packet of cigarettes. 'Mind if I smoke?' She shook her head as he lit up and inhaled deeply. 'I was there to talk to your dad, not to hurt him.'

Ava suddenly frowned. 'How did you know about it? If it wasn't you, how do you know?'

He laughed. 'Calm down, detective . . . no, that's your other half, ain't it? Tony?'

She bristled. She didn't like the thought of this man knowing about Tony, or anything to do with her life for that matter, when she had no idea who he was. 'Who told you about my husband?' She frowned.

'I know a lot about you. Like I said, I'm a friend of your dad's.' Yet again he shrugged and held her stare. 'And if you must know, it was one of your dad's neighbours who told me, when I went round there. Sorry, Sherlock, that's as exciting as it gets.' He winked.

There was something too smooth about him, and it wasn't just the arrogance. As much as Ava wasn't afraid of him, she was having a hard time trusting all that he was saying. 'It still comes down to the fact my dad flat out denied he knew you.'

Ben squinted his eyes as the cigarette smoke went into them. 'And he always tells you the truth, does he?'

Ava glared at him, then grabbed her trainers and slipped them on. There was no way she was going to admit to him that her dad had lied to her all her life. 'Why is it that I don't believe you?' She looked at him. 'Why don't I believe that you haven't got something to do with what happened to my dad?'

He took another puff on his cigarette. 'You know what, I think you *do* believe me. Maybe you don't want to, but you do. Otherwise, you wouldn't be so calm with me being here. You'd be trying to get out of the room, trying to save yourself, if you really thought I'd tried to kill your dad and knocked you unconscious too . . . Don't you see, babe, one of us is lying – and it ain't me . . .'

18

It was only when Ava went out of the door, along the corridor and down the stairs that she realized where she was. The house in Meard Street.

Her humiliation was complete.

'Don't you want to know what happened last night?' Ben asked as they made their way into the marbled hallway.

She looked straight into his eyes. Ava knew the eyes often betrayed the true emotions of a person, and she'd expected to see confirmation that he was taunting her. Instead she saw only warmth and genuine concern.

While she was curious about how she'd wound up back inside the house, she wasn't sure she wanted to hear right now. Especially when it involved her ending up in bed with only her shirt and pants on, and him in the bedroom with her. 'Why would I need to ask? I already know what happened,' she lied.

'Is that right? You can remember exactly what went down?'

She saw the glimpse of a smile, but it wasn't unkind. That didn't stop it triggering her. 'Yeah, I can.'

His smile grew. 'Have it your way, but if you do want to fill in any blanks – and I'm not saying there are any – you only need to ask.'

Ava fumed. It was clear that Ben knew she wasn't telling the truth, but she wasn't going to give him the satisfaction of hearing her admit it. 'I won't. My memory is crystal clear, thank you very much. Anyway, let's get back to you . . . you didn't answer me earlier when I asked if you'd been following me . . . So come on then, did you follow me all the way from Nottingham?'

Ben raised his eyebrows. 'Oh, come on, what do you take me for? You're going a bit over the top now, ain't you?'

'Then why are you here, at my dad's house? And don't tell me it's a coincidence.'

'I wasn't going to – well, I kind of was, with you being here . . .' Ava detected the slight pause before he continued: 'Your old man asked me to look after the place. I keep an eye on it for him, while he's travelling or up in Nottingham.'

'So when are you going to call the police?' Ava folded her arms.

'The police? What the hell are you talking about?'

'The break-in.' She frowned. 'When I arrived yesterday, the door had been prised open.'

Hearing what Ava had to say, Ben seemed to relax. 'Oh that – it's pointless. The Old Bill won't do anything. It'll be a waste of their time.'

'How will it be a waste of their time? That's what they're there for. They might be able to take fingerprints or something.' She shook her head. 'Fine, if you won't call them, I will.'

'No,' he blurted.

She tilted her head to look at him. 'Why not?'

It was the first time she'd seen Ben ruffled.

'Go on, why not?' she pushed.

'It's . . . it's a waste of time, that's all.'

She pulled out her mobile from her back pocket. 'I don't think it is. Who knows, it might be connected with what happened in Nottingham.'

'There you go again, playing detective. Leave it, won't you?' He rubbed his head.

Ignoring him, Ava punched in 101, and was about to press dial when he gently took hold of her mobile. 'No, don't. Harvey wouldn't want you bringing the Old Bill round.' His words rushed out. '*Please.*'

She stared at him. 'Harvey? Are you talking about my dad? Why did you call him Harvey?'

'What?'

'You said "Harvey".'

Ben's face darkened. 'Did I?'

'Yes, you did, and you know you did.'

Seemingly regaining his cool, Ben leaned against the wall. 'Slip of the tongue. I'm not great on names at the best of times, and when I'm tired, it's even worse . . . Look, I need a glass of water.' His eyes darted around, and Ava wondered what he was trying to work out, then she watched him march towards a closed door and open it. It led into a large drawing room.

She strode down the hall and stepped in front of him. 'I thought you said you knew this place? If you look after this place for him, how come you don't know where the kitchen is?'

'What are you talking about?'

'You, being a liar . . . How about you tell me what's through there.' Ava pointed at a closed door across the hallway. 'Or what's through that door over there?'

Ben's face reddened. 'I don't need to play your fucking games,' he growled.

'I'm not playing games, I'm merely asking you: what's through there? All you're doing is lying to me, over and over again . . . I want to know what the fuck is going on, but first off you're going to tell me what's behind that door.'

His eyes skimmed over Ava's face.

'No.' He shook his head. 'If you want to play this game, why don't you tell me? Go on, tell me.' He turned the spotlight on her, something she was used to her clients trying to do when they knew they were in the wrong or lying.

Keeping her cool, she shrugged. 'It's no secret that I don't know, I've never been here before.'

Ben looked genuinely surprised. 'Oh, come on, don't give me that shit.'

'It's true, I had no idea this place existed until . . . well, until the other day.' Ava suddenly felt emotional, and hated the fact that her vision was blurred with tears. She wiped them away. 'I also had no idea that my dad isn't called Billy Fields. I don't even know who he is. Is that enough truth for you? Imagine that, not knowing what your own fucking dad is called.' She ran across to her suitcase, which was still where she'd left it yesterday, flicked it open and grabbed the envelope she'd hidden under her clothes.

Rushing back across to Ben, she pulled out the handful of passports, and pushed them into his chest. 'Here . . . see . . . look . . . all different names. The police don't even know who he is. Do you know how it feels to know all he's ever done is lie to me?' Why was she telling him this? She wanted to stop but she couldn't help herself. 'So if you want to call out bullshit, start with him.'

Ben silently thumbed through the passports, then threw them down on the hall table.

Ava watched him closely. It crossed her mind that, showing him the passports, and telling him the little she knew about what was going on, could well be a big mistake. Not that she'd planned to open her mouth. It felt like everything was out of her control.

He sat down on the stairs and took out another cigarette. He lit it slowly, then smiled up warmly at Ava. 'He's called Harvey Fletcher. That's what I've always known him as.'

'Really?' She sounded childlike.

'Yeah. That ain't bullshit – and I'm sorry he's been an arsehole about things.'

'But why has he got all these passports?'

'Your guess is as good as mine.'

Ava started to pace. 'I think you know more than you're letting on.'

He leaned back on the stair. 'I don't know anything. I really don't . . . but I do have a confession . . . It was me who broke into the house.'

Puzzled, she turned to him. 'Why?'

'Stupid, really . . . I left the keys at my place, and I didn't want to have to go back home. It would've been a five-hour-plus round trip.'

'So you broke in?'

'You make it sound bad. I was going to get it repaired.'

'And what about the stuff everywhere?' It occurred to Ava that he seemed to have an answer for everything.

'I'll tidy that up. I didn't know you were going to be here, did I?' He shrugged. 'Sorry, but I was looking for the details of . . . of the housekeeper who comes and cleans. She has a spare set. I thought I could use hers. I only broke the one lock, so I reckoned it would save having to call a locksmith. They fucking cost a fortune, that lot . . .' He trailed off.

'So why not just tell me that?'

He drew on his cigarette. 'Well, I was going to, but you were too busy trying to call the Old Bill.'

She sat down next to him, took the cigarette out of his hand, put it to her own mouth and took a deep long drag.

Still trying to work out how much of what he'd told her was true, she chose her words carefully. 'So, where did you meet my dad?' She gave him a sideways glance.

'Here . . . London, at a bar . . . I can't quite remember . . . Yeah, I think we got talking one night and played a bit of pool. He beat me, of course.'

That much rang true to Ava; she'd never known her father to lose to anyone. He was proud of that fact.

'Then we stayed in contact,' Ben continued. 'And I guess we've been mates ever since. Bit of a boring story, really.'

'And how long ago was that?'

Ben took the cigarette back from her. 'If you're trying to catch me out, this isn't anything to trip me up with. I've known him ten years, give or take.'

'And what exactly does my dad do? What's his line of work?'

'Jesus! Why all the questions, babe?' There was a slight irritation to his voice.

'Well, he's never told me, so I was hoping you might.'

Ben sighed. 'He's in property, that's all I know . . . Look, it feels as if you're trying to find something on him . . . on me, and there isn't anything. I swear.'

Her eyes rested on the passports. 'Then why the fake names? Why tell me all his life his name was Billy Fields, when he tells you that his name is Harvey Fletcher?' She shifted to look directly at him. 'How do you know?'

'How do I know what?'

'That Harvey Fletcher is his real name? How can you be sure if you've only known him ten years? He could've called himself anything before that.'

'I don't know. Maybe your old man just wanted a fresh start. I'm sure even you have skeletons in your closet you don't want other people to know about.'

Ava wasn't able to hold his stare. It made her feel uncomfortable, and she chewed on her lip. 'I think the person who will really hold the answers is my mum. Well, she would if I knew where she was.' Then as if to answer Ben's unasked question, Ava added, 'She walked out on us when I was two or three. Haven't heard anything since . . . That's life, hey?' For some reason Ava felt emotional and she stood up and dusted the cigarette ash off her clothes. 'But before I do anything, I need to call my husband.' She looked sheepish as she turned back to Ben. 'I told him I was at a work conference.'

Ben got up as well.

He gave her a half smile, and let out a chuckle. 'Ah, I see, so now you're going to play the good wife . . . It seems like we're all lying, doesn't it?'

19

In a small top-floor flat on the other side of London, Dean Burling watched Jed Carter, a man who he'd trust with his life, bring his foot down into the stomach of Sam Walters. The weight and severity were so great that immediately Sam began to cough, screeching out in pain as blood oozed from the wounds he'd already sustained from the beating Jed had dished out.

Dean's weathered face bore the marks of a life well lived, with deep wrinkles, a crooked nose, and a deep scar across his cheek. With cold, calculating eyes, he slowly walked over to the middle of the room where Sam was lying. A well-worn couch faced the television on a sturdy metal stand and a coffee table sat in the middle holding a remote control and a couple of books. The walls were adorned with framed photographs, and light filtered through the sheer curtains.

He looked down at Sam's battered face, then raised his foot and booted him in the mouth. Blood spurted out, along with another scream from Sam.

'Stop with all the noise, mate, it's starting to do my head in . . . Now, I'll ask you again, what has your brother told you about the money? What has Ben said about it?'

'I . . . I don't know anything about any money . . . I swear, I don't know.' Sam's words were barely audible.

'Well, that's going to be a problem for us and for you, because we need you to help us.' Dean pulled a tissue from his pocket, bent down and wiped Sam's face.

'I can't, because I don't know.' Sam breathed heavily. 'You need to ask him.'

Dean grinned. 'Why didn't we think of that?' Sarcasm dripped from his words. 'We prefer to ask you, because we reckon you might be more willing to tell us than Ben.'

Sam stared at him. 'I can't tell you something I don't know.'

'I'm not sure you're taking me seriously, Sam. Do I look like I'm someone that's joking?' Dean growled out his words.

Sam looked back at him, eyes wide with terror, and shook his head.

'No, that's right. At least we agree on something. So, a word of advice: start remembering everything he's told you, or you're going to know what pain really is.'

Tears of agony and fear ran down Sam's cheek. 'Please, you've got to believe me, I don't know, I haven't seen him for a while. I spoke to him last week, and that's it.' His words were muffled as he struggled to speak through broken teeth and swollen lips.

Dean looked up at Jed, then back down at Sam. His eyes were dark and impassive. He pulled back his sleeve and checked his watch. 'I tell you what I'm going to do, I'm going to give you one minute to remember. If you don't come up with a better answer than "I don't know", I'm going to get Jed here to start doing some serious damage. Do you understand me, Sam?'

With blood pouring from the side of his face and the gash on his forehead so deep the flesh underneath was exposed, Sam spluttered, 'Please . . . look, I'll do anything. But I just don't know.'

'Where's your phone?'

Sam swallowed. 'It's in my bedroom.'

'And the passcode?'

'It's 1889 – but you won't find anything on it.'

Dean gestured with his head. Jed immediately left to search for the phone, while Dean, who was several inches shorter than his sidekick but much stockier, turned his attention back to Sam. 'Can't you see, mate? It really is in your best interest to tell me. It'll save that pretty face of yours.'

Sam closed his eyes.

Dean's mop of unruly red hair was flattened by sweat. 'Suit yourself, if that's the way you want it, so be it. Don't say I didn't try and help you . . .' He trailed off as Jed walked back through carrying the mobile.

'Give it here,' Dean snapped. He had thought that Ben's little brother, from what Jed had found out about him, would be an easy touch. There was no way Ben hadn't confided in his brother; by all accounts they were close, even if Sam was a law-abiding citizen, making a living as some sort of music teacher. Yet here he was, refusing to divulge anything, as though his life didn't depend on it.

'Call him.' Dean pushed the mobile into Sam's hand. 'Call your brother and ask him about it.'

Sam struggled to talk. 'He . . . he won't say anything . . . He'll know something's wrong if I ask.'

Dean prodded him in the side of his head. 'I don't care how you do it, Sam. One way or another, I want you to get him to tell you about the money. *Now do it!*'

With one eye partly closed, Sam stared at Dean. 'No.'

'You what?'

Sam licked his bloody lips. 'I said, no.'

Dean let out a scornful laugh. He glanced at Jed, who looked surprised. 'You're either brave or fucking stupid. I'd say it's probably the latter.'

He grabbed a clump of Sam's hair, twisting it in his hand. Then he smashed Sam's head hard against the floor, once, twice, three times. '*Call him.*' Dean spat the words through his teeth. '*Now.*'

Sam gave the tiniest shake of his head. 'Go to hell.'

Hearing those words, Dean swung his fist hard, battering Sam's face, feeling his teeth on his fists as he pushed them into the back of his mouth.

Panting, Dean stood and wiped his hands on his trousers. He looked down at Sam, who wasn't moving. 'Come on, let's get out of here.'

'You don't want me to finish him off?' Jed asked.

Dean stared down at Sam. 'No, pick him up and put him in the car . . . I've got another idea, let's show Benjamin and Harvey we're not playing games . . .'

20

'Hey, it's me. I'm so sorry I didn't call you yesterday, everything got so busy.' Ava sipped the triple-shot latte she'd just bought from the Italian coffee shop in Dean Street. Finally, she was starting to feel human again. 'I've been rushed off my feet, this conference is a bit full on for my liking.'

There was silence on the phone.

'Hello?' Ava frowned. 'Are you still there.'

'*Yeah, it must be the signal . . . So you didn't you get my messages yesterday?*'

Fuck, she'd forgotten to listen to them.

'No, sorry . . . I actually didn't get them . . . I think it's this phone, it's really temperamental, I might need to get another one . . . Was it something important?' She took another sip of coffee, careful not to burn her lips as she watched Ben walk out of the deli opposite with a couple of sandwiches.

Was she being foolish, speaking to him about her dad? Because of the job she did, she'd become sceptical of people and what they had to say. Yet here she was, with a complete stranger, discussing things she'd never told Tony about. The irony didn't escape her. That was exactly what her clients did with her. Instead of speaking to family and friends, they felt more comfortable paying her.

But it was crazy that somehow, in less than twenty-four hours, she'd gone from thinking that Ben was some unhinged chancer, possibly even responsible for the attack on her dad, to a guy she was about to have breakfast with.

Why wasn't she doubting her wisdom in believing him? Perhaps it was because everything he'd told her had a ring of truth to it. She was still uneasy about the way he'd strolled into her office, and her father's denial that he knew him. But for the time being she was setting those doubts aside. Right now, she was desperate to find out the truth about her father. And she knew only too well that desperate people did desperate things.

'. . . *No, nothing important . . . nothing to worry about.*'

Ava snapped herself out of her thoughts to listen to Tony. She didn't want him to think she wasn't interested in what he was saying. 'Oh good,' she replied, trying hard to muster up some enthusiasm.

'*I was checking how the conference was going, checking in with you really.*'

Ava's gaze followed Ben as he gestured to her that he was going into another shop. She nodded and continued to talk to Tony at the same time. '. . . Are you all right, Tony? You sound a bit distant. A bit low?'

'*Oh, I'm fine.*'

'Well, you don't sound it . . . Is this because of how we left things? Look, I'm sorry – I should never have treated you like that. I couldn't face having to speak to the police. It's all been a lot to take in . . . Which reminds me, I was hoping you could do me a favour.'

'*Another one?*' The bitterness dripped down the phone.

'I'm sorry, I wouldn't ask if it wasn't important. I swear, Tony, once this conference is over and done with, I'll take some time off work, and maybe we can book ourselves a holiday. Somewhere hot, celebrate our anniversary in style. You and me. What do you reckon?'

'Sounds good but, like you say, you need to get that conference over and done with.'

Ava didn't say anything for a moment. She could hear how much Tony was trying to rein in his temper. 'I really am sorry, Tony . . . I know I've been a bit of a nightmare lately. What with work being full on and then all this crap with Dad, it's kind of made me question my whole life. I'm so angry with Dad. And I know, when he comes round, nothing will change. He won't tell me anything and I'll be in the dark again. That's why I want you to help me trace my mum.'

'Are you serious?'

'Absolutely. I've thought about it for a while, and now, after everything, I feel I don't have any other choice. I can't just go back to how things were . . . If there was any way I could do it without involving you, I would. And yes, I realize how much trouble you'd be in if you got caught doing this, but I can't go through the proper channels. Dad's got all the birth certificates and document tucked away somewhere, and I wouldn't know where to start looking for them . . . So if there's a chance that, well . . . if there's a chance she might be on your central computer, then it might be a way of finding out who my dad actually is . . . *Please, Tony.'*

Ava closed her eyes, taking a deep breath as she waited for him to speak.

'Fine, I'll do it. What's her name?'

'Claudia Davies.' She saw Ben walking towards her. 'Look, I need to go, Tony, but I'll text you everything I know about her. Age – or the age I think she is – and the address we used to live at before she left. I don't know, maybe those details might help narrow it down a bit? I'll speak to you later.' She clicked off the phone as Ben arrived in front of her.

'Who was that?' he asked.

'Tony. I couldn't get through before, so I was checking in now. I thought it best.' She pushed the mobile into her jacket pocket and took the sandwich Ben had bought for her. 'Thanks.'

'So how long have you been married?'

'Why do you ask?'

Ben stepped out of the way of a group of tourists. 'No reason. You just don't seem . . . how can I put it? Well, the way you are, you just don't seem . . .'

'Like a good wife?' She stared at him, projecting how she felt about herself.

'No! Fuck, no . . . I wasn't going to say that, babe.' He laughed. 'Although, now you come to mention it, darlin' . . .'

'Go to hell,' Ava growled. 'You don't know anything about me.'

'Hey, I was joking. And you were the one who said it.'

'Has anyone told you, your jokes aren't funny?' Ava fumed, even though there was a part of her that felt like she was being unreasonable. It was clear Ben was just enjoying a bit of what he thought of as 'chirpy banter'. Her father was the same; perhaps that's why it was a pet peeve of hers.

'I was actually going to say—'

'Whatever it was, Ben, I'm not interested,' Ava cut in. 'Like I say, you don't know me, and let's keep it that way, shall we?'

He nodded, and Ava couldn't quite work out what the look on his face meant. For a while neither of them said anything, just sat eating their sandwiches and watching the Soho traffic crawl by.

'You didn't tell him anything, did you?' Ben asked. 'Tony. You didn't mention anything about me or the house? He is the Old Bill, remember. If your dad is involved in anything . . . dodgy, you wouldn't want Tony finding out, would you?'

'He is also my husband.' She glared at him.

'Yeah, I realize that.' There was a slight impatience to Ben's voice. 'But I can't see your dad thanking you for discussing his affairs.'

Ava was on the verge of telling him she didn't care what her dad did or didn't thank her for, but she decided it was none of his business how she felt about her father. Neither did she tell him she'd asked Tony to trace her mum. Again, it had nothing to do with Ben. Nothing at all. It was her business how she went about things. The only thing she wanted from Ben were answers.

'No, I didn't say anything to him – I'm not stupid. We just had a chat about our anniversary, that's all.' She held her smile.

Ben took a bite of his roast beef sandwich. He stared at her, his handsome face marked with doubt. 'You ain't lying to me?'

'I've already said, I didn't. Besides, lies have a way of catching up, don't they?'

Tony stared at the mobile he held in his hand. Why the hell hadn't he called Ava out on her bullshit? Why hadn't he told her he knew about her not being at the hotel or the conference? He was angry with himself. But maybe he'd been hoping that she would come clean, and there'd be an innocent explanation . . . Maybe there still was.

Or perhaps the truth was he'd been too afraid of the answer to ask the question.

Sighing, Tony rubbed his head and looked down at the piece of paper he'd written the name on. *Claudia Davies.*

He turned off his computer and yawned.

He hadn't got back to Nottingham until late, but he'd decided to come into work after all, better that than stay at home with his imagination working overtime, as it was now. 'Hey, Joe, can you do me a favour?' He called across to his colleague, who was sitting at the opposite desk.

'Sure, what's up?'

'I need you to trace a name for me. I'll give you more details later, when I get them.'

Joe raised his eyebrows and shrugged his shoulders at the same time. 'Why can't you do it? You've got access.'

Not wanting the officers at the other end of the room to get wind of what he was saying, Tony stood and walked across to Joe.

'The thing is, mate, between you and me, it's personal, I don't want it to come back on me, especially as they're already looking into Billy Fields. It wouldn't look good if I'm searching names connected with him. But if you do it, there'll be no connection with you . . . All this shit with her dad has made Ava want to try to find her mum.'

Joe seemed surprised. 'What about birth certificates and stuff? Wouldn't that be easier?'

'She's not sure where her dad kept them. I know it's a long shot, but who knows, her mum might have a record or something. Sorry for asking.'

'It's no problem.' Joe sounded casual. 'I know you'd do the same for me. Well, you have done.' He laughed and reached out for the small piece of paper. 'I'll see what I can do. I won't be able to do it until later though, I need to get a report in to the super first.'

'That's fine, no rush, mate.' Tony took a deep breath. 'But there is one other thing.' He grabbed a pen off Joe's desk and scribbled something else down. 'I need you to trace this as well, but I'd rather you did that first, before looking up her mum.'

Joe looked at the paper and popped a mint into his mouth. He sucked on it, rolling it around with his tongue. 'What is this?'

Tony brought his voice down to a whisper. 'It's my wife's mobile number . . . I want to know where the fuck she is . . .'

21

Ava sat in the passenger seat of Ben's Range Rover. The rain was hammering down now, and she was grateful for the warmth of the car. 'For someone who house-sits, you've got a really nice car.' She turned to him. 'What is it you *actually* do, Ben?'

Finishing off his cappuccino, Ben turned to look at her. Hands down, she was probably one of the most attractive women he'd laid eyes on in a very long time, but Christ it was clear she had major problems. Fuck knows how she dealt with other people when she had so much shit going on herself.

Last night was messy, that was the best he could say about it. He didn't know what he'd expected when he'd followed her, but given all that, there was something about her, and it wasn't just to do with the way she looked. She was smart and sassy, and he respected that she wanted answers and was determined to get them, even though he wasn't completely sure if that was in his best interest.

He stared at her intently. 'You mean, how can I afford this car? That's what you really mean, isn't it?'

'No . . . no . . .'

'Oh, come on, don't lie, I can see it in your face.' He winked at her. 'If you must know, it's my brother's car. Sam has a big plush job in the city, and I think he takes pity on me, so he lends me his cars and takes me on holiday a couple of times a year.' It was a complete lie, but where he got his money from was his business. Although, as it happened, Ben was proud of the fact that Sam hadn't gone down the same route he had. Yes, there were several years between them, but it still amazed Ben how Sam had kept on the straight and narrow, gone to university, become a teacher, and was an all-round good guy. Ironically, someone Ava would probably approve of.

Ava grinned. 'Was it that obvious?'

'Yes, it was.' He laughed. 'Next time, just ask me and I'll tell you the truth. As I say, I've got nothing to hide, darlin'.'

'Yeah, me neither.'

They both fell silent. The only sounds were the quiet hum of the car heater and the rain tapping on the roof.

Flicking the windscreen wipers on, Ben pulled out a cigarette, lit it and opened the window slightly, so as not to fill the car with smoke. 'I know I haven't said it before, doll, but I am gutted about what happened to your old man.' He sounded sincere.

'Thank you.' Ava smiled, though inwardly she was wondering if Ben was genuinely concerned about her dad. For some reason, she wasn't entirely convinced.

Ben shook off the intensity of the moment and took another drag on his cigarette. 'So where are you going to start? Have you any idea where to look for your mum?'

Ava wasn't about to share that, as they spoke, Tony was hopefully looking her mum up on the police database. She shrugged. 'Well, my dad is hardly the scrapbook and photo album sort of guy. I've no idea what she looks like. She could walk past me in the street and I wouldn't know. God knows where he's put all the documents.'

'You sound angry.' He squinted at her.

She shook her head. 'I am so pissed off with him – isn't it obvious?' She laughed at herself, then sighed loudly. 'When I was younger, I used to blame her . . . Mum. Every problem I had as a kid, I always put it down to her leaving . . . Stupid, I know.

I used to imagine what it would be like to have a mother, what it would feel like. Especially when I watched my friends' mums. And even though I didn't know anything about her, I convinced myself I was going to be the total opposite of her.'

'Like how?'

He handed her his cigarette, which she took, taking a puff before answering. 'Stay loyal to my family, work hard and provide for them . . . be a good mother eventually, be a good wife . . .' She raised her eyebrows. 'But of course, now, I realize it wasn't about her at all. It had more to do with how I felt about Dad – his arrogance, his bullshit, his excuses . . . Though my job would tell me relationships are complex and everything isn't a matter of being one thing or another.' She peered at Ben through the smoke. 'But I reckon Billy Fields – sorry, should I say, *Harvey Fletcher* – might just be the exception to the rule.' She let out another self-deprecating laugh, and reflected not only on her dad, but on Tony. Her relationship with her husband was complicated, on her side anyway. Then she shrugged and smiled at Ben. 'Sorry, you don't want to hear my shit . . . Do you reckon I'm too old to have daddy issues?'

Ben winked at her. 'I wouldn't like to say . . . How old are you, anyway?'

'Thirty-nine.'

Ben's face blanched. 'Thirty-nine?'

Once again, Ava couldn't read Ben. He was good at covering up what he was really thinking. She supposed she'd met her match. 'You sound surprised. How old did you think I was?'

'I didn't, but . . . I mean, how didn't I know?' It sounded more like he was speaking to himself than her.

Ava opened her window slightly. 'Why would you know how old I was, and what does it matter?' She didn't add that he seemed to have a problem with it.

'It doesn't matter. I'm surprised, that's all . . . So you were born when he was . . . So Harvey, he must've been twenty years old, give or take . . . Have you always lived with him?'

'Sorry, am I missing something here?' Ava wondered.

Ben ran his fingers through his hair, and Ava picked up on his agitation. 'No . . . no, not at all.'

'Are you OK?'

'I'm good.'

For a moment Ava didn't say anything. Ben's body language made it clear how ill at ease he was, yet his words kept up the illusion he was taking it all in his stride. 'Look, if you want to get back home, I'll tidy your dad's place up. I don't mind paying for a locksmith, either. Then we can get a set of keys made, in case you can't get hold of the housekeeper.'

'Housekeeper?'

Momentarily, Ben seemed puzzled, which only piqued Ava's interest all the more.

'Oh yeah, sorry . . . er, no, I broke it, I'll pay for it. And actually, I thought I might stay down in London for another day or so. That way, if I can be of any help to you, you only have to ask. The only thing is, I usually stay at your dad's when I'm down here – that's not going to be a problem is it?'

Every part of Ava wanted to say it was. She wanted to be alone to gather her thoughts, try to work out what was going on. She wanted to look around her father's house without anyone else there, particularly Ben, although the conversation had certainly made her more curious about how much of what he was saying was true.

'No, it's fine, stay . . . It's your job and I don't want to get in the way.' She was cordial.

Ben nodded. 'Good, that's settled then. I can cook you something tonight, if you fancy . . . or is that too weird?'

'Yeah. Too weird.'

They both laughed, but Ava sensed how hollow it was. She peered out of the window for a moment, and as she watched the rain, she decided that perhaps it wasn't only her mother who might hold the answers to her father's past. She had a strong suspicion that there was much more to Ben's connection with her dad than he was letting on. She supposed only time would tell, and right now, time was all she had.

22

It was the next morning when Ava woke up, still fully dressed in the clothes she'd been wearing the day before. She hadn't been planning to sleep that much, but yesterday after the conversation with Ben in the car, she'd laid down for what she thought would only be a couple of hours to sleep her hangover off.

Stretching over to look at her mobile, she noticed that Tony hadn't called her, which was strange, because even if he didn't have any news on her mum, which was certainly a long shot, she would've expected him to text her. Clearly, he was still upset from the other day. She didn't blame him. She'd put him in an awkward position. She wasn't proud of that, but everything had happened so quickly.

'Knock, knock, sleepy head . . . can I come in?' Ben's chirpy voice – perhaps a little too chirpy – boomed through the door.

'Yeah, sure. Nothing to see here,' Ava called back to him.

A moment later, the door was opened. 'I come bearing gifts . . . I thought you might like a cappuccino and an egg sandwich to start off the morning.'

'I'll have the coffee, but maybe I'll take a rain check on the egg sandwich, if that's all the same with you.' She smiled and watched Ben, who'd showered and was dressed in a pair of dark denim jeans topped off with a navy hoodie and expensive trainers, saunter across the room.

It had been obvious from the first time she set eyes on him in her office that he prided himself on the way he looked. He was handsome and had the muscular frame of someone who worked out, but Ava couldn't help thinking that everything about Ben was a little too good to be true. There was something behind the Mr Nice image that rankled with her, and while he was here, she was determined to watch him closely.

'Thanks.' She took the coffee, and proceeded to fire off a text to Jude, checking in that everything was fine in the office. Even though she wouldn't be going in for a while, she was open to having phone meetings or Zoom calls if her clients needed them. It felt very strange not being at work or preparing for work even. And although it had only been a few days, she felt lost without the daily routine of going into the office.

Work had been her anchor. It felt like the one thing that defined her. The one thing she was good at. The other labels in her life had never felt like they fitted. The good daughter, friend, wife – all those roles she'd never believed she could quite live up to. She was a mess, and she was the first one to admit it.

Pushing that thought aside, as it would only bring her down, Ava wrote a quick text to Tony while listening to Ben chat away.

'How are you feeling this morning?'

She glanced up. 'Mmm, much better, maybe I'd go far as saying I feel almost human.'

Ben sat on the end of the king-size bed. 'Well, I'm glad, because I wondered whether you'd fancy going on a little car ride?'

Pressing send, Ava placed her phone to the side. 'And why would I want to do that?' She had hoped that Ben might go out today, do whatever it was he did, leaving her alone to go through her father's things, and have some time to think.

'What you were saying yesterday, it got me thinking: maybe some of your dad's old friends would be able to give you some answers. Perhaps they'd know where your mum was, or at least give you a few more clues about her. I know a couple of his mates, the ones that knew him from back in the day.'

Ava swung her legs off the bed. 'Why are you being so helpful?'

'Am I?' Ben feigned an innocence which Ava didn't buy. Her clients were forever trying to pretend they'd had no idea of the consequences of their actions, when in fact they were manipulating everyone around them, and knew *exactly* what they were doing. Just like Ben, in her opinion, knew what he was doing. But why he was doing it, that was the real question.

'Not that I don't appreciate it,' Ava added with a warm smile.

He shuffled closer to her. 'I know this is weird, and I can imagine you're trying to work out why I'm doing things like . . . getting the lock fixed.' He dropped a set of keys on the cream bedside table. 'For you.' He tilted his head. 'But I don't know what else to do.'

'How do you mean?'

'Your dad and I are good friends; we have been for ten years or so. I work for him.'

'So you said. But doing what?'

'This and that.' He shrugged.

It didn't go unnoticed by Ava how vague he was being.

'And he's been really good to me,' Ben continued. 'He's helped me out on many occasions. Look, I'm not a big one for sentiment and all that shit, but I'm worried about him.' He shrugged. 'So, keeping busy suits. And I know from what you've said that there are issues between you and your old man, but I also know he loves you – I'd put all my money on it. Besides, if I didn't keep an eye on you, he wouldn't be too happy with me.'

'Well, I can't imagine he'd be too happy about me wanting to poke around in his past.'

'Maybe not. But looking for your mum ain't poking around in

his business, is it? It's personal. What you choose to do is down to you. If you want to track down family, I say crack on.' He held her stare, and Ava's nose tickled as his powerful cologne filled the room. Was she being paranoid? Maybe things weren't too good to be true. Maybe Ben was genuine, and her problem was that being a psychologist made her too suspicious of people's intentions. Shit, she didn't know what to think. He was so . . . so . . . *convincing*. Yeah, that was the perfect word for him, which made it hard for her to trust her judgement.

Ben stood. 'So, are you up for it? Meeting some of your dad's mates?'

Ava didn't answer immediately. Until Tony got in touch with her mother's details, she was at a loss how to move forward. It was possible that Tony wouldn't be able to trace her mother. As things stood, Ben was her best chance. But it came back to the same old question: could she trust him?

'How do you know them?' she asked.

'The usual thing. Over the years, mates of mates in the pub, or in the pool hall, become mates, don't they? Like an old school version of Facebook.' He laughed and winked at her, something he'd been doing a lot; Ava guessed it was part of the routine he used when turning on the charm with women. Using his charisma, his gift of the gab to get them into bed . . .

God, what was wrong with her? She had to stop this. She didn't know anything about him, yet she was quick to be cynical when, in reality, he hadn't put a foot wrong since she'd been in London. Perhaps that was the problem: he seemed too good to be true.

'And they'll speak to me?'

'Yeah, I'm sure of it. I hope you didn't mind, babe, but I gave them a quick call already, and said we might drive over.'

'OK, I'll jump in the shower and get ready . . . And thanks, Ben.'

He wandered over to the door. As if it was an afterthought, he turned to her: 'I forgot to ask, you do know your mum's full name, don't you?'

Ava stared straight into his eyes, trying to ignore the voice in her head that said something wasn't right. 'Yes.'

He nodded. 'Good . . . Good . . . Well, I'll see you downstairs then.'

She waited for him to leave. Certain that Ben was gone, Ava knelt down and pulled her suitcase from under the bed. She opened it and grabbed her clothes for the day. Then she unfolded one of her thick jumpers and stared at the gun she'd brought from her father's house.

She paused to listen, making doubly sure Ben wasn't coming back up the stairs, then slipped the gun into her handbag. After all, she might be too judgemental, but that didn't mean she couldn't be too careful.

Ben closed the door in the kitchen, waiting to hear the sound of the shower from upstairs. He gave it a moment or so, then pressed dial on his mobile.

After a couple of rings, it answered.

'It's me.' Ben spoke roughly down the phone. 'She's agreed to come. I'm bringing her over later, and she knows the name of her old girl . . . Who knows, maybe it'll help us.'

'*You mean, help you.*'

'It's talk like that which will fuck everything up. Anyway, I already told you, you'll get a touch if this works out.'

'*And what about Harvey?*'

'What about him? Don't start thinking you owe him any loyalty. Remember what happened: the only person who owes anything is Harvey. So, keep it shut, you understand me?'

'*Perfectly . . . But why not get her to tell you the name? Seems a lot fucking easier.*'

Ben wandered over to the black marble island in the middle of the kitchen and hopped on a stool. 'First off, I don't want to fucking push her, do I? If I keep asking questions, sticking my beak into her business, she might shut down on me. Already I reckon she's on the alert. Plus, she might want to ask me questions, and I can't answer them, can I? I'm as much in the fucking dark as she is.'

'And what am I supposed to say if she asks how long you've known Harvey?'

Ben listened to make sure the shower was still running. 'She won't fucking ask. I've told her, ten years, and she seems happy with that . . . Now, I'll see you later – and remember what I said . . .'

23

'Good morning. You look like you had a late one, and for once it wasn't me. I actually went for a jog this morning. All right, I only got as far as the greasy spoon, but the intention was there.' Joe walked into the office and grinned at Tony.

'I had a couple of whiskies last night.' If truth be told, it was more like half a bottle. He'd wallowed in self-pity, and if it wasn't for the fact that the battery had gone on his mobile, he probably would've drunkenly called Ava and admitted how he felt, admitted that he was angry and let down by her. Thank God he hadn't.

'Anyway, look . . .' Joe continued. 'I wanted to have a word . . . In private.'

'Yeah, of course, what's up?'

Joe nodded towards the empty office at the end of the room. 'Let's talk in there.'

'Sure.' Tony frowned and followed Joe across the open-plan room, which was overly stuffy today. Although Tony wasn't sure whether that was just because he was feeling like crap right now.

'Close the door, mate.'

Tony did as he was asked but spoke at the same time. 'Now you're worrying me. What's going on?'

With the sun streaming through the window, Joe turned to him. 'It's about what you asked me to do.'

Tony put his hands up in the air. 'Oh, listen, I understand if you'd rather not get involved. I'm sorry I put you in that position. Forget I ever asked. Sorry, mate, I was taking the piss.'

Joe shook his head. 'No, no, it's not that. I told you yesterday that it wasn't a problem.'

'Then I'm not following you.' Tony rubbed his head. He wasn't usually one for getting wasted, especially on his own, and now he was regretting it. His headache was making its way behind his eyes, and he felt like at any moment he was going to throw up. 'Is this about her mum?'

'No, I haven't had time to trace the name you gave me yet. But the number . . . Ava's number.'

'You know where she is?'

Joe paused. 'I wish I did, mate. Something else came up before I managed to start the trace on her location.'

Tony had known Joe for a long time, but he'd never seen him look so strained. He was always the guy in the office who kept everyone upbeat, even in the most serious situations.

'Take a seat, mate.' Joe pointed to the chair by the desk he was resting on.

'Jesus, Joe, when someone says that to me, I start getting really worried. I'd rather you spat it out.'

'OK, sure, sorry . . .' Joe took a deep breath, adding to the tension Tony was already feeling. 'The number.'

'Yeah, what about it?'

'It flagged up.'

Tony frowned. 'What are you talking about?'

'Her number was on Danny Oliver's call log . . . He's well known, always in and out of prison. They raided his place recently and confiscated a load of burner phones. Unit two asked me to download and cross-check all the numbers. See who he's phoning and who's phoning him . . . Like most burners, the numbers were stored without names, so it's hard to identify who's who – which of course is the point.' He paused again and shrugged.

'So what are you telling me?'

'Ava's number came up several times. Obviously I wouldn't have known it was hers, if you hadn't given me her mobile. I'm really sorry, mate.'

'Wait, hold on . . . Who exactly is this Danny Oliver?'

'Danny Oliver is a middle-of-the-road drug dealer. He likes to think he's in the big boys league, but he isn't. Though he still floods the streets with his shit – coke, mainly. He's based over in Derby now, but he deals over here as well. He's got a long history – plus he's a nasty piece of work.'

Tony shook his head. 'There must be some mistake.'

'There's no mistake. I cross-checked it and . . .' Joe trailed off.

'And what? And fucking what?' Anger surged through Tony.

'OK, don't have a heart attack. When I cross-checked Ava's number with a couple of Danny's associates who sell for him, her mobile popped up there too.'

Tony tried to process this information. He didn't say anything for a moment, then banged his fist on the table. 'Is this some sort of bad joke? Who's put you up to this? Was it Luke? Did he think this would be funny?'

'No, this has nothing to do with any of the guys . . . Tony, I'm not joking. I wouldn't do that to you – not about Ava. And I haven't told anyone else. I'm going to bury this. It'll stay between you and me, all right? I swear it won't go any further.'

'So, wait, let me get this straight, you're telling me that Ava, my wife, is linked to this scum . . . Danny Oliver?'

'Yeah, that's what I'm saying.'

Tony rested his head in his hand. What the hell was going on? It felt like he was trapped in a nightmare. Ava. Ava and coke. No, those two things didn't go together. He would've known if she was taking drugs.

He looked up. 'I've just had a thought . . . what if someone else was using her phone? Jude – she works in Ava's office. She seems the kind of girl that might be scoring.'

'OK. Does Ava usually leave her phone in the office? Are you saying it's a work phone?'

Tony sighed and shook his head. 'No, I'm not saying that. She never leaves it anywhere.' His voice was quiet. 'What about Bill, her dad? Maybe it's to do with him?'

'Tone, I think if someone like Billy Fields wanted to score, he wouldn't be asking his daughter? Look, mate, in all fairness, it's not going to be anyone else besides her making those calls.'

Tony wasn't listening. 'Maybe he's a client. Danny Oliver could be one of Ava's clients. Maybe he's got something to do with her practice.'

'Mate, this is all bullshit.' Joe sounded and looked sympathetic. 'You don't really believe that, do you? There are loads of calls between them – mainly from Ava, lasting no more than a minute. But that's all you need when you're asking, *Have you got any gear?*'

'Fuck off, Joe.' Tony stood up, furious. 'You are bang out of fucking order to say that.' He pointed at him. 'You don't talk about her like that.' Then he stormed across to the door.

'Wait, Tony.' Joe ran in front of him, blocking Tony's way. 'Keep your voice down, you don't want anyone hearing . . . Look, I'm on your side, you know that.' He paused. 'So, Ava toots a bit. It's not a big deal.'

'Not a big deal?' Tony raised his voice, but then immediately lowered it, hissing through his teeth. 'You're telling me that Ava has a drug dealer's number on fucking speed-dial, and you don't think it's a problem? She's my wife.'

'I know, and she's a good one, and we both know that. Tony, it's not the end of the world. So she likes a few lines. You hear stuff about those doctors all the time. Under pressure, stressful job . . . Look, before you go off on one, maybe you should talk to her? See what she has to say.'

'Is that before or after I find out where she fucking is?'

'Tony, everyone goes through shit with their missus. It's just your turn this time.' He gave a sympathetic smile. 'I'm telling you, you need to do what I never did to my ex-wife: talk to her.'

Tony stared at Joe. He rubbed his temples as he thought of Ava. 'To hear more lies coming out of her mouth? No way. The person I need to speak to is Danny Oliver. Let's see exactly what that bastard has to say.'

24

Ava followed Ben up a flight of wooden stairs in the East End warehouse. Like the rest of the place, the stairs were strewn with rubbish.

'Sorry about the mess. They've just bought this place and, as you see, it's a bit of a shithole right now. But they're planning to do it up and turn it into a private member's club. Bar, restaurant, gym. All that kind of stuff . . . You'll have to come back when it's up and running.'

Ava didn't say anything. Not for the first time since she'd got out of the car, she wondered if it had been sensible to come to a place like this with Ben.

Ben stopped and looked over his shoulder. 'You're quiet. Is everything all right?'

'Yeah, I'm fine. A bit nervous, that's all.'

'Understandable, it's not every day you get closer to finding out about your mum.'

She smiled and was surprised again by Ben's warmth, which only served to confuse how she felt. For a moment, her mind wandered to Tony. He still hadn't been in contact with her. After she'd finished here, she'd call him to make sure he was all right.

At the top of the stairs, a corridor stretched out in front of them. It was enclosed by cold, grey walls. Dim bulbs flickered overhead, casting a weak glow on the concrete floor. The place seemed completely deserted.

As they made their way along the corridor, Ben spoke quietly: 'You'll like them, and I'm sure they'll be interested in meeting you.'

'Why?'

He shrugged. 'Because you're Harvey's daughter.'

Which didn't really answer her question.

'But, a word of advice: maybe don't mention the different names Harvey has been using. He'll have had his reasons, but I reckon it's your old man's business who he tells, and no one else's. There'll be time enough for you to ask him about that when he wakes up.' He gave a smile and knocked on the door without giving Ava time to reply. Then, not waiting to be invited, he opened the door and walked into the room, which turned out to be much larger than Ava had expected.

It had bare wooden floors and floor-to-ceiling windows which looked out across the docks. Apart from a couple of tatty leather chairs and a desk that was full of paper, magazines and what Ava thought looked like rubbish, there was nothing else in the room.

'Guys, this is Ava. Ava, meet John and Terry, or Tel to his friends.' Ben did the quick introductions.

Terry, a small, bald-headed man, who looked like he was hitting his seventies, and John, who was tall and appeared to be of Italian descent, stood up. The cigar Terry was smoking hung out of his mouth. 'It's good to meet you, darlin'. Who'd have thought Harvey . . .' He broke off, looked at Ben and looked slightly awkward. 'Anyway.' He hurriedly filled the silence. 'I'm sorry about what happened. Sounds nasty . . . But knowing Harvey, he'll pull through. He was always a fighter.'

Ava shook hands with them both. 'So how long have you known him, Terry?'

'Call me Tel, darlin'. . . . A long time. Years.'

'Ten? Twenty? *More?*' Ava asked.

'Oh, more . . . yeah, a lot more.'

Ava couldn't help but think that he seemed uneasy.

'And when was the last time you saw my dad, just out of interest.' She tried to make it sound casual, rather than it being some sort of inquisition.

Again, Terry looked uncomfortable, but the question was, why. Why would a simple question that any normal person could answer easily, make him so uneasy? Ava studied his eyes, but there was nothing there apart from apprehension.

'God, your guess is as good as mine, darlin', I've never been all that great with times and dates. One year runs into another – well, it does at my age.' He laughed loudly but it was hollow. 'So.' He clapped his hands together. 'Ben here says you want to ask us a few questions to see if we can help you.'

'Yeah, fire away.' John took over the conversation as he walked around to where Terry and Ava were standing.

'If you don't mind, that would be great.' She answered politely while wondering if they thought it was strange that she was here, wanting to quiz them, instead of waiting until her father was awake. Or even why she hadn't asked her dad before this moment. Although, if they did think that, they weren't showing it.

'Not at all, darlin', we don't mind. Happy to help – if we can remember anything, that is. It's going back some, ain't it.' Terry relit his cigar, which had gone out. He sucked on it furiously to get a glow on the end.

'Well, I'm thirty-nine.' Ava offered up the information.

'Thirty-nine?' Terry had the same reaction as Ben – puzzled. Ava looked to Ben for some kind of explanation.

There was a slight beat then, as usual, Ben winked, and launched into a cheerful dialogue. 'Oh, she looks pukka for it, doesn't she . . . ? I thought that myself, Tel.' He rushed out his words, clearly trying to gloss over Terry's reaction. 'You look ten years younger, babe. That's why everyone's surprised.' He smiled at her, but the way he was behaving made Ava ill at ease.

Ben nodded to the two men. 'Ava was telling me before how she always lived with her old man as a kid. That's something, ain't it?'

The men exchanged glances, which Ava couldn't work out the significance of.

'But then Harvey has always been a family man, hasn't he?' he added.

Terry pointed to his garish gold watch. 'Listen, I've got a meeting later, so hopefully I can answer everything before then.'

Ava took the hint and sat on one of the rickety chairs. 'Ben's probably told you that I'm looking for my mum. I've been wanting to for a while, but you know how it is: sometimes events trigger you into doing things . . . Anyhow, I was hoping that you could help me trace her. Or if not, maybe you can remember something about her. I don't know anything.' She paused to reflect, and added by way of explanation, 'I think it was hard for Dad to talk about her. He never wanted to. She left when I was two or three, you see, and if I was to take a professional guess, I'd say she hurt him. But being a macho guy' – her stare worked its way between all three of them – 'I'd say he buried it, pretended he wasn't bothered.'

'Either that or he was fucked off with her, and happy to see the back of her. Could be he just didn't want to be reminded of someone who did his nut in.' Terry shrugged. 'Just a thought.'

'Yeah well, maybe Ava doesn't want to hear that shit,' Ben growled at him.

'Sorry, darlin', me and my big mouth. Ignore me. It just makes me think of all my exes, when they left me. Fucking hell, the minute I heard them walk out of the front door, I wasn't calling them back, I was calling for a taxi.' He grinned, then cleared his throat, and became more serious. 'But that's me, I didn't mean to sound insensitive.'

Ava smiled at Terry. 'It's fine. And you might be right.' She took a deep breath. 'Her name was Claudia Davies.' She looked at Terry, whose face stayed blank.

He shook his head. 'Nothing springs to mind, and it's not like it's a common name, but from what I remember, he never talked about anyone called that. I'll give it him; he kept it quiet. I didn't even . . .' Terry stopped talking.

Ava frowned. 'You didn't even, what?'

Terry rubbed his head and puffed on his cigar. 'I don't know what I was going to say, only that Harvey was always private. Or rather, he became that way . . .' Terry trailed off with a frown.

'That name does ring a bell, actually.' John, who'd been silent, suddenly spoke up. 'Yeah, if it's who I'm thinking of, I know who you mean . . . Claudia Davies, fuck me, you must remember her, Tel. She was that tart . . . Sorry, Ava, I didn't mean that. What I meant to say was, she was a bird who used to work in that sauna on Ferry Street. You must remember, Tel, it was opposite the Red Lion, always being raided.' He laughed warmly.

'Oh, fucking hell.' Terry's face lit up. He wagged his finger. 'Yeah, I do now. That place was a fucking dive, but it was where we always ended up.' He looked wistful. 'They were good days, mate . . . You would've had a right crack, Ben – shame you weren't . . .' He stopped.

'Around?' An irritated tone jumped into Ben's voice. 'It was a shame I wasn't around, wasn't it?' He shook his head. 'And we know why, don't we?'

'Look, mate, I didn't mean anything by it.' He stared at Ben and gave an apologetic nod.

'Forget about it – I already have.' Ben glowered.

Ava picked up on the tension between the men, but she didn't want it to distract from what she was here for. Instead, she moved the conversation on. 'So what else do you know about her?' she asked.

'God, well she was larger than life. She always wore this short blue feather dress, and by the end of the evening, she was always be standing on the table, singing away. It's coming back to me now, but I had no idea that your old man and her were an item,' Terry said, sounding somewhat surprised.

'Is the Red Lion still there?' This was the most she'd ever talked about her mum, and she wasn't sure how she felt that she'd had to wait all these years to do it, with two strangers. She looked at Ben, who was listening intently.

'No, it closed down years ago. It's a block of offices now. But I know Claudia and some of her mates went to work in the saunas down near Kings Cross. Fuck knows if they're there now – everything's changed so much. But it's a lucrative profession, so who knows.'

'A lucrative profession?'

'Claudia, she was a brass . . . I take it you didn't know that.'

'No, I didn't . . . but it's fine . . .' Ava tried to smile, but she couldn't quite manage it. She didn't care what her mum was or wasn't – God knows she wasn't in a position to judge people's lifestyles – but it was bringing up feelings she thought she'd buried long ago.

'Yeah, she ran a lot of the hookers. I wouldn't quite say she was a madam, but she was heading that way. She earned a cut of what the other girls earned – how and why, I don't know . . . But that's why I was surprised when you said Claudia. I didn't think your old man would touch her with a bargepole, unless of course he wanted to catch a dose—'

'Tel!' Ben shouted Terry down. 'What the fuck's wrong with you?' He turned to Ava. 'Sorry, babe, you'll have to excuse Terry, he can be a bit of a wanker at times, and that's putting it fucking mildly.'

Ava said nothing. As before, she studied the men. Her stare moved behind John, to the pile of papers. Her heart leapt as she caught sight of the nozzle of a gun hidden underneath some files.

'I have to go.' Ava got to her feet. 'But thank you for everything. I appreciate it.'

Terry glanced towards where she'd been looking and pulled a newspaper over the gun to hide it. He gave her a tight smile and looked her straight in the eye. Ava wondered if he was challenging her, waiting to see if she'd say anything.

'I'll make a few calls, see if I can track anyone who knows of Claudia's whereabouts . . . and I am sorry, darlin', if I upset you.'

Ava hurried out without a word. Whatever their business was, she didn't want to stick around to find out.

'Ava, wait up.' Ben hurried after her. 'Are you OK?' He caught up to her as she was walking out into the parking area at the back of the warehouse. 'Was it what Terry said? Look, ignore him, all right.'

'No . . . no, it wasn't. It's a bit much, that's all.'

He stared at her, and moved aside the strand of hair which was blowing in her eyes. 'You want me to take you home?'

She shook her head. 'No, I fancy a drink.'

'You sure that's a good idea?'

'No, I'm not. But right now that's all I can think of.'

As they got to the car, Ben opened the door for Ava. He looked up at the window and saw Terry looking down, then he got into the driver's seat. If Terry thought he'd forgotten about what happened, he was more of a fool than Ben took him for. He might not have been around back then, but he was definitely going to make up for it now. And one thing he was never going to forget was that people owed him . . .

25

They drove back to Soho in silence. Ava had given up trying to strike up a conversation with Ben when all she got in response were grunts. Having nothing better to do, she'd slept most of the way. She jolted awake when Ben slammed his fist on the horn.

Yawning, she turned to him. 'Is everything all right?' Clearly it wasn't.

Ben clicked off the call button on the steering wheel. 'Sorry, babe, didn't mean to wake you.'

'Tends to happen when someone has road rage right next to you,' she joked.

He gave her a sideways glance, and Ava saw the tension in his face. 'I'm actually trying to get hold of my brother, Sam. It annoys me when he doesn't get back to me. We were supposed to meet up, but he's proper dropped me out.'

Ava watched a cyclist out of the car window. 'That makes two of us: Tony seems to have gone underground as well.' She turned back to him. 'You look worried.'

Ben turned right into Wardour Street. He pulled a face, and Ava thought he was trying his best to appear nonchalant. 'No, not worried. I always check in with him. He's got a new job over in Bromley and I think the kids are playing him up a bit. He's a soft touch, wouldn't say boo to a goose.'

'I thought you said he worked in the City?' She frowned.

Ben held her gaze. 'Er, yeah, yeah, he does . . . but . . . but there are some company offices over that side of the woods, he often goes there.'

Ava nodded, digesting this information. 'How many kids has he got?'

'Three.' The way Ben answered was a closed response, and Ava didn't push to get any more out of him.

'Anyway, what about you?' He changed the subject at the same time as overtaking a van parked up on the side, blocking the traffic. 'How do you feel about what Tel said? He's a bit of a wanker – opens his mouth when he shouldn't – but he's got a lot of contacts, and he owes me one, so I'm sure he'll put the feelers out.'

'Why?'

Ben pulled up in Greek Street, expertly reversing into a tight space. 'Why what?' He grabbed a packet of cigarettes from the inside pocket of his coat. 'I'm not following you.'

'Why does he owe you?'

Ben shrugged. 'It was a throwaway remark.'

'It didn't sound it.'

Ben tilted his head, and it was a moment before he spoke. 'If we're going to spend any more time together, could you do me a favour, could you stop with the Dr Psychology show – it's starting to do my head in. Not everything has a deeper meaning, babe.' He got out of the car, slamming the door behind him.

Surprised by Ben's reaction, Ava got out as well.

It was stupid, but she was offended, and as much as she tried to hold her temper, she couldn't. 'For your information, being concerned for someone is not a bad thing.' She raised her voice, not caring about the passers-by giving her strange looks. 'And if you think that, you need to take a long hard look at yourself.'

Ben swung around to stare at Ava, at the same time locking the car with the remote he held in his hand. 'What is your problem?'

Ava was amazed by his attitude. 'With you? Wow, where should I start?'

He stepped towards her, his piercing green eyes flashing with anger. 'Turn it in, will you? The last thing I need right now is someone like *you* telling me anything.'

'What's that supposed to mean?'

'I don't want to get into this, but you need to wind it back.'

Ava's gaze moved over his face as she tried to work out why he was behaving like this towards her. 'Whatever is going on right now, I don't think it's anything to do with me. This is all about your issues.'

'*My issues?*' He laughed loudly and scornfully. 'There you go again.' Then, as was his habit, he took a deep drag of his cigarette to buy himself time to think.

Ava shook her head. 'If that's how you want to play it, I'm going for a drink.'

'No, you're not.' Ben stood in front of her. His towering frame blocked her way.

'Excuse me?' She blinked, not quite believing what she was hearing.

'You heard me . . . I am *not* going to pick you out of the bar again and have a stand-up row with a bunch of geezers who think they're on a fucking promise.'

Ava felt herself blush, and angrily she pulled up her coat collar against the early November chill. 'What the hell are you talking about? That's rubbish.'

Ben snorted. He leaned in towards her. 'I thought you said you could remember what happened?'

'I can.' Defiantly, Ava stood staring into his handsome face.

'Then why deny what happened? Let me tell you, if I hadn't come along when I did—'

123

'I would've been fine,' Ava snapped. 'I've managed all this time without you, so I think I would've been all right, don't you?'

'Well, if what happened in the bar is what you usually do, darlin', I'd say you haven't been managing, you've been lucky to get away with it. You need to tell your husband to keep a tighter rein on you.'

'Piss off.' It began to drizzle again, and Ava blinked away the raindrops. 'Don't you dare speak to me like that.'

'All I'm doing is telling you my opinion, sweetheart, based on what I saw.'

'I'm not listening to this. Who are you to judge me?' She turned to go, but Ben grabbed her by the arm.

'I've already said, you ain't going anywhere. Not today. I've got more important things to do than be your bodyguard.'

Ava tried to pull free of his grip, but he held on to her. 'Are you serious?'

'You better believe it, babe. Deadly. So even if I have to put you over my shoulder and carry you back to your dad's gaff, there's no way you're going anywhere.'

Right then Ben's mobile rang in his pocket. His striking face curled up in irritation. 'Saved by the fucking bell.' He pulled it out and answered as he glowered at Ava.

'*Yes?*'

Ava watched him nodding while he listened intently to the person at the other end. Finally, pressing end on the call, Ben threw his cigarette down, and put it out with his foot. 'That was Tel . . . He's come up trumps already . . . He thinks he's been able to locate your mother.'

26

It was the following evening, and as it was a Thursday, the traffic had been particularly bad and the journey from Nottingham to Derby had taken much longer than Tony had anticipated.

It was dark and there was a hint of snow in the air as Tony and Joe got out of the car and made their way across the estate on the north side of Derby. It was run-down and graffiti was sprayed across the walls of the bleak blocks of flats.

'Have you spoken to her?' Joe asked as they walked down a narrow alleyway that smelled of piss.

'No. No fucking way. I can't.' He'd deliberately not texted or called Ava; he couldn't trust himself not to say something that he'd later regret. 'She's called me a few times though.'

'You think that's a good idea, to ignore her? Won't she get suspicious or think something's up?'

Moving aside for a small woman hurrying along, who Tony thought looked like a smackhead, he answered quietly, 'Something *is* up . . . very up.'

They fell into silence and Tony followed a step behind Joe as they made their way into the Old Bell pub.

The place was a dive. It stank of sweat and alcohol. Groups of drinkers sat huddled around the various dirty tables and as Tony continued to follow Joe, he felt the sticky floor underfoot.

'He's over there.' Joe discreetly nodded towards Danny Oliver. 'He's as regular as clockwork; every Thursday and Friday he's here, selling his shit or getting someone else to sell it for him. He's a lowlife, but you still have to be careful. Operations have stopped following him, but he's still a person of interest. Remember, there's an active case open on him, and you really don't want this to come back on you.'

'Will he recognize you?' Tony asked, keeping his back to Danny.

'No. Don't forget I've been with digital forensics several years now, and even before that, I was never one of his arresting officers.'

'So, why don't we get a pint and wait until he leaves, then I'll have a word with him,' Tony said as he gestured to the barman.

'Are you sure you want to do this, Tone? Maybe we should just get out of here, and you can have a word with Ava.'

'Two pints of your best larger, please,' Tony addressed the barman before he answered Joe. 'I don't reckon my good wife is up for telling me anything apart from a pack of lies . . . Look, if you're not up for this, that's fine. I understand if you want to go. This is my mess, not yours, so don't feel you have to do anything you don't want to.'

Joe took a sip of the pint as Tony handed a twenty-pound note to the barman. 'Nah, I'm happy to stay. Come on, let's sit down and wait for that prick to leave.'

Tony found an empty table in the corner of the pub, and they sat under the dim light while inconspicuously watching Danny.

'He doesn't care who sees him selling his shit,' Joe muttered. 'He might as well put out a sign saying he's doing it.'

Tony turned slightly to see Danny giving a couple of wraps to a man in a long trench coat with a tattoo on his neck. He looked around him and tried not to let his thoughts return to Ava, and what the fuck else she'd been lying to him about. Perhaps it was as Joe had said: maybe she was just doing what head doctors did to relieve the pressure: taking coke and lying to the people closest? She must really think he was a mug.

'Looks as if he's going.' Joe gently nudged Tony, who turned in the direction of Joe's stare.

'Perfect.' He got up, trying to appear casual, and walked quickly to the entrance. He used his jacket sleeve to open the door. The whole place was filthy, and once again, he thought of Ava.

They followed Danny quietly, keeping their distance so as not to raise suspicion. Once they reached the estate's underground car park, they quickened their steps.

'Let's speak to him here.' Tony looked around. 'Seems the perfect place.'

Joe nodded and moved forward. 'Hey, Danny! Danny, we just need a word.'

Danny Oliver, a tall, lanky man in his mid-thirties, turned. His thin features strained with suspicion. 'What about?' He didn't move but continued to speak. 'Do I fucking know you?'

Joe flicked a glance at Tony. 'We were given your name. Heard you might be able to sort us out.'

Tony watched Danny look around him. 'Yeah, and you could be the filth for all I know.'

Joe sauntered across to Danny where he was standing by a stairwell. Tony hoped he wasn't going to make a run for it.

'Well, I'm not.' Joe grinned. 'I'm just looking to have a good night.'

Danny eyed Joe up and down, and something told Tony that, when it came to money, Danny put caution to the side, which probably explained why he ended up in prison so often.

Tony approached Joe and Danny. He felt his temper beginning to rise but he held it down.

Joe stepped in close to Danny, assuming an air of menace.

'What the fuck are you doing?' Danny looked suddenly ill at ease.

'My mate here wants a word with you.'

'Fuck off.' Danny spat his words out, earning him a fist in the side of the head from Joe. 'Watch your manners.'

'Who are you?' Danny was panting now, a veil of fear crossing his face.

'It doesn't matter who the fuck we are. We're not here to answer your questions. You, however, are going to answer ours.'

Danny tried to move away, but it was pointless as Joe stood in front of him.

Joe booted him in the shins, causing his knees to buckle slightly.

'Going somewhere, are we?' Joe glared at him. 'Well not until my friend here has a word with you.'

'I'm not usually one for violence, but if you don't give me a straight answer, the way I'm feeling, you'll regret it.' Tony stared into Danny's brown eyes. 'I want you to tell me about Ava.'

'Who?' the dealer sneered. 'Who the fuck is Ava?'

'My wife.'

Danny burst into laughter, causing Tony to grab him under the chin and squeeze his face hard as Joe held Danny's arms. 'You think this is funny? Do I look like I'm laughing?'

Danny gave the smallest shake of his head.

'No, that's right.' Tony was furious now. He'd given up trying to deny that Ava hadn't had anything to do with this creep. 'So now, Danny, we're going to try again. Why have you been in touch with my wife?'

'I don't know any Ava.'

Tony grabbed hold of a clump of Danny's hair and banged his head against the concrete pillar he was standing in front of. 'I told you to answer my question.'

Danny, clearly in pain, stared at Tony. 'Whoever she is, I don't make a habit of exchanging names with people I pick up. Fuck them and leave them, and don't look back is my motto.' He grinned nastily.

It was all Tony could do not to batter Danny senseless. 'I'm not talking about sleeping with her, I'm talking about selling to her.'

Danny shrugged. 'Then I definitely won't know her name. Most people buying gear don't give me their name, or if they do, it's not their real one.' He leaned into Tony's face. 'So, I can't help you, *mate.*'

Tony reached into his pocket and pulled out his phone. He went into his gallery and scrolled through the photos. 'Here.' He showed Danny the picture of Ava. 'This is my wife.'

Immediately, a wide grin lit up Danny's face. 'Oh, yeah, Lucy Lush. If you're married to her, mate, my condolences.' He roared with laughter and Tony immediately brought back his fist and punched him hard in the stomach.

Danny started coughing and Tony brought up his knee and slammed it into his face. Danny collapsed to the floor.

'Not so funny, now, is it?'

'Just tell me what the fuck you want.' Danny's breathing was laboured as Tony stood over him.

'I want you to tell me everything. How long, how often, how much.' Tony wiped his mouth with his hand. His heart was racing, and anger surged through him. Ava had put him in this position. What the fuck was she thinking?

Danny tried to sit up, but Tony had other ideas. He pressed his foot on Danny's face. 'Tell me.'

Even though he was in pain, Dany managed to smirk. 'Are you sure you want to know? It's not pretty.'

With his foot still on Danny, Tony put more pressure on it. 'Stop messing me about.'

'OK . . . OK, don't say I didn't warn you . . . Your wife,

Ava – though we call her Lucy Lush – comes she comes in every Friday night, sometimes on Thursdays, and she always buys a couple of grammes of coke.'

'You're lying.'

'Believe what you like, mate.'

Tony gazed at Joe, who looked back at him and shrugged sympathetically.

'Go on then, carry on.' Tony balled up his fists, digging his fingernails into his palms. He could hardly stand to hear any more, but he knew he had to. He could feel hatred unlike anything he'd known before rushing through his being. Hatred, jealousy and humiliation. A lethal combination.

'Like I say,' Danny continued, 'she comes in here most Fridays, and more often than not she stays to have one drink, two drinks, before ending up being the Friday night entertainment.'

'What the fuck are you talking about?'

'I'm talking about *Ava* getting so pissed she ends up being somebody's lucky night.'

Tony shook his head. He stepped back, putting his hands on his head. What the fuck was he hearing? 'No, no . . . I can tell you're trying to wind me up, but let me tell you, it's not working,' he snarled at Danny, although it was more than working. He wanted to put his fist through a wall, or better still, through Danny. 'How long has she been coming to you?'

'I dunno, I don't count . . . Maybe a year, two . . . a while. She snorts up that shit like there's no tomorrow.'

Tony closed his eyes. Fridays. How was that even possible? Fridays she always had late-night clients, while he always went across to his mother's for the night, ever since his dad had passed away a few years ago. It was one of the reasons he'd been pleased to come to Nottingham; Cardiff had been too far away from her to make it easy for him to visit her over in Birmingham, although eventually he'd persuaded her to move to Nottingham too.

He shook his head. Ava wouldn't lie to him so blatantly – would she? Christ, he didn't know what to think.

'Phone her.' Tony was adamant. 'I want you to phone her and ask if she's coming down tomorrow . . . Ask her that, but keep your mouth shut about us being here.'

Danny looked between Tony and Joe.

'You better do what he tells you.' Joe glared at Danny, but it took a moment before the dealer reached into his pocket to get his burner phone out.

'She'll think it's strange, you do know that, don't you? Me, calling like that.'

'Then you need to make it sound normal.'

Danny shook his head, although he didn't say anything. He scrolled down a list of numbers.

'How do you know which is hers?' Tony asked.

'I have my regulars stored in my phone. She's stored under, LL . . . Lucy Lush.'

'I should kill you,' Tony hissed through his teeth.

'Then maybe I shouldn't bother phoning her.' Danny waved the phone, taunting Tony.

Joe prodded Danny with his shoe. 'Don't take the piss.'

Danny shrugged, and proceeded to dial Ava's number. He didn't have to wait long for her to answer.

Tony mouthed, *put it on speaker*, which Danny did.

'All right, gorgeous? It's Danny.'

'*Hi, what's up?*'

Tony's stomach tightened as he heard Ava's voice. He hadn't spoken to her since the other day, and now here he was, listening to her speaking to some scum.

'I was wondering if you were coming down tomorrow? It being Friday and all that . . . It's just that I've got some nice powder in.'

There was a long pause before Tony heard Ava's voice. *'Is this a new service?'* She let out a gentle laugh which did nothing but infuriate Tony.

'Yeah, you could say that. You know me, I like to look after my best customers.'

'I'm not sure how to take that. So no, I won't be around tomorrow, but thanks . . . I suppose.'

'No worries, I'll see you around.'

'Yeah, bye.'

The phone went dead, and Danny stared at Tony. 'Now do you believe that your wife is a regular?'

'Oh yeah, I believe you, all right.' And with those words, Tony looked over his shoulder, checking there was no one around, before beginning to boot Danny hard in the sides, his screams filling the empty car park.

'Tone, that's enough . . . Tony, leave it now . . . *For fuck's sake, Tony!*' Joe pulled Tony away. He stood, panting heavily, while Joe crouched to take a closer look at Danny, who was covered in blood. Reaching out a gloved hand, Joe touched Danny's neck. 'Oh shit, he's not breathing.'

'What?'

Joe turned to stare up at Tony. 'No pulse. Nothing.' Then, as Tony had done, he looked around. Scooping up Danny's burner phone from where it lay on the floor, he told Tony, 'You need to go and get the car, I'll stay here.'

'What are you talking about, we need to call an ambulance.' Tony's face drained of colour. This couldn't be happening. What had he done? Christ!

'Yeah, because calling an ambulance is a clever idea.'

Tony struggled to speak. 'Are you listening to what you're saying?'

'And have you seen what you've done?' Joe growled.

Tony covered his face with his hands while Joe continued:

'Don't forget who he is, Tone, and what he's done. Getting him off the street is the best thing that can happen.'

Tony dropped his hands, swallowing down the bile in his throat. 'Not like this.'

'Yeah, just like this – unless you want to serve time for scum like that . . . Well, do you?'

'No, of course I don't. But . . .'

'But nothing.' Joe grabbed Tony by his sleeve, pulling him towards the stairwell. 'I know for a fact that there aren't any CCTV cameras around here – not ones that work; it pissed off Operations no end. Which means we can either load him into the car and dump him, and no one will be any the wiser; or we can stay here and ruin our lives. So, go and get the fucking car, you hear me?'

Tony flashed a hard look at him. Panic sounded like a roar in his ears.

'Tony, do you really want to mess everything up because of him?' Joe stood waiting for a reply.

Tony looked again at Danny, who lay motionless. Then he thought of Ava, imagining her drunk and *someone's lucky night*. He clenched his fists and nodded slowly. 'OK . . . OK . . . I'll go and get the car.'

Joe stepped close to him. 'You're doing the right thing . . . We'll dump him deep in the woods, over near the river, let the animals get him. By the time they find him – if they find him – all trace of the fight will have long disappeared.'

27

Ava stood in the kitchen in Meard Street and frowned. Danny didn't usually call, unless she'd left a message, which she rarely did. She preferred just to phone him without leaving that much of a trail, that was one of the reasons she went across to Derby, it was more anonymous, he knew that, so it was odd that he was calling around. Although, maybe business wasn't as good as it usually was. She'd heard there was a new dealer, selling in the same area as Danny. Perhaps that was it. Maybe the people who usually bought from him were fed up with him cutting up his coke so much, it was like buying talc most of the time.

She sighed, moving her thoughts away from Danny as Ben walked in.

'Are you sure this is going to be all right?' She cupped the mug of coffee in her hands. She hadn't spoken to Ben since yesterday, which she had no doubt suited him just fine.

She'd heard him pop out late last night and return a few hours later. She was curious where he'd been, but she wasn't going to ask him. Her first guess would be at his brother's. Even though he'd denied it, it had been very clear how worried he was. Quite why, she had no idea.

'Who knows.' His reply was curt, and it reminded Ava of Tony when he was sulking.

He wandered to the coffee machine. Although it was the afternoon, he was freshly showered. His shirt was unbuttoned, showing off his muscular chest. For some reason, Ava found herself averting her eyes and focusing on the now lukewarm coffee.

'Like I told you yesterday, Tel's contact says your mum's working out of a house in South London. Whether that turns out to be right or not, it's worth checking out.'

Ava felt sick. She'd been waiting for this moment for as long as she could remember, but now it was actually here, she wasn't sure if she could go through with it.

She'd wanted to go yesterday, the moment they'd found out. Get it over and done with before she lost her bottle. But according to Tel, on Wednesdays Claudia worked in Essex. So there'd been nothing for it but to wait.

Ava told herself to get a grip. This wasn't just about her mum; it was the only way she was going to find out who her father really was. When it came down to it, this was her chance to put the pieces together.

Ben walked up to her, stopping inches away. He reached for the sugar on the shelf behind her. She caught her breath, quickly becoming self-conscious.

'Are you nervous?' he asked neutrally.

'No, why should I be?' Her reply sounded sharper than she'd intended. 'Sorry. I didn't sleep very well, and I'm a bit tired. And I haven't been able to get through to Tony, so I'm starting to worry – but that doesn't mean it's all right to snap at you.'

He stepped away from her, sugar container in hand, and smiled. 'I've had worse.' He stared at her, and once again, Ava found herself having to avert her eyes.

'Well, I'm sorry.'

'Apology accepted.' He laughed warmly. 'So, how come Tony's not answering?'

She poured her coffee down the sink. 'I'm not sure, it's not like him . . . What about you? Did you get through to your brother?'

'No.' He shook his head. 'But I'm sure he's fine.' Ben looked anything but sure of his brother's well-being. 'I was thinking, after we've seen Claudia, I could drop you off here and then swing over to see him.' He finished doing up his shirt and grabbed his jacket from the side, and his car keys. 'Right then, let's go.'

The journey took much longer than expected. As soon as they crossed Waterloo Bridge they hit traffic; every shortcut they tried ended in gridlock, adding an extra hour to the journey. But eventually they arrived at a nondescript terraced house off London Road.

Ben pulled up, parking in a resident bay. He turned off the engine and glanced at Ava. 'Are you all right?' It was about the tenth time he'd asked the question since they set off, and each time she'd replied with the opposite of how she was really feeling.

'Yeah, I'm great.'

He nodded and got out of the car, waiting for Ava to join him. Then they walked without speaking to the house on the corner. The door was painted a deep navy blue, and the small front garden was pristine.

Ben stepped up to the front door and knocked. He looked at Ava while they waited and for a moment, she thought he was going to ask if she was all right, but he said nothing.

Getting no reply, he rapped harder on the door.

'*I'm coming! Fucking hell, where's the bleedin' fire?*' A shrill voice came from the other side of the door before it was swung open.

'Yes?' A woman in her late sixties, maybe more, with her hair in rollers and her make-up caked on, stared at them suspiciously with brown beady eyes. She was dressed in a pink frilly dressing gown, tightly tied in the middle of her bulging waist.

She held a cigarette in her hand. 'What can I do for you?' She sniffed haughtily. 'If this is about the fucking drains, you can tell the council they're being sorted.' She looked them both up and down. 'Though, come to think of it, you don't look like you're the type of people who deal with drains.'

'No, drains have never been my thing, though I can think of other things that are.' Ben grinned at her and immediately winked at the woman. It had the desired effect, and she gave him a small smile. For some reason it irritated Ava, and she shot him a stare.

'So go on, what's a good-looking bloke like you knocking on my door for? Is it my lucky day?' She licked her red-painted lips suggestively.

Ben roared with laughter, and Ava tried her hardest to smile.

'I'm looking for a Claudia Davies. We've got a mutual friend, and I just wanted to pick her brains.'

At that moment, a very rotund man waddled down the hallway. The woman turned her head to look at him, breaking out into a grin. 'I hope Bonny has looked after you.'

The man was red-faced and flushed, and Ava could see a film of sweat covering his forehead. 'She did. Very well,' he chortled.

Over the years, Ava had learned not to judge people on first impressions. But that didn't stop her getting a feel for what they were like. And the feeling she had was, this guy was a creep.

'I'm glad to hear it, darlin'. So shall we say, same time next week?'

He nodded, and slapped the woman's backside as he walked out. She broke into laughter as he waddled away, but the moment he'd disappeared from view, she rolled her eyes. 'What would life be like if there weren't arseholes in the world . . . Anyway.' She turned her attention to Ben again. 'What were you saying, sweetheart?'

'I'm looking for Claudia – one of Terry Oldham's mates said we might find her here.'

'Oh my God. That's a name I ain't heard for years! How is Tel?'

'The last time I checked, he was the same wanker he's always been.'

The comment brought the woman to genuine tears of laughter. She held onto the door frame, letting out a deep belly laugh.

With her face lit up, she gestured with her head. 'Come on in . . . and I'm Claudia, by the way.'

It was now Ava's turn to grip the frame of the door. She took a deep breath. This was her mother. She had no idea how to feel, how to think, what to do, and she caught Ben giving her a quick look.

'I'm fine,' she replied, before he had a chance to ask. Then she followed him and Claudia down the hallway, closing the door behind her.

'Come into my lounge, it's private so no one will disturb us. The girls are all in their rooms and we've got no more clients today, so I'm all yours . . . that's if you want me.' She roared at her own joke and went across to the small chest of drawers which had several bottles of spirits standing on it. 'What's your poison, darlin'?'

'I'm driving, thanks, so I'll take a rain check,' Ben said as he took a seat on the red velvet couch.

'I'll have a whisky, if you don't mind,' Ava said, ignoring the look Ben was giving her.

'That's what I like, a girl after my own heart.' Claudia poured a generous tumbler of whisky and passed it to Ava, then proceeded to pour herself one.

Ava went to sit down on the chair opposite and took a gulp of whisky. She felt the burn of the alcohol and welcomed the taste of it, even if Ben was giving her daggers from the other side of

138

the room. She was counting on the whisky to give her Dutch courage. And right now, that was something she needed.

Claudia slumped into the nearest armchair. 'So, you're not here just to let me know you're mates with Tel, are you?'

'No.' Ben shook his head. 'But it's a bit of a delicate matter.'

Once more, Claudia burst into laughter. 'I don't think you should worry about that . . . The nearest I get to delicate these days is making sure my teeth don't bite down on someone's cock.' More giggles fired out of her, and she took another drink and smiled at Ava and Ben. 'So go on, I'm intrigued.' She caught a glimpse of Ava's almost empty glass. 'What sort of hostess am I? You want a top-up, love?'

'No, she doesn't.' Ben answered for her, and Claudia raised her eyebrows at him. 'Hark at you . . .' She looked at Ava. 'Does he always play the protective boyfriend?'

'Oh God no, he's not my boyfriend – I'm married.'

'Poor you! But it's nice to see you've got a bit of on the side.'

As Ava went to open her mouth, Ben intervened. 'What she's trying to say, Claudia, is, we're not together. Not now, not ever.'

'Whatever you say, darlin'.' Claudia smirked. 'Keep telling yourself that . . . But if you don't want him, send him over to me, anytime. It's been a while since I've had anything other than a geriatric on top of me.' Claudia was about to laugh again but it turned into a coughing fit. Red-faced, she waved her hand. 'Don't mind me, I'm only dying.'

'Can I get you a drink?' Ben asked, concerned, to which Claudia raised her glass of whisky and knocked it back. A few seconds later she smiled.

'That's better.'

Ben, clearly ignoring the comment about him and Ava, launched into what he was here for. 'Look, it's not just Tel we've got in common, there's someone else . . . Harvey Fletcher.'

She shook her head, and her face looked blank. This wasn't the reaction Ava had expected. There was no sign of anything like recognition, and she was certain Claudia wasn't faking it. But maybe, as with her, her father had been using a different name, like some kind of con artist.

'No, sorry. Can't help you.'

Ben pushed some more. 'We're going a long way back now. Thirty-odd years. Thirty-nine years?'

'Bloody hell, I'm hard-pressed to remember last frigging week.'

'There are some things you don't forget,' Ben said firmly. 'Like having a kid.'

Claudia's eyes widened. 'Having a kid? Who? Me?'

'Oh, come on, don't mug me off.'

Ava watched Claudia flash with irritation. 'Listen, mate, I think I would remember pushing a kid out, don't you? Look, if that's all, I'd like you to go now.'

'Not until we get some proper answers,' Ben growled, and Ava, worried that he'd completely alienate the woman, stood up and went to sit on the arm of the chair next to her.

'You'll have to excuse him.' Not for the first time, she threw a glare at Ben. 'I appreciate you letting us in like this. The only reason we're asking is that we were told . . .' Ava stopped to take a deep breath. 'Basically, I was told *you* were my mother.'

Claudia blinked. She began to laugh but abruptly stopped. 'You're being serious, ain't you?'

Ava nodded. 'Yeah, I was told from the time I can remember that you were my mum.' She felt the wave of emotion start to come over her, but somehow she got herself under control.

'Maybe there's been a mix-up. Another Claudia.'

Ben shook his head. 'It seems unlikely. It's not such a common name that Tel would know two Claudia Davieses.'

'But I don't know a Harvey, so it must be someone else,' Claudia insisted.

'Well, according to him, he knows you very well,' Ben continued. 'Apparently, he used to hang around with you . . . thirty-nine odd years ago, and you left the family home . . .' He turned to Ava to fill in the blank.

'. . . Thirty-six years ago.'

Ava watched Ben frown. 'That doesn't make sense. Are you sure?'

'Yeah, when I was three.' Ava's voice teetered on the brink of emotional. 'Not that I can remember that far back. When any kid has trauma that young, like a parent leaving, it creates gaps in their memory.' She turned to Ben. 'What doesn't make sense?'

Looking in deep thought, Ben shrugged. 'Nothing. The whole thing, I guess.' He smiled at her, but it didn't reach his eyes.

Ava grabbed her phone from her jeans pocket. 'I'm sorry to ask you again, but are you sure that you don't know a Harvey . . . Look, maybe this will help. It's an old photo of him and me, but we aren't really the photo-opportunity father–daughter duo.' Ava noticed the pain in her own voice, and tried to keep her attention on showing Claudia the phone, which she took after putting her whisky down. 'Harvey?' Her brow furrowed as she sat holding the phone, staring at it, then her face suddenly changed. 'Oh, my fucking God! Harvey . . . Yes, yes, of course. How is he?'

'OK.' Ben got in before Ava had a chance to say anything, and she saw what seemed like a warning stare from him to keep her mouth shut.

Claudia looked between the two of them. 'But he doesn't know you're here?'

'No, it's not that,' Ava said. 'I'm actually estranged from him, and I just fancied finding the other side of my family. So, I thought I'd start with my mum.' She shrugged. 'I'm sorry to waste your time. Thank you.' She got up to go.

'You didn't waste my time, but if I was you, I'd thank your lucky stars, girl, that I ain't your mum. I think you got a lucky escape there.' Claudia smiled at her and then impulsively reached out and gave Ava a tight hug. 'Take care of yourself. And if you ever want a job . . .' She gestured upstairs. 'A gorgeous-looking woman like you, you'd be raking it in here.'

'There is one other thing though.' Ben got up. 'How long did you know him for? When did he stop being in contact with you?'

An expression that Ava couldn't work out crossed Claudia's face. 'We used to have a laugh, that's all. There was never anything between us – more's the pity. But then he had so many women to choose from, it's no wonder he didn't look at me. I think he preferred getting his blow jobs for free. But, as I say, Harvey was a laugh. He was quite the life and soul of the party – larger than life, in fact. Everyone loved him.' She stopped and Ava felt she was watching the memories pass in front of her eyes. 'Then for some reason he started hanging around with a different crowd, and everything changed.'

'What kind of crowd?' Ava was puzzled.

'They were . . .' Claudia searched for the words. 'Let's just call them a bad crowd. I didn't want anything to do with them, so we parted company. That was . . . oh fucking hell . . . it was a few months or so before all that shit went down with Tel, when he went—'

'Don't worry about what Tel did – we ain't here to talk about him,' Ben cut in. His reaction was so extreme that both Ava and Claudia stared at him.

'Excuse me for breathing.' Claudia's voice dripped with sarcasm, and she shifted her attention to Ava. 'It must have been thirty-six years ago, I guess.'

'And who was this crowd, then?'

Claudia shook her head, and Ava thought there was something like fear in her eyes. 'I've said more than enough.'

'Not from where I'm standing, you haven't.'

Claudia crossed her arms. 'I ain't saying anything more.'

'Not good enough.' Ben moved closer to Claudia, but Ava grabbed hold of him.

'What's wrong with you?' she snapped at Ben, then began backing towards the door. 'Thank you, Claudia, I appreciate you helping,' she said, opening the door and stepping out into the street, where it was beginning to snow. Ben followed, and they set off for the car.

'Why were you like that with her? Anyone would think we were looking for *your* mum, not mine.'

'Sorry, I just want to help.'

'Bullying people isn't my idea of helping.' Angrily, she strode ahead, shivering in the cold wind. When they reached the car, she spun round. 'Why do you think Dad used Claudia's name?'

Unlocking the car, Ben held the passenger door open for Ava. 'I don't know, your guess is as good as mine, but perhaps it was the first name that came to him when you asked what your mum was called. Or maybe he used it because he knew he wouldn't forget it, and he assumed that no one would find out.'

'But why? Why not just tell me the truth? And if she isn't my mother, who is?'

28

'Oh fuck.' Ben started to frisk himself down as he sat in the driver's seat.

'What's the matter?'

'I think my phone must have dropped out at Claudia's . . . Give me five minutes and I'll be back . . . Keep the door locked.'

Ben jogged down the street, turning round to make sure that Ava had done what he'd asked her to. Then, confident she had, he picked up his pace. Ava had accepted his involvement more readily than he'd anticipated, given her headstrong nature. Though, given that Harvey was the same and had been since the day he'd met him, it shouldn't have come as any surprise that she was a chip off the old block.

With the snow getting heavier, he knocked on the door and blew on his hands. It was freezing, although for the first time in years he was going to be able to enjoy winter in a warm environment, unlike the past thirty-odd years.

He clenched his jaw, allowing the feeling to wash over him. Holding on to anger wasn't going to help the situation, but getting what was his, what was owed to him, well, that was altogether a different thing.

The door was opened by Claudia. 'Back already?'

'Sorry, darlin', I think my phone dropped out of my pocket.'

Claudia grinned. 'And there's me thinking you were coming back because you couldn't resist me.'

Ben laughed. 'There is that, of course.'

'Come on in.' She gestured, and like earlier, Ben followed her down the hallway, walking into Claudia's private lounge.

'It's probably over there on the sofa.'

'Let's take a look, shall we?' Claudia was cheerful.

'Thanks, I appreciate it.' Ben quietly closed the door behind him.

'I can't see it, are you sure you didn't drop it on the pavement outside?'

'No, and actually I remember now, it's still in my pocket.'

Claudia looked at him. 'Is this some sort of game? Because if it is, I charge for role-playing.' Her voice became hostile.

'It's not a game – far from it. But now it's only you and me, you can start telling me the fucking truth.' Ben's whole demeanour changed as he walked towards her. 'And I don't want any bullshit, understand?'

The look of shock was quite apparent on Claudia's face. 'Get out.'

'Save your breath, babe. I'm not going anywhere until you tell me everything you know about Harvey.'

'I don't know anything. Now I won't tell you again: I want you out.'

Ben shook his head. 'I'm not sure who you think you're talking to, but I'd save your breath, unless you're volunteering to pick me up and throw me out . . . No, I didn't think so. So you'd better start telling me what I want to know . . . Who the fuck was this crowd that Harvey was knocking about with?'

Claudia pursed her lips. 'I can't remember.'

He stepped towards her, taking in the deep lines of age on her face. 'I don't usually go around threatening old women, but this time I'm going to make an exception. And if you don't want me to do that, and you want to keep this nice and stress-free, stop the shit, all right? Soon as you tell me what I need to know, I'll walk out the door, and you'll never have to see me again.'

Without warning, Claudia spat in his face. He stared at her in disgust, then he roughly grabbed the collar of her dressing gown to wipe his face. 'Now that was very fucking silly of you, because that has *really* pissed me off.' His voice was low and threatening, and slowly he reached into his pocket and brought out a small handgun, which he placed at the side of Claudia's temple.

'So, shall we start again? This is how it's going to go. I am going to ask you, and you are going to answer. That way, you won't get hurt and I won't get my hands dirty. Deal?'

Claudia – no doubt regretting her outburst – gave the tiniest of nods.

'Good. See, that's better . . . now, who were these people, and why, after all this time . . . thirty-six years, are you still keeping your mouth shut about them?' He pushed the gun into her temple as a reminder.

Claudia took a deep breath. 'Because I heard through the grapevine . . .' She sounded breathless but Ben knew it was fear tightening her chest '. . . they're still around.'

'Names.'

'I don't know – I swear, it was Harvey who was hanging around with them. I don't understand why, because he never seemed that type of bloke, but then, people can hide all sorts, can't they. Once I found out, I didn't want any part of him. That was the last time I saw him. Not long after that I heard that he'd disappeared clean off the face of the earth. But no one was paying that much attention back then, they were all too shocked by what had gone down with Tel and his crowd.'

'And with me.'

'You served time as well?'

Ben nodded; the bitterness flowed through him. 'Yeah, a lot of time. It made what Tel did seem like nothing. Thirty-six years, three months, two weeks and one day, is a fucking long time.'

'Oh my God, you're Ben? . . . I had no idea. Harvey was always talking about you. He had so much respect for you.'

He pushed the gun into the side of her head. 'Stick to the subject.' Ben glared at her. He was surprised that he hadn't met Claudia before. After all, unlike the story he'd told Ava, he'd actually known Harvey since they were kids, which was why a few months ago, when he'd found out about Harvey having a daughter, he'd been more than a little surprised. He'd been friends with Harvey thirty-nine years ago, when they were twenty, and that was when Harvey had first become a parent, but he hadn't said anything to Ben. He hadn't uttered a word. Nothing. Not to him or anyone else around him. Looking back, there'd been no signs either, but then that was Harvey, wasn't it?

No matter how close they'd been, Harvey had always been a closed book when it came to his personal affairs. He'd compartmentalized his life, keeping groups of people separate from each other. Clearly, that was what had happened in this case. For reasons of his own, Harvey had decided not to let him in on it.

The secrets had been there, on Harvey's side at least, but Ben hadn't seen them. And those secrets had had far-reaching consequences – like him spending the past thirty-six years locked up.

Switching back to what Claudia was saying, Ben felt the beginning of a tension headache.

'He was hanging around with this guy who I do remember the name of – Ash Barker. You might have heard about him – he was all over the news.'

Ben knew exactly who Ash was – the whole of the country probably did. Ash was a nonce, but thankfully he was still banged up. He'd also had the misfortune to come across the guy a few times.

'Anyway, it turned out Ash was connected to the men Ben was

hanging out with. They used to have a place over by the docks. They still have, I think. Not sure exactly where, though. They lie low, under the radar . . . Nasty fuckers.' She looked at Ben. 'Fuck knows why Harvey decided to become mates with him, or any of them for that matter . . . Ash was a sadist, a fucking pervert. None of my girls wanted to be around him, although they were probably too old for him anyway – he liked them young . . . But Harvey must have been attracted to that side of life too. I'm not a prude, darlin', but that lot were sick fuckers.'

'What are you saying? You think Harvey was a nonce as well? No fucking way! I would've known.' Although, the moment he'd said it, Ben immediately had his doubts. Would he have known? He'd had no idea what Harvey had in store for him thirty-six years ago; if he had done, he wouldn't have spent more than half his life inside. So why would this be any different?

'We only know what people want to show us, darlin'. . . And it seems like Harvey didn't want to show you everything. I'd say anyone who lies to you the way he has over your girlfriend—'

'She's not my girlfriend.'

'Whatever.' She smirked. 'There's clearly a side to him that you don't know anything about. And let me tell you something: no one hangs around with nonces unless they're a nonce themselves.'

'What the hell are you doing?' Ava stood at the door. She stared at the gun in Ben's hand. Although he was less concerned about her seeing the firearm than he was about her having over-heard the conversation he'd been having. 'I was just having a little chat with Claudia here, and she's been really helpful.'

He slipped the gun into his pocket and headed out of the door and into the street. Ava ran behind, grabbing his arm. 'What the hell was that about?'

Ben didn't answer her directly. 'How much did you hear?'

'What are you talking about?'

'In Claudia's, what did you hear?' Ben stood facing her, although he leaned forward and gently pulled up Ava's collar to stop the snow from falling down her neck.

'I didn't hear anything. But I saw you with a gun against her head . . . Jesus Christ, Ben, a gun? Seriously . . .' She was angry and bemused all at the same time. This went way beyond him trying to help her. 'Who the hell goes around doing that? Do I need to be worried?'

'About what?'

'About you. Do I need to be afraid of you?' She stared at him.

'Afraid of me? Why would you say that?'

She blinked as the snow blew into her eyes. 'I'd say a man holding a gun against someone's head isn't your average guy.'

Ben shook his head and turned away. 'I was only trying to help.'

'That's an extreme way to do it.' She stared directly into his eyes. 'What is it you're not saying? And you better start by telling me what's *really* going on.'

Claudia Davies sat down with the whisky bottle next to her. She hadn't thought about Ash Barker for all these years. He was a twisted sadist and anyone in their right mind would've stayed well away from him. Like she'd said to Ben, she'd never understood why Harvey had all of a sudden changed. She'd liked him, liked him more than she'd ever let on to him, but the minute Ash had come onto the scene, all feelings for Harvey had disappeared.

She took a sip of her drink, but hearing a noise, she glanced up. 'Who the fuck are you?'

Jed Carter and Dean Burling stood at the door of her lounge.

Jed regarded her, a look of disgust on his face. 'I want you to tell me exactly what Ben wanted . . .'

29

Tony stood in the shower, letting the hot water scold his skin. He'd washed his body with a mixture of bleach and soap, making sure all trace of Danny Oliver was washed from him, although that was more about the way he was feeling than anything else. Joe had been right, the place where they'd dumped him was remote and deep in the woods, so the likelihood of anyone coming across Danny's body was slim to zero.

Exhaustion swept over him, and he looked down at his hands. What the fuck had he done? He was so far from the kind of guy who'd resort to violence . . . to beating someone up . . . to killing them. But that's exactly what he'd done, wasn't it? Without thought, he'd battered Danny senseless.

Leaning on the shower wall, he took a deep breath and thought of Ava, and within seconds the hatred he'd felt for Danny in that moment rose again inside him, but this time it was aimed at Ava, or rather for what she'd done to him.

She was the one who had put him in this fucking position. She was the one who'd lied, and it seemed like her lies went a long way back. All those times she'd pretended she'd had after-hours clients, she'd been busy snorting up the whole of Bolivia. Jesus Christ! And what else? What else had she been lying about?

Stepping out of the shower, he grabbed the towel from the side. She'd probably been lying to him for the whole of their marriage. Then a thought came to him. A thought that made him feel sick to his stomach . . . The mark on her neck the other day. He'd questioned her, but she'd vehemently denied it. Oh God. He covered his face like he'd done earlier. He couldn't even go there.

Then a surge of anger rushed through him, and he swiped the bottles and lotions off the top of the cabinet. 'Fuck.' He yelled and punched the mirror, and immediately he felt a shot of pain in his hand as the glass cut into it.

'Shit.'

The blood dripped onto the floor, and Tony grabbed a towel, wrapping his hand up in it. He heard his phone vibrate and he saw it was Joe.

'Hey, mate, how are you?' He kept his voice as even as he could.

'*You all right? You sound out of breath.*' Joe's voice was calm, as though what had gone down earlier hadn't happened.

'Yeah, I'm good.' Tony looked around him at the mess in the bathroom. 'Oh, right, yeah . . . I've just come back from a jog . . . What can I do for you?' They'd decided not to talk about Danny, especially on the phone. If something cropped up that they needed to discuss, then they'd meet somewhere away from prying ears and eyes.

'I thought you'd like to know; I've got a trace on Ava's number.'

Tony felt dizzy. He was incapable of speech.

'*You still there, mate?*'

'. . . Yeah, sorry. How close is the trace?'

'*It's a good one. At first I thought we'd only be able to work out the nearest phone masts, but I was able to narrow it down to a couple of streets . . . I got Brian to help me. Don't worry, he won't say anything.*'

'Are you sure?' A slight panic came into Tony's voice.

'*Yeah, I am. There are a few things I know about Brian that he wouldn't want anyone else to find out about.*'

Tony didn't ask what, and it crossed his mind that he wouldn't want to make an enemy of Joe.

'Brilliant. Thanks. I appreciate your help, mate . . . Hold on while I go and get a pen, it's better than texting it, I don't want it on my phone.'

'No worries . . . and then get yourself down there and see her, sort this shit out. And Tony, forget about what happened earlier . . . I know I have.'

'Yeah, you're right . . . And don't worry, I'll go and see her, then me and my good wife will have a little chat . . .'

30

'I got some croissants; I thought it was my turn to get breakfast this time. Oh, and a cappuccino.' It was the next morning and Ava yawned as she pushed the coffee towards Ben.

'Thanks. Did you sleep OK?'

'I did.' Which was a lie; she'd spent most of the night tossing and turning. She'd ended up calling the hospital; it had come as a relief to hear that her dad was stable, and they were thinking of bringing him out of his induced coma. 'Anyway, did you?' she asked warmly.

'Like the dead.' He sat on the stool opposite her.

'You would tell me if Claudia had said anything, wouldn't you, Ben?' They hadn't talked last night, not really. She had been angry with him at first, then she'd tried a different tack, being non-judgemental. Neither of those approaches had worked, though. She hadn't got any information out of him, and in the end, she'd given up.

By rights, she should be throwing him out, especially after his behaviour with Claudia. She hadn't bought his excuse that it was purely about helping her find her mum. She'd have to be a fool to think that. It was obvious that she should've trusted her initial instinct about him. He was a liar, and clearly had an ulterior motive. What it was, she didn't know, or even how to start guessing what it was. But it all came down to the fact, anyone who was a friend of her dad was not to be trusted.

Sighing, she rubbed her head. Why then didn't she just send

him packing and have nothing to do with him? That part was on her, and she couldn't actually understand it . . . Was it because she thought Ben was her last hope of finding the truth? Or maybe the whole situation was so overwhelming she needed someone by her side. Although, if that was true, why didn't she just ask Tony?

Taking another sip of her coffee, Ava fell into deep thought.

Ben grabbed a pain au chocolat off the plate and stared at her as he ate. What was it about her? She was such a mess, for someone so beautiful, who had such a great career. He'd thought it before: everything about her spelled trouble. And yet, as crazy as it was, he couldn't help being drawn in by her.

Yeah, of course there was the immediate physical attraction, but as strained as the past few days had been, he'd actually enjoyed her company. Christ, what was he even thinking! He needed to stop this shit. He was just being an idiot. Of course, he'd enjoyed her company – she was the first woman he'd hung around with since he'd got out of prison. Yes, for the first couple of weeks he'd shagged every single one-night stand he'd come across – after thirty-six years inside with only hairy-arsed men for company, anything with a female pulse would have satisfied his need. But being with Ava had felt different somehow.

Pulling himself together, Ben shrugged. 'I would tell you, if there was anything to say.' There was no way on earth he was about to spill to her that Claudia thought her old man was a nonce; no way at all. There was also no way that he was going to tell her that he didn't know Harvey well enough – although he'd thought once upon a time he did – to rule it out.

'I'm going to have a root through Dad's things in a bit. There are a couple of boxes in the back of his walk-in-wardrobes, and I'm going to have a look around the attic as well.'

Ben gave a tight smile. He hadn't even realized there was an attic. He hadn't had the chance to take a proper look around before Ava had arrived. Contrary to what he'd told her, the other day had been the first time he'd set foot in Harvey's gaff. And the last thing he'd been expecting was for Ava to show up. That had, as it was doing now, complicated matters. 'I'll do that, you don't have to bother.'

Ava gave him a long look. 'It's fine. He's my dad and—'

'I don't mind.' Ben pushed a little more.

'And I said, *it's fine.*' Her voice was firm, and Ben got the message loud and clear.

He took another bite of pain au chocolat and noticed a text from Terry on his phone which he'd put on the table in front of him.

Call me.

He frowned. Terry wasn't one to get in touch unless it was absolutely necessary. He had an aversion to phones, mainly because he'd been caught out twice by the Old Bill, who'd nabbed him based on evidence gathered from his mobile. Not that Ben had much sympathy; anyone who was that stupid, deserved all they got.

Taking the pastry with him, he picked up his mobile and moved towards the door. 'I have to make a call.' He didn't wait for Ava to reply, just sloped off into the hallway, dialling Terry.

On the third ring, it was picked up.

'*Hello?*'

'I got your message.' Ben didn't bother with niceties.

'*Can you talk?*'

Ben glanced across to the kitchen, making sure Ava wasn't in listening range. 'Yeah, what is it?'

'*It's Claudia.*'

'Oh, don't fucking tell me she'd been on the blower about what happened yesterday? What did she expect me to do? Walk away and accept that she wouldn't tell me what was going on? Fuck that.'

There was a pause. '*No, it ain't that . . . Claudia's dead.*'

'No, you're having a laugh.' Ben walked into the lounge, shutting the door behind him.

'*So, I take it from your reaction, you didn't do it?*'

'Are you taking the piss? Of course I didn't fucking do it. What do you take me for?'

'*I had to check.*'

'No, no, you didn't, mate. I don't go around killing women – that's not my style,' Ben growled. Then he reined in his temper and asked, 'So what happened? Did anyone see anything?'

'*She was shot. And no, no one heard or saw anything. When I spoke to Reg, he said there were so many geezers coming in and out of that place, it was like a doctor's waiting room. And you and I both know it's easy to disguise the sound of a bullet.*'

Ben didn't reply. He didn't want to go there. Not now, not ever. For his own sanity, some things had to be left in the past. He did not dwell on them.

'*Did she say anything to you? Did you have any luck?*'

'If you mean, did it turn out Claudia was Ava's mum, no. Harvey was giving her a whole pack of bullshit . . . and even when I put some pressure on her, she still came up with fuck-all.' There was no way he was going to spill what Claudia had said to Tel. Like Ava, he was best kept in the dark. But Ben couldn't get his head around what had happened to her.

'*If it wasn't you, who was it? That's what you need to ask yourself . . . Was it Claudia they were after, or was it you?*' Terry mused.

'What are you talking about?'

'*Come on, Ben, you must've thought about it: they'll be after you*

156

now that you're out. They'll be thinking you have some questions to answer. You and Harvey.'

Ben's temper flared. 'You mean, they'll have some questions for Harvey, *not me.* I served the fucking time, don't forget, unlike him. He just vanished off the face of the earth.'

'But now you've found him. Maybe they did too, because what . . .'

Ben had stopped listening to Terry. He was wondering if it was possible they could have followed him. He'd been careful – overly careful, he'd thought. Coming out of prison, then heading to a remote location in Scotland where he'd laid low. Because, after thirty-six years, what was another few weeks? Only then had he followed up on the information he'd gathered over the years, the money he'd spent to find Harvey, all while sitting in his cell.

Not that anything had come up during those years of putting out feelers. Harvey had vanished without trace – or so it seemed, until luck had fallen Ben's way for once.

'. . . The Old Bill, as you can imagine, are sniffing round.'

Ben pulled himself out of his thoughts to tune back in to Terry.

'It always gets messy when something like this happens. But then—'

'Do you know where Ash Barker's crew hangs out?' Ben interrupted. 'I heard a rumour that they've still got their place down the docks. Do you know anything about it?'

'Why are you asking?'

'Don't answer a fucking question with a question.' Ben was irritated and he let it be known. 'Do you know or not?'

'The only thing I know is that about ten years ago they were still operating in that area. Word has it their places have been raided more times than you've had the proverbial hot dinner, but they never find anything. Ash Barker's lot, they know exactly what they're doing. It wouldn't surprise me if Ash was still pulling the strings from inside.'

Ben heard Terry give out a long sigh.

'*To tell you the truth, I don't want to know any more about them . . . Has this got something to do with Claudia?*'

'Of course not,' Ben lied. He didn't want to raise Terry's suspicions, although it wouldn't be long before Terry put two and two together. For now though, he was going to keep his mouth shut. 'I met some bloke inside, and he was talking about Ash. He mentioned a club, and the people who used to hang around with him. I didn't know anything, so I was wondering, that's all. You know how it is – blast from the past and all that shit.'

'*Sickos, the whole fucking lot of them.*'

It was clear to Ben that Terry had no idea Harvey had been an acquaintance of Ash's. How much of an acquaintance was anyone's guess.

'*Anyway, like I say, Ben, the Old Bill are all over Claudia's, so if I were you, I'd stay well away.*'

'Oh, don't fucking worry, I've got no interest in being done for a crime I didn't commit . . . *again*.' And with those words, Ben clicked off the phone angrily.

'Everything all right?' Ava popped her head around the corner. She smiled.

'It's all good, babe . . . Couldn't be better.' Ben gave her a wink as he kept the lies rolling in.

31

'Does this mean anything to you?' An hour later, Ava walked into the front room and dropped a small, tatty notepad on the coffee table next to him.

Frowning, Ben picked it up, shaking his head. He sat up in the chair. 'No, should it?' He flicked through the pages.

'It's obviously one of his old notebooks, but there's a whole lot of addresses in there. I've done a few Google searches on my phone; most of them look like they're shops or restaurants, but there are a few which are down the dock, across near Tilbury.'

Hearing Ava talking about the docks made Ben's blood run cold. This is what he was dreading: Ava getting a head start on things.

'Most of the stuff is no good to us,' Ava continued. 'But I thought those addresses might be of some help. It's strange because I have a memory . . . it's not completely clear, but I remember when I was little, being down the docks with Dad.'

'Are you sure?' It piqued Ben's curiosity, but he was careful not to push her. She sounded hesitant, and it was important that she open up rather than clam up under pressure.

'Yeah, I have so few memories, but this one, for some reason, I can recall quite vividly.' She rolled her eyes. 'But, who knows, it could all be in my imagination, or I'm remembering it wrongly. I mean, I've spoken to enough clients who have false memories.' She shrugged and laughed at herself, waiting for Ben to join in.

Ben watched her and decided not to react to the address Ava

was showing him. He had no idea if it was where Ash Barker and his crew had their underground club. If it was, why the hell would Harvey have taken Ava there? It wasn't the sort of establishment he'd take an adult to, let alone a kid. Unless . . . Ben's stomach turned at the thought that had made its way into his head. There was only one reason anyone would take a child there. One reason alone.

'Are you all right?' Ava came and sat next to him. 'You look pale.'

'No, I'm fine, but it's a lot.' He gave her a tight smile.

'What's a lot?'

'Everything, *everything* that's happening . . . Look, do you mind if I keep this? Check out those places down the docks.'

He held the notebook, but Ava gently pulled it from his grasp and took it back. 'Actually, I'd rather keep them myself, if it's all the same to you.'

'Yeah . . . sure, of course, but I'll write down the address, go and have a recce.'

Ava stared at him. 'When were you thinking of going?'

He shrugged. 'No time like the present.'

'Good.' Ava stood. 'Then I'll come with you.'

He laughed in a condescending manner. His handsome features scored with irritation. 'I don't think so, darlin'.'

Ava raised her eyebrows. 'First off, in case you haven't noticed, I'm the one holding the address. Secondly, it's fine if you don't want to take me – I can always go by myself. And thinking about it now, maybe you should be the one who doesn't come. After yesterday's shit with Claudia, I don't know if it's such a good idea to have you tag along.'

Ben's hackles went up. 'I told you already, I was trying to help . . . I'm sorry I got carried away.' It crossed Ben's mind Ava was like a dog with a bone.

'Carried away is raising your voice, losing your temper. It doesn't begin to cover putting a gun to someone's head.'

Ben had to take a deep breath. He wasn't used to having to explain himself. That wasn't the way prison life went. It was simply a matter of telling someone to do something and, if they didn't, then making sure they reaped the consequences. In prison, patience was not a virtue.

'Look, I know it wasn't ideal, but people like Claudia will never talk unless you can apply some kind of pressure.'

'Well, it didn't work, did it?'

He spoke evenly to her. 'No, I guess not.' He didn't add what had happened to Claudia. He didn't want to freak her out. She was already spooked, and he needed to reassure her, not make the situation worse.

'OK, I can see that I'm not going to win this round, so come along, if that's what you want. But you need to stay in the car.'

'After what happened yesterday, I'd say it's the other way round, wouldn't you?'

32

As usual, the traffic through London slowed them down. They headed through Whitechapel, and through Bow, which seemed overly busy, most of it bumper to bumper, until Ben finally hit the A13, driving slightly faster than Ava would've wished, although she didn't let on.

Her mind was elsewhere, as it had been most of the morning. She needed to know what was happening with Tony. Could he really be this angry with her, that he was ignoring her calls? Sighing, she gazed out of the window, watching London fade into the distance.

Suddenly, she frowned. Another, unformed memory made its way into her mind as Tilbury Docks came into view.

'You're quiet.' Ben looked towards her.

'I could say the same for you.'

'Touché.' He fell back into silence. Bringing Ava here was a mistake, but what choice did he have? She'd left him with no option but to agree. She held the cards, and if he wanted to find out *anything* that might help him get what was owed to him, he had to try to keep her sweet.

Who knew, maybe he was going down a rabbit hole, and chasing these leads would turn out to be nothing more than a distraction, a waste of time, when he should be focusing on his main objective. Although, not being able to speak to Harvey had limited his choices; at least this way he was making some progress, even if only to eliminate false leads.

The other thing that was preying on his mind was Claudia. He hoped it was merely a coincidence, but when had he ever believed in coincidences? And if she had been targeted, then what Terry had said about Ash Barker's people looking for Harvey – and looking for him – had a ring of truth to it. No matter how much he'd tried to convince himself that what happened to Harvey was merely a house robbery gone wrong, he'd been afraid all along that it was connected to what had gone down thirty-six years ago.

Driving down an unmade road, Ben slowed. They were away from the main part of the docks, which had been transformed beyond recognition in the years he'd been locked away. None of those high-rise offices had existed when he was here last. But there were other areas, like this one, which had been left untouched. It felt like a ghost town: disused shipping warehouses, half-erected buildings, and row upon row of cargo containers, giving it an eerie feel, especially on a grey, drizzly day like this.

He checked the satnav, and turned in to one of the old ship-repair facilities which had closed down years ago, driving parallel to the water. There was a remoteness to it; nothing but rusted cranes and derelict warehouses silhouetted against the sky. The place was desolate, a forgotten corner, away from prying eyes.

'Does this seem like the right place to you?' Ava asked.

'That's what the address says, but it looks as though it was closed down a long time ago. Don't forget, that notepad was years old. All we can do is try though.'

Ben parked alongside a rusting shipping container. He took out a packet of cigarettes, lit one up and took a deep drag before stepping out of the car.

The chill November wind hit his face straight away. If this was the place that Ash Barker and his crew had worked out of, and still did, he could see how perfect it was for them. It was isolated, with wide-open spaces, and the road which led to it was the only approach. Day or night, they would be able to see anyone approaching when they were still a long way off.

He wasn't surprised that, when it was raided, the police had found nothing. In the time it would have taken them to cover the ground, Ash and his lot could've easily dipped out, either via the river, with a boat on standby, or simply by heading on foot through the warren of containers into the docks beyond.

Sighing, he walked around to the passenger side and opened the door for Ava. 'Look, why don't you stay here, just so I can take a look around.' He nodded towards the warehouse, which had two vans parked up outside it, as well as a very muddy Range Rover.

'You think we've come to the right place?' Ava didn't sound convinced.

'Yeah, and there isn't anything else around here.'

He wasn't going to tell her what he'd been thinking: that this was exactly the sort of place Ash and his crew would hole up in.

'Look, Ava, stay here until I know the coast is clear, then I'll come and get you.'

She gave him a suspicious look. 'We're only checking out an address. Why do you think there's going to be a problem?'

'I don't.' He shrugged. 'Force of habit.'

'What habit?' She frowned. 'What do you know that I don't? It's an odd thing to say, otherwise.'

Not for the first time, Ava was testing his patience. 'I'm only saying, if it turns out there is a problem, I don't want you to get caught up in it.' He rubbed his face, feeling his stubble. He hoped that there was no one around, that they could drive away with Ava thinking there was nothing worth seeing. Then he could come back without her and ask the sort of questions he needed to.

Ava took a 360-degree look around her, focusing for a moment on the two vans and Range Rover. Then she turned back to Ben. 'I think we need to stick together on this – strength in numbers.'

He rolled his eyes. 'Well, it all depends on who's making up those numbers, doesn't it?'

Ava didn't bother replying; she just grabbed her scarf from the back seat and got out of the car, making her way across to the warehouse, followed closely by Ben.

Everything told him that they were about to open a can of worms . . .

33

Tony was grateful to get off the train. He'd booked a seat in the quiet carriage, but he'd ended up sitting crammed against the window, while four unruly children screamed and ran about, their mother happily ignoring them as she watched a Netflix movie all the way to London.

Walking through the station, Tony, dressed casually in jeans and a hoodie, checked his phone. Joe had promised to call him if there was any news about Danny. He knew he was being paranoid about the whole situation, and Joe had had to reassure him several times that it wouldn't be an issue, no one would find Danny, although Joe had covered their tracks by putting in a report.

Joe had called by early this morning to let him know he'd filed a report stating that they'd come across Danny Oliver and he'd recognized them. Danny had immediately started mouthing off, so they'd tried to bring him in but there'd been a scuffle and Danny had flashed a knife and run off . . .

In the event anyone did discover the body, that would explain any traces of their DNA found on Danny. Just a precaution, Joe had said. He'd also said there was nothing to worry about, so why then was Tony feeling worse?

Blowing out a long breath, Tony hailed a cab. Instead of stopping, it sped past.

The location of Ava's mobile, along with her IP address, had been narrowed down to three streets which, judging by the map, wouldn't be too difficult to cover. There were a variety of offices and shops, which he wouldn't rule out completely, but he planned to try the residential addresses first.

'*Cab!*' Tony yelled, waving down a shiny black taxi. It pulled over.

'*Where to, mate?*'

'Soho.'

Tony stepped into the cab, sinking back into the seat. He watched the sleet running down the windows and tried to push the image of Danny's lifeless body out of his head.

'Business or pleasure?' the cabbie asked, grinning at him in the driver's mirror.

'Sorry?'

'I was just wondering if you were here on business or pleasure.'

Tony turned back to look out of the window. Ava's face flashed into his mind. His wife. His good wife, who had been the reason he'd done something really bad.

'Well, let's just say it's definitely not pleasure . . .'

34

'Who the fuck are you?'

Following Ben through the entrance of the derelict warehouse into a corridor lined with doors on either side, Ava spun around to come face to face with a small, craggy man. On his cheek was a raised scar, and from the looks of his nose, he had either boxed in his youth or been in a lot of fights.

'Sorry, we were—'

'Lost.' Ben interrupted her. His answer surprised Ava. Maybe she was being naive, but she'd assumed he would tell the truth. 'Sorry, mate, we were looking for the export office.'

The man stared at Ben, looking him up and down. 'Well, it isn't fucking here, so you can turn the fuck around right now.'

Ava watched Ben's jaw clench and she wondered if he was going to do something that might escalate the situation, but he just said, 'No problem . . . We'll go.' Then he'd taken Ava's arm and steered her towards the entrance.

'What's going on, Dave?' The door opened at the end of the corridor. Four men appeared, blocking their way. Instinctively, Ava took a step back.

One of the men – tall, olive-skinned, with a face that spelled trouble – stepped forward.

'Apparently, these two are looking for the export office,' Dave told him.

The tall man tilted his head, and Ava noticed how he kept one of his hands in his pocket. 'For what company?' He spoke gruffly and, like his colleague, seemed full of suspicion. It was clear to Ava that he wasn't buying Ben's lie.

'Wetherby's.' Ben spoke without hesitation.

The men turned to look at each other.

'Wetherby's? Hey, Dave, do you know a Wetherby's?' The olive-skinned man spoke while keeping his eyes on Ava and Ben.

'Nope, never heard of it meself.' Ava could hear the mocking tone in his voice.

The tall man addressed Ben again. 'You see, there isn't a Wetherby's here. And as far back as I can remember, there never has been.'

Ava stared at Ben, and something about the way he looked at her told her not to say anything.

'Then that's my mistake. Apologies, mate. We'll just head off, and I'll make sure that I have a word with my satnav.' He winked at the men, turning on the charm which, in the short space of time Ava had known him, he'd used at every opportunity.

'Not so fast, mate. Why don't you tell me exactly what you're here for.'

'Like I say, I was looking for Wetherby's, no more no less.'

The man flicked a toothpick in his mouth. 'And like I say, I need you to tell me what you're doing here.'

'Get out of my fucking way, all right?'

Ava knew from the way Ben had reacted – not just in what he said, but in the way he'd said it – that he was not faking the anger or that threatening tone underneath his words. It was real, and everyone in the corridor knew it. Which made Ava wonder how safe they were going to be now. These men didn't seem the sort to play games.

'I tell you what, why don't we go and have a nice cosy chat. There's a room just down there.'

The man gestured with his head for Ben and Ava to start

walking, which they did. As they made their way towards the stairwell, Ava noticed that one of the doors was slightly ajar. She sneaked a look inside, expecting to see an office. Instead, she saw a minibar, some chairs upholstered in deep red velvet . . . and oddly, a bed. But the strangest thing were the walls, which were decorated with wallpaper intended for a child's bedroom.

'Get a move on.' She was pushed in the back by one of the men.

'Don't put your fucking hands on her,' Ben snapped.

'It's fine,' Ava said calmly. She didn't want him to make this situation worse than it already was.

'If I was you, mate, I'd listen to the lady. She's talking sense.'

They fell silent again, and Ava focused on breathing deeply, trying not to let her nerves get the better of her.

At the top of the stairs, they were taken into an open-plan space. The grey, tinted windows stretched around all sides, giving far-reaching views of the docks. Like the room downstairs, it had a bar in the corner. Chairs and tables were dotted around, and Ava thought anyone could be forgiven for thinking they were in a Manhattan night club.

The door in the corner opened, and a woman dressed in a high-end designer suit appeared. Ava struggled to put an age to her; she guessed somewhere around the late sixties mark.

'Take a seat.' The woman spoke politely, very much at odds with the way the men had addressed them. 'Can I get you a drink?'

'No, but I'd appreciate it if you'd call off your goons, and let us get on with our day.' Ben stared at her with open hostility.

'I can see how this is an inconvenience for you, but I'm sure once we've had a little chat, everything can be sorted.' She smiled, and Ava thought how much more menacing she was than the men.

She walked across to the bar, and poured herself a tonic, slowly and purposefully dropping in ice and lemon. 'So, how about we start off with your name. That always helps.' She tilted her head.

'Fuck you!' Ben spat out the words.

The woman placed her drink on the bar, and with the same, slow casual pace, she strolled across to where Ben and Ava were standing.

Stopping in front of Ben, she stared at him for a moment, then slapped him hard across the face, the force of the blow making Ben's head jolt to one side.

'Rudeness is one of my pet peeves.' She smoothed down Ben's shirt collar, then turned her back on them and went to pick up her drink.

Ava glanced at Ben, who was breathing heavily, no doubt trying to curb his temper as a red, angry mark appeared on his cheek. Much to Ava's relief, he remained silent.

The woman turned her attention to Ava. As they held each other's gaze, Ava was unexpectedly struck by a distant memory she couldn't quite grasp. There was something familiar about the woman . . . it was her green eyes, as though she'd looked into them before. Shaking off her confusion, Ava waited for the woman to speak. Her profession had taught her that rushing to fill silence was a sign of weakness; she was determined to maintain her composure.

'Maybe, you'll be more forthcoming.' This was directed at Ava. 'The sooner we sort out the misunderstanding, the better.'

'It's like we told your colleagues, we were looking for an export firm and we'd been given this address . . . To tell you the truth, this feels like a very bad joke that we're not in on.'

The woman nodded. 'I'd like to see some identification.' Her tone was flat.

Ava shook her head. 'You have no authority.'

'And you have no authority to be wandering around my warehouse.' The woman shrugged. 'I think it's only fair, don't you, that I check to see who you are. You could be anyone.' She nodded at Ava's bag, which she'd placed on the chair next to her. 'I'll do the honours.' She turned her gaze away from Ava for a moment and nodded to one of the men, who immediately grabbed the bag.

Ben went to make a move.

'That would be very silly.' The woman's voice cut through the air. 'Take a seat, both of you.'

Ava watched Ben hesitate, then they both sat down while the man began to rummage through her bag. A phone was brought out, packet of tissues, her wallet – which they went through, although she never kept her driver's licence in it.

'Give that here.' The woman reached out for the wallet and removed one of Ava's bank cards.

'Dr Ava Barclay . . . well, well. I didn't realize that I was due a health check-up.' She tilted her head to one side. 'I wouldn't have put you down as a doctor.' She passed the card back to the man just as he was bringing out another item.

Ava's heart sank.

The gun.

'What the fuck!' This from Ben.

'I was about to say the same thing,' said the woman. 'Now, I wouldn't say it was common for people to walk about with a gun, unless they're looking for trouble or expecting trouble.'

'It's neither,' Ava snapped. 'I took it from someone I know, and . . .' She trailed off, not only did it sound empty, but this wasn't going the way she'd hoped. She felt a rising fear.

The man dropped the gun back in her bag, although it was the woman who was doing all the talking.

'Why don't you start telling me the truth about why you're

here. Otherwise, I will have no option but to force it out of you – starting with him.' She nodded towards Ben. 'And I don't think that would be pleasant for anyone . . .' She paused, but neither Ava nor Ben said a word. 'Have it your own way then.'

She didn't need to give them a cue; all four men strode across to Ben and set about dragging him out of the chair.

'It's about Harvey,' Ava blurted out.

'Shut up, Ava.' Ben gave her daggers, which Ava ignored.

'Harvey Fletcher . . . that's why we're here,' she continued. 'That's the only reason we came. He's my father, and I wanted to . . .' She searched for a pretext, and not being able to come up with one, settled for the truth: 'I'm piecing together my child-hood, trying to find out more about his friends and life when he was younger.'

A quiet descended on the room. The woman stepped out from behind the bar and gave a nod. The men immediately released Ben.

'Harvey Fletcher!' Her face broke into a smile. 'You don't mean Big Harve, as in Ash Barker's mate, do you? Now that's a name I haven't heard in a long while. Fuck me!' She licked her lips. 'There were a few people not too happy with him, I do remember that.' She cackled. 'How is he?'

'He's dead.' It was Ben's turn to get in. 'He passed away, and like my wife said . . .'

Ava gave him the quickest of glances.

'. . . I was helping her,' he continued. 'She wanted to find out a bit more stuff, you know, all this family tree shit that women like to do.'

The woman glanced between them. 'I'll have my men show you out.' She passed Ava the bag. 'I'm sorry for your loss.'

'Thank you.' Ava got up and began to follow the men.

'I'm sorry I can't help put your tree together.' There was a mocking tone to her voice. 'I haven't seen Harvey in well over thirty years.' She laughed nastily, which made Ava turn. 'Though I do know one thing, Dr Barclay . . . He liked them young as well . . .'

35

Ava almost ran out of the building, sucking in the fresh air, but the wave of nausea overwhelmed her and she vomited, closing her eyes, trying not to hear those words in her head: *He liked them young as well.*

'Why did you go and do that?' Ben came out of the building a few moments later, and Ava hurriedly stood and wiped her mouth.

'Excuse me?'

'Why did you go and tell them. Have you any idea what you could've done back there? Opening your big mouth like that could have caused endless grief.'

'Wait, what? I've just saved you from getting a beating or whatever else those knuckleheads were going to do to you, and you're complaining?' Ava was amazed by Ben's attitude.

'They were bluffing. You could tell.' He sounded exasperated.

Ava shook her head furiously. 'Really? And you knew that for sure, did you?'

Ben clenched his jaw and didn't say anything else as Ava ranted.

'Next time, I won't bother, I'll just leave you to it . . . And what did she mean: *He liked them young as well?*' Ava's heart raced as she said the words out loud. 'What did she fucking mean?'

Ben looked away. 'I don't know. They were winding you up. You saw what they were like. That's who they are.'

Ava narrowed her eyes as she stared at him. 'Wait a minute . . . What do you know about them?'

Ben was aggressive in his reply. 'Fuck all.'

'You can't look at me, can you . . . Avoidance of eye contact, Ben. The classic tell-tale sign that someone's lying or hiding something. I'd say you're doing both right now, wouldn't you?'

'No, I wouldn't.' He stomped across to the car, and only then did he turn round to face her. 'But it's pointless telling you that, isn't it? Because you're the one who's got the degree in psychology, not me.' His voice dripped with scorn.

She stepped closer to him, ignoring the wind-driven sleet. 'Oh no, don't turn this on me, or try to deflect what I was saying . . . You *knew* where we were going, didn't you? And I don't mean the address. I mean, you knew what we were walking into.'

Ben wiped his face, though Ava guessed the gesture had more to do with her venting her frustration than the weather.

'Don't be stupid. Do I look like I want to be jumped on by a crew of geezers?' he yelled. 'And yeah, I thought I'd take you along for the ride.'

Ava let her rage get the better of her. She pushed him, angrier for the tears she felt threatening to come. 'Don't you dare condescend to me! And just so you know, I'm not being *fucking* stupid. Though I have been, trusting you.' She burst into bitter laughter. 'Oh God, that's why you were so keen to come here with me, wasn't it? You know exactly who these people are, and you didn't want me to talk to them without you, in case I found out some information about you and Dad . . . I'm right, aren't I?'

Ava was nearer the truth than Ben would've wanted.

'No.' He closed his eyes for a moment and sighed loudly. 'I didn't know what we were walking into, I swear. Yeah, I thought they might be a bit off, but I would've never brought you, if I'd known.'

'There you go again, treating me like I'm your sidekick. It's you who came along with me, remember . . . But what's so weird is how you reacted. Maybe you're telling me the truth when you say you didn't know what we were walking into, but you know something about those people, otherwise why shut down what I was saying about Dad?'

'Jesus Christ, I'm not big on telling people our business. That's just the way I am – old school. I've said it before, Ava, you don't need to look for an ulterior motive in everything. I'm trying to look out for you.' His gaze wandered over her face. 'I don't want anything to happen to you.'

'No, sorry, I don't believe you. We both know there's more to it than that.'

Ben made to open his mouth, but Ava cut him off.

'I don't want to hear any more of your lies, all right?' She fiddled with the button on her leather jacket. 'And FYI, never pretend I'm your wife again.'

'That won't be hard to do, darlin', because fuck knows, if I had a ball and chain, it wouldn't be you.'

'What's that supposed to mean?' Ava could've kicked herself; what difference did it make what he meant? He didn't know her, his opinion meant nothing, but she'd given him the invitation to carry on now.

'What it means, sweetheart, is if I were fool enough to get hitched, I'd want myself a good wife.'

She was so angry, she didn't trust herself to speak.

'So can we go now?' He adopted a softer tone. 'And on the way home, I think you need to tell me about that gun in your bag, don't you?'

Ava returned his smile with a scowl, breaking off when her phone buzzed. She pulled it out of her bag, and saw it was Jude.

Walking away from Ben, she answered. 'Hi, stranger . . . I'm so sorry I haven't called you, it's been crazy – and trust me, that's no exaggeration! Is everything all right with you?' Ava reeled off her enthusiastic greeting. It was a relief to speak to someone familiar . . . someone she could trust.

'*Actually, I'm calling about, Tony.*'

Ava's stomach turned. 'Oh shit, is he all right? I haven't heard from him, and I was beginning to worry. What's happened?'

There was a long pause. '*He's all right . . . but . . . he came around here, and he was asking some really weird questions, I didn't say anything, but . . . I'm really sorry, Ava, but it sounds like Tony knows, and he wasn't happy about it.*'

Ava was puzzled. 'Knows what?' Watching a boat in the distance, she spoke cautiously, not really wanting to address which of her many secrets he'd uncovered. Christ, there were a whole heap of possibilities.

'*About the conference,*' Jude said matter-of-factly. '*He knows you weren't there . . . which came as news to me. Why didn't you tell me?*' She could hear the hurt in Jude's voice. '*You could've trusted me.*'

'I know and I'm sorry, I didn't want you to be part . . .' Ava took a deep breath. What was it she always said to her clients: speak it out loud, that's the only way to break the power of it. '. . . part of my lies.' Shame washed over her, and she was relieved to hear another call coming in. 'Jude, can I call you back?'

'*Sure, no problem.*'

'I'm sorry . . . and thank you.' She ended the call with Jude and connected to the other call.

'Hello?'

'*Dr Barclay?*'

Ava didn't recognize the voice. 'Speaking.'

'*It's Staff Nurse Walters, I just wanted to let you know your father's woken up . . .*'

36

'Tony, it's me . . . But you probably already know that. I was hoping to catch you, but as I haven't, I wanted to make a confession . . . it's silly really, I don't know why I didn't simply tell you, maybe it was because I was feeling a bit guilty for not being able to cope, given my job, or maybe I was feeling I shouldn't want some time alone. That sounds awful when I say it out loud, but anyway, there it is . . . But basically, I didn't go to the conference, I was going to, but . . . all the stuff with Dad and me being attacked, I didn't really process that, and I woke up that morning and just needed to get away . . . Not from you, that's not what it's about . . . Anyway, I checked myself into a nice Airbnb in the Dales . . . I'm so sorry. Look, I'll try again later, and maybe I could check out of here and we can meet up, have something to eat, and talk about going on holiday to celebrate our anniversary in style . . . I love you and, like I say, I don't know why I didn't just tell you the truth.'

'Because you're a lying bitch.' Tony spoke out loud as the message came to an end. He pushed his mobile into his pocket and continued walking down Meard Street. He'd knocked on doors in the surrounding streets, flashing his badge to encourage people to answer his questions, and showing a photo of Ava.

He hadn't told them anything, only asked if they'd seen her, but he was fully aware that it would give the impression it was a police matter.

Walking up a couple of stone steps, Tony knocked on the door.

He waited patiently, but there was no answer. He made a mental note of the number so that, if he had no success, he could return later.

He strolled past freshly painted railings, wondering how much the houses on this street went for. At a guess, he reckoned anything from four million upwards. Again he wondered what the hell was Ava playing at. And, more to the point, who she was playing with.

Until recently the possibility of Ava being unfaithful hadn't even crossed his mind. Now, it was the only thing in his head. Her with another man: kissing, caressing . . . *shit*. It was torture. The possibilities of who she was with, what she had done . . . Oh my God. He stopped in his tracks. Had she used precautions? Or had she put them both at risk? Christ Almighty, now he'd have to take a trip to the clinic.

Tony's heart was racing now; he had to lean against the railings for support, and it took a good minute or so before he felt able to continue.

He walked up another set of stone steps and rapped on the door. Unlike the last three, this one opened. He found himself facing a shaven-headed man. Handsome. Piercing green eyes, looked to be in his late fifties, but in good shape, the muscles set off by his expensive shirt and jeans.

'Look, mate, I'll cut to the chase. I ain't religious, and I ain't going to change my mind,' he said, grinning amiably at Tony.

'I'm not here to help you find God.' Tony's voice was hard and sharp. 'I'm looking for someone.'

'And what's that to do with me?'

Tony reached into his back pocket and pulled out his warrant card, which he flashed quickly. Then he pulled out his mobile. 'I'm looking for this woman. She's a person of interest and I believe she's been staying in this area. I was wondering if you'd seen her.'

'No, sorry, mate. What's she supposed to have done?'

Tony tried to sound cordial, but the man's Jack-the-lad attitude had put his back up. 'I'm not at liberty to say, sir. Are you sure you haven't seen her?'

'Positive, mate. I think I'd remember a sort like her, don't you?'

Without saying another word, Tony stomped off, leaving Ben on the doorstep watching him.

Ben went back inside and closed the door. He hadn't been quick enough to catch the name on the badge, but he didn't have to. He knew exactly who it was. Tony Barclay. When he'd been watching Ava, he'd seen her with Tony. On first appearances, they'd looked the perfect couple. Clearly, he knew different now. A lot different. But for Tony to chase her down, that was fucked up.

One thing he'd always thought he'd missed out on when he was banged up was not having the chance of forming a relationship. After all, he'd gone inside when he was twenty-three, and thirty-six years later, here he was. Then again, if Ava and Tony's relationship was typical of a happily married couple, he was grateful to be single.

He wasn't actually sure where Ava had gone. They'd driven back from the docks in silence, and the minute they'd parked, she'd stormed off, but not before he'd taken the gun from her. Walking round with a loaded weapon was not only stupid it was dangerous.

Ben looked up at the kitchen clock. She'd been gone a good few hours. As much as he was pissed off with her relentless questioning, he got how difficult this must be for her. He couldn't help worrying whether she was all right, and now on top of everything else he needed to warn her that her husband was on the hunt.

Fuck! Ben slammed his hand on the counter. He'd been meaning to take her mobile number down, but he hadn't, and now he couldn't even warn her, or check that she wasn't holed up in a bar somewhere getting pissed.

He was about to sit down and pour himself the beer he'd bought earlier, when an image of Ava dancing in the bar, surrounded by those idiots he'd had to slap about a bit, rushed into his head. He sighed and grabbed his jacket, heading out of the front door to see if he could find her before Tony did.

The bar Ava had found herself in was on the edge of Soho. She'd wandered round for a while before taking the flight of stairs that led down from the street into the club. Thick red velvet drapes covered the walls, the tables and chairs were matt black and disco balls hung from the ceiling. There was a low hum of music, but the place was quiet at this hour. A couple sat in the far corner, a man stood at the bar, and the bar staff looked bored as they played on their phones.

On the table in front of Ava were four empty glasses. Each had contained a double shot of whisky, but she could still hear the words ringing in her head: *He likes them young.* Christ, she'd dealt with enough victims, and seen enough in her life and her career, to know there was only one possible meaning.

Shaking, she grabbed the fifth glass, knocking back the remainder of the whisky. The room was spinning, but not enough, not enough for the way she was feeling, and she didn't care right now if she was wallowing in it, because that's exactly what she wanted to do.

In her drunken haze, she frowned. That woman had said a name . . . God, what was it? Ava peered into the gloom around her. It wasn't helping that the whisky was blurring her thoughts. Think . . . what was it?

She stumbled to her feet and swayed across to the bar to get another drink. 'Same again, please.' She waved to the barman, who nodded and measured out a double.

Still trying to think of the name, she took the glass, sauntered back to her table and sat down. Taking a sip, in her drunken state, she tried the exercise she used on her clients when they struggled to remember things. Picture the scene, recall the smells, how were you feeling, what sounds did you hear, the voice . . . Albert. Was it Albert . . . ? No. That didn't sound right. Arthur, no it was shorter than that, but she thought it began with the letter A.

She took another sip of whisky, feeling the burn, and it crossed her mind that right now she could really do with a gramme or so, to take even more of the edge off.

Sighing, she tried the exercise again: she pictured the woman, the scorn on her face, in her voice, the smirk, the laughter when she'd said the words: *He liked them young as well* . . . Ava sat bolt upright. That was it! Ash. That was the name the woman had said . . . Yes, Ash Barker.

She had no recollection of her dad mentioning that name. But that didn't mean anything, did it – he never mentioned anything to her. And now she understood why. Had Ben known the name? Was that why he'd reacted so quickly, cutting her off before she could say anything else? Had he been trying to prevent her from hearing more about her dad and this Ash whoever he was?

Ava fell into deep thought for a moment, then jolted herself out of her drunken trance and reached for the phone in her bag.

Although she wasn't on social media herself, it was her go-to when researching people. It was amazing what people put up on the net, a permanent digital footprint for all to see.

She typed the name into the search engine.

Ash Barker. London.

The signal was bad in the club, and she waited for the search to load . . .

Oh my God.

Her breath caught in her throat.

Holy shit . . . She looked away from her phone, blinking rapidly. This wasn't what she was expecting. Not even close . . . There were several different Ash Barkers, but *one* stood out . . . Only one came up page after page.

She covered her mouth, swallowing hard to stop herself from screaming. Tears blurred her vision, and she roughly wiped them away, squeezing her eyes shut, but it didn't make a difference. What she'd just read was emblazoned on her mind.

Ash Barker, Paedophile, jailed for life.

Jesus, she couldn't even pretend that this was a mistake, or the wrong Ash Barker, because it'd said, hadn't it? It mentioned the docks: Tilbury Docks. Working out of there . . . Others involved, but they hadn't caught them, and Ash hadn't given anything away. He'd been sentenced without saying a word . . .

And what of her dad? God, she felt sick.

He likes them young *as well* . . .

There was no getting away from those words. Was that why her dad had disappeared? Changed his name? Because they were looking for him? Was that why he never attended any events with her when she was a child? Was it because he didn't want to be spotted by the police? Was that why he'd been so set against her marrying Tony? He'd never supported them being together, but he'd always made out it was to do with him not believing Tony was good enough for her – which of course wasn't true. All this time, it had been about him.

She laughed out loud, not caring whether people were looking at her.

And then it came to her. That's why he'd never reported anything to the police, wasn't it? When his brand-new car had been stolen, when his house had been broken into, he'd just ignored it.

She began to shake, and she felt cold sweat running down her spine.

'Ava? Hey babe, are you all right?'

Ava looked up to see Ben.

'Ben . . .' It was all she said, but in that moment she was overwhelmed with huge relief that he was here. She didn't want to be alone with her drunken thoughts.

He came to sit by her, and he spoke warmly. 'I've been looking for you, darlin'. I was a bit worried about you. But I also wanted to say, I'm sorry – I was out of order with the way I treated you.'

She stared at him. 'Did you know?' Her voice was slurred, and she felt the tears rolling down her face. 'About Dad, did you know about him and Ash? About their *tastes*?'

In her alcohol-fuelled haze, Ava thought she saw a flicker of concern cross his face. 'I don't know what you're talking about, babe. How about we save our chat for the morning . . . Look, how about I take you home, get a coffee inside you, and put you to bed.'

'I'm happy where I am.' She knew she sounded petulant, but she was past caring. She took another gulp of whisky. 'If you need to go to bed, go right ahead.'

Ben gently took the glass out of her hand. 'Look at me, babe, I just want to make sure you're all right.' He smiled; his dazzling green eyes stared intently at her. 'Come on, let's go.'

Ava looked back at him, and she smiled, holding his gaze. Then, without thinking, she leaned forward, kissing him on his lips.

Immediately, Ben pulled back. 'No. You've had too much to drink, darlin', and it's not really my style to take advantage, no matter how beautiful you are.' He swept back the hair that was falling across her face and tucked it behind her ear. 'But I really am flattered, darlin'.' There was genuine warmth in his voice.

The humiliation Ava felt was like a bucket of cold water being thrown over her. 'God . . . I . . . I don't know what came over me . . . I . . .' She sprang to her feet, and before Ben could stop her she raced up the stairs and out into the night air. Hail pounded her face, blocking out all noise, but it couldn't block the image that flashed through her mind.

She stopped dead in her tracks, trying to hold onto her thoughts before they disappeared . . .

. . . She'd been young, *very young*, and there were men around her . . . *lots* of men . . . She remembered being scared, terrified, and yes . . . her dad was there . . . just standing there . . . oh my God . . . Ava shut down the memory. Then she vomited.

37

Early the next morning, Ava made her way along the corridor. She'd spent a restless night, and had woken with a massive head-ache. But far worse had been the massive humiliation. Unlike the many times before, when she hadn't been able to remember any-thing, every moment of her mortification lingered in vivid detail. The way he'd looked at her when she'd tried to kiss him kept playing over and over in her head.

She'd got up way before the sun had, and long before Ben. Knowing that she couldn't face him, she'd crept out of the house. She needed to get away. One-hundred-odd miles away seemed perfect.

Wincing at the memory, Ava pressed the bell for the ICU unit and waited for it to be answered.

'*Hello?*'

'Hi, it's Dr Barclay, I'm here to see my father, Har—' She stopped herself saying the name she'd come to know. 'Billy Fields. I know it's not yet visiting time, but I called, and they said it would be all right if I dropped in.' She rubbed her throbbing temples, wishing the pain would stop.

'It was me you spoke to . . .' The voice was chirpy, and the door lock was pressed open. Ava walked in and found herself face to face with the nurse she'd seen before, and it struck her how so many things had changed since the last time she'd seen him. Her life would never be the same. Though she'd been a mess before, she'd been an oblivious mess, unaware of any of this shit. Actually, it was more than just shit . . . it was her worst nightmare.

Her hospital and prison work had brought her into contact with paedophiles, lots of them, and she'd struggled with her role in their rehabilitation. She had found it impossible to remain neutral. Everything about that part of her job had turned her stomach.

'How is he?' Even to herself she sounded listless. Emotionless. It was an automatic question, one she'd asked thousands of times before when she'd worked in psychiatric units.

'He's doing well. Of course, he's tired.' The nurse smiled as he talked. 'Which is to be expected. The good news is, he says he can remember everything, and his speech isn't slurred, so we're hoping he's through the worst. He'll have to undergo more tests, and it's still early days, but we're pleased with his progress.'

'That's great news. Thank you.' Ava battled not to show her emotions.

'Would you like me to take you to him, or can you remember which room he's in?'

Ava smiled back. 'Oh, don't worry, I know where he is.' She walked away, and tried to pretend her stomach wasn't in knots and her heart wasn't racing.

When she got to the room, Ava pushed open the door.

'Hello.'

Her father turned his head. Looking weak, he grinned, although a slight look of surprise crossed his face. 'All right, darlin'? It's good to see you, babe. I had no idea you were coming – they didn't say. Typical, they tell you fuck-all in this place. Mind you, I have been out of it for a few days.' Even though his face was bruised and swollen, and he had two black eyes, he winked, reminding Ava of Ben. Another wave of humiliation washed over her at the thought of him. 'It's good to see a friendly face, I've had the Old Bill quizzing me. The way they were going on about things, anyone would think I did this to myself. Fucking hell, they were a right pair of muppets! They even tried to put the feelers on you. I put them straight, all right . . .' He grinned. 'I'm rabbiting on like a woman, ain't I? Come and sit down, you look like you're the one who needs this bed . . . You all right?'

She crossed the room and sat on the chair next to his bed. 'It's good to see you awake, Dad . . . or should I call you Billy? Oh no, silly me. What I should really be calling you is Harvey, isn't it?'

'What the hell are you talking about?' He tried to move further up the bed and Ava saw a look of pain cross his face, but she didn't move to help.

'Are we really going to do this, Dad?' Her voice held so much scorn, but she wanted to keep calm, that was the only way she was going to get through this. She needed to view her dad the same way she viewed her clients, that way it was easier to remain detached. She needed to protect herself.

'I swear—'

'I wouldn't bother,' Ava cut in. 'I know. In fact, do you know where I've spent the past week?' She tilted her head. 'Go on, guess.'

'You know I don't like guessing games.'

She shook her head. 'That's the thing, Dad. I don't know anything, not really. I mean, I thought I knew nothing before, but now . . . Jesus, this gives a whole new meaning to the word *nothing*.'

Harvey's face flushed. 'What the fuck's got under your skin?'

'Maybe it's the bang on the head I got when I woke up and found you unconscious.'

'What?' He frowned. 'What the fuck are you telling me?' He grimaced as he moved, but this time his anger helped him push through the pain. 'You were hurt?' He clenched his fist. 'Tell me they didn't hurt you.'

'They? So, there was more than one?'

'Yeah . . . yeah.' He sounded distracted. 'Ava, tell me, what happened?' His breathing was heavy and there was a look of distress on his face, although Ava could see it was mixed with anger.

'No.' She was firm. 'I'm not here to answer your questions. I want you to answer mine.' She stared at him, noticing the heart monitor he was plugged into changing numbers. 'So, are you going to guess where I've been, or am I going to have to tell you?'

'If this is what I'm waking up to, I'm going to ask them to put me back in a fucking coma.'

For a moment, Ava didn't say anything, then she sat up straight in her chair and took a deep breath. 'You give up?' Her tone was even. 'OK, fine, I'll tell you, shall I? I've been in London. That's right, in your house. Or should I say, in my house, because it is my house, isn't it?'

'You've been snooping in my stuff?' he growled at her. 'You've got no fucking right.'

'Is that all you can say?'

'No, there's a lot more I can say, but I won't, cos I don't want to upset you.' He wiped his hand across his chin. 'But . . . but I never told you about it because it was a surprise. I wanted you to have something of your own, nothing to do with that arsehole you're married to.'

Ava shook her head and then laughed out loud. Loud and bitterly. 'Oh my God, you are so good at this, Harvey.'

She watched his fist clench, but he stayed silent.

'Two weeks ago, I would've believed the bullshit that came out of your mouth so easily . . . Was everything a lie?'

'Ava, you may be my daughter, but you're starting to do my

fucking nut in. Maybe that bang on your head has done more damage than you thought.'

Although Ava's heart was racing, her outward demeanour remained calm. However, her voice was louder than usual. 'Aren't you wondering how I know the name Harvey? Because none of the passports were in that name, were they? Remember that envelope of passports you had?'

Harvey cricked his neck. He kept his voice down. 'Wind your neck in, Ava. What are you trying to do to me? So, I had a few fakers. It ain't the end of the world. Now drop it, you're starting to sound like that husband of yours.'

'You can't stop the lies, can you?' She smiled. A cold, steely smile. 'I've also been spending time with Ben. In fact, last night I kissed him. Not my finest hour, mind, but hey, under the circumstances, it could be worse.'

She watched the colour completely drain from her father's face. He looked ill, more than he had previously. 'What the fuck did you say?' His voice was no more than a whisper.

'Ben. Ben told me. We've been spending a lot of time together . . .'

'Whatever he's said, you can't believe a word that comes out of his mouth.'

'Then that makes two of you.'

He was growing more agitated. 'He knows nothing . . . he might think he does, but he doesn't. Ava, are you listening to me?'

She stared out of the window, watching the sleet hit the glass. Then her eyes shifted to her father. 'Tell me about Claudia. Claudia Davies. Mother dearest.'

He shrugged. 'There isn't much to tell. She walked out when you were little. You know that. Why are you bringing her up?'

'Because I went to see her. Yep, that's right, I've been busy, Dad.' She mocked him scornfully. 'But she says she isn't my mum. Fancy that. Then again, that probably comes as no surprise to you, does it?'

Harvey squeezed his eyes shut for a moment. 'You have opened a can of worms.' He said it almost to himself, then he glared at her. 'She would say that, wouldn't she? She's a whore, she only cares about money. You going to see her, probably put the frighteners on her. What the fuck did you think she was going to do? Greet you with open arms?' Ava watched the pulse in his jaw quicken, something she'd noticed in the past when he was under pressure. 'I didn't even know she was alive . . . where the fuck did you find her?' He shook his head. 'You know what, I don't want to know. You have to stop this now. Ava, please, babe, you are going down a road you don't want to.'

'You mean I'm going down a road that *you* don't want me to. That's more the point, because you don't want me to talk about Ash. Ash Barker.' Her stomach twisted into a knot, and she felt sick. 'Tell me about these *particular tastes* of yours.'

'Nurse! *Nurse!* Nurse!' Harvey yelled angrily. He stared back at Ava. 'You've got it wrong, darlin', so wrong.'

Tears flooded her eyes. 'I don't think I have, though. I know—'

'You don't, you don't fucking know . . . *Nurse.*' He yelled again for assistance. 'I need to get out of here. *Nurse.*' He pulled at one of the needles in his hand, pulling out the drip and causing it to bleed.

'Is everything all right?' The nurse, with a worried expression on his face, came running in as Ava got up from the chair and began to walk away.

'Ava, wait!' He turned to the nurse. 'I want out. Take me off this shit,' he bellowed, waving the tubes and wires about.

'Mr Fields, we can't do that . . .'

'Ava! Ava! Come back. You don't know what you're messing with. Ava!' He cut the nurse off to shout after Ava again, panic and terror in his voice. 'You've got it wrong, babe . . . You hear me? . . . I ain't like that . . . Ava! And you stay away from Ben; do you understand? *Stay the fuck away from him.*'

Harvey watched her disappear through the door; it was as if he'd been slashed with a knife. He turned to the nurse. 'I need a phone . . . get me a fucking phone, *now!*' He had some business to deal with, and that was going to start with killing Ben.

38

Ava had gone back to the house she and Tony shared in Nottingham. She'd needed to think, and going straight to London wasn't something she could deal with. Not right now, anyway. She couldn't face Ben, and she certainly didn't trust him.

Paranoia wasn't something she was usually given to, but the sense of not knowing what was really going on, of only knowing part of the situation with her dad, was tearing her apart. She had no idea who she could turn to. And maybe it was wrong, but she wanted to see Tony. Sit down and talk to him: not about this, but about the everyday stuff. Try to forget, even if it was for one evening only. The safety of the familiar.

She'd tried to call Tony a few times, but he had his phone turned off. She knew his shift pattern, though, and by her reckoning he was due to be home soon. While she waited, Ava made some phone calls to her old work colleagues and pulled in a few favours.

She was going to find out exactly what her father had been doing and, once she had, if she found evidence that pointed to him sharing the same *tastes* as Ash, she would report him to the authorities herself, even if that meant him spending the rest of his life behind bars. One thing she would never do, could never do, was be complicit in crimes of that nature. It made her sick to her stomach to think he'd been getting away with it all these years.

Stifling a yawn, she got up to go to the kitchen and make herself another coffee. She wasn't feeling 100 per cent, although that had little to do with her hangover and everything to do with the revelations she'd been trying to process. God, so often she'd listened to her clients talk about their lives, and although she knew hers was far from perfect, she'd felt grateful for it. But now, her life seemed even worse than her clients'.

She didn't know what to think or feel, and she didn't, or rather she couldn't, go back to the memory which had flashed through her head. She didn't want to start going down a path when she didn't know where it would lead.

Rinsing out her cup, she heard the front door open and close.

'Tony?' She called through to the hallway, and she was surprised to feel so happy to hear him come home. She rushed through just as he was walking into the lounge. She smiled. 'Hi, you have no idea how happy I am to see you. I hope you got my message about the conference; I am so sorry that I just didn't tell you the truth. It's ridiculous. But I thought we could perhaps go for something to eat, or maybe I could run you a nice hot bath.'

Tony nodded and held her gaze. 'Ava.' He moved towards her. 'My good wife.' He smiled, then without warning, he drew back his hand, and hit her so hard, she went flying across the room.

Ava screamed and scrambled up, feeling the blood trickling from her lip, and a burning heat in her eye. She shielded her head as Tony advanced towards her again, grabbing her hair and then crouching down, his face red and taut with anger. He spat his words. 'I know . . . I know everything.'

Ava's breathing was ragged as pain shot through her scalp. She was shocked and scared; this was the first time he'd ever hit her. 'What . . . what are you talking about? What the hell are you talking about? Is this about Dad? I can explain . . .'

He banged her head against the walnut sideboard. 'No, it's not fucking about him . . . it's about *you*.' He stank of alcohol and his eyes were wide and wild. 'You're a slut. A coke-snorting little slut, and you have made me do things that I would never do.' He pressed his lips against hers, and she fought and struggled to get him away from her.

'Stop, stop. Tony, *stop it.*'

'That's not what you say to all those men, every Friday when you're pretending to work late, you're not telling them to stop, are you? You're behaving like a little whore . . . Oh, Danny told me all about it . . . Yeah, that's right. How you're easy meat, how you're someone's lucky night.'

He was pushing his weight against her. 'Tony you're drunk, let's talk later . . . Tony, *please.*'

'Do you know I've been looking for you?'

She gave the tiniest shake of her head.

'Well, I have . . . you'd be surprised how many places I've been to, just so I could find you.'

'Tony.' She spoke in a whisper. 'Please get off me.'

He was looking at her like she was a stranger. His stare was full of hate, then she felt his hand roughly go between her legs.

'Don't . . . Tony, don't, please, don't do this.'

'You're my wife.' He snarled at her and began to pull at the jeans and knickers she was wearing.

She tried to break free but her strength was no match for his. 'Get off! Tony, get off!' she screamed, and he slammed one hand over her mouth, pushing her down. Although she continued to fight, she felt his erect penis. Terror rushed through Ava.

He was pulling at her, and he sneered as she continued to struggle. The next moment she felt him enter her.

'Don't . . . don't!'

'You're my wife, I'll fucking do as I like, you understand me?' he shouted as he thrust harder into her.

Ava bit down on his hand. He pulled it away, and she seized the chance to twist to the side, causing Tony to lose his balance.

She scrambled to her knees, and even though she felt him grab at her, she managed to get up on her feet, pulling her pants and jeans up as she staggered to the sofa, then ran into the hallway and out through the front door.

'Ava . . . Come back here. *Ava!*'

Back in London, Ben was worried. He had trouble on his mind. Two lots of trouble, and two lots of shit he didn't need. He had to focus on getting what was his, but the fact that he hadn't been able to reach his brother, either by phone or when he'd gone to his place the other day, had him worried. Of course, there was the possibility Sam could've gone away on holiday, people did, but Sam would have told him, sent him a text at least. The more he thought about it, the more his gut was screaming at him not to ignore it.

He'd have to pop over later. In the meantime, he needed to find out what was going on with Ava. For all that she was strong-headed, fiery and everything else that would drive him crazy in a woman, there was a vulnerability to her. Even though he didn't really know her, she was becoming distracting. He was genuinely worried about her, which pissed him off. This hadn't been part of his plan.

When she hadn't come downstairs, he'd checked her bedroom, but there'd been no sign of her. She'd definitely slept in her bed. He'd looked in on her during the night and she'd been fully dressed and sound asleep. He had no idea what time she'd left the house, but it must've been in the small hours as he'd been up at dawn. He'd wanted to talk to her, he'd wanted to tell her that what happened last night wasn't a big deal. Not for him. He wouldn't tell her that not only did he find her beautiful, but he was attracted to her, and it had taken everything he had not to go down that road with her. Although, in the cold light of day, he was glad he hadn't, not when she was in that state at any rate.

He started to fiddle with the coffee machine, but decided to make a tea instead. Right now he was in no mood to start messing about with coffee beans.

His phone rang, and he frowned. It was a private number.

Picking up, he pressed answer as he gazed out of the frosted-glass window into Meard Street. 'Yeah?'

'*Ben.*'

He knew immediately who it was, but that didn't stop his surprise at hearing that voice. 'Harve, I didn't know you'd woken up . . . Does Ava know?'

There was a long pause. '*Does Ava know? Are you being a funny cunt . . . of course Ava fucking knows – she was with me earlier.*'

'Ava?'

'*Am I speaking another fucking language, mate? Ava has left here, and the way she left, I don't know if I'm going to see my girl again, and that is because of you.*'

Ben had to move the phone away from his ear as Harvey yelled down it.

'*What the fuck have you been saying to her? Why the fuck is she talking about Claudia? Fucking Claudia, what are you trying to do? I already told you to leave her alone. Don't mess with her, otherwise you're a dead man. In fact you're a dead man anyway, you understand that? When I get out of here, I'm going to put a bullet down your fucking throat. You have messed with the wrong person.*'

That was when Ben lost his temper. 'No, mate, I'd say you were the one who've been messing with the wrong people. Whoever put you in hospital meant business, and we both know who they are. The question is, who's going to get to you first? Me or them? And I've no doubt that last time was a warning, to make sure you start to remember. I played nice when I saw you, and all you did was play games. It would be a real shame if I had to start getting nasty . . . As for your daughter, she's proper messed up. Not as happy as you think. Her perfect, shiny life is just a mirage. It would be shame if I were to make her life worse, wouldn't it?' he snarled down the phone, but his heart wasn't really in his words.

'*Listen to me . . . You fucking listen to me, you leave Ava alone . . . you stay away from her. I'm warning you.*'

'Warn away, cos from where I'm standing there's fuck all you can do about it. Unless, of course, you tell me where my money is, then I'll back off. You will never hear from me again. I'll just disappear.'

'*There is no money, I already told you that.*'

'And I told you that I served thirty-six years . . .' Ben's voice cracked with emotion. 'And I didn't once open my mouth. I served my time for something I didn't do, while you vanished . . . You fucking vanished, Harve. We were mates. Best mates.' He wiped his face with his hand, trying to stop his emotions getting the better of him. Taking a deep breath, he continued. 'For all those years, I was trying to work out why you'd do that to me, and now I know.'

'*You don't know what you're talking about.*'

Ben took a cigarette from the packet lying on the counter, he lit it and took a deep drag before he answered. 'I know exactly what I'm talking about: Ash. It was something to do with Ash, wasn't it? When he got pulled, you were worried that they'd be after you too. You sick fuck. That's why you ran, ain't it? It was on the same day that you were supposed to meet me that Ash got nicked. That ain't a coincidence. You knew the Old Bill was going to come for you too, so you made sure you cleared off. You took your daughter and cleared off, then you set yourself up with a new life using our money – and left me to take the fall for you.'

'*Ben . . . mate, it wasn't like that.*'

'Then tell me what it was like.' Ben wiped away his tears. 'It was exactly like that. You were my mate. I loved you. I would've given my life for you . . . I did give my life for you. Thirty-six years of my life, and thirty-six years of getting people to track you down. Well, now I've found you, *mate*, and now you owe me.' He clicked off the phone, and sat down on the chair, head in hands. He wept, something he'd never done in his entire life, not even when he'd been jailed for life.

39

It was early the next day and Ava looked into the mirror in the bathroom of McDonald's. She winced at the sight. Her face was swollen, and even the make-up she'd put on this morning wasn't able to cover the bruises. Her injuries were probably going to take a couple of weeks to heal, and in the meantime she hurt like hell.

She'd had several calls from both her dad and from Tony, all of which she'd rejected. Right now, she wasn't sure she'd ever want to speak to either of them again.

Was she being unfair to Tony? She hadn't recognized him; he'd been so angry last night. More than angry – he'd been hateful . . . No, that wasn't the right word either . . .

But was it unreasonable that he'd wanted to punish her after finding out the way she'd behaved? She stopped that train of thought dead in its tracks. If any of her clients had tried making those kinds of excuses for their partner, she wouldn't accept it. So why, even when she knew how wrong it was, did she feel partly to blame? She'd lied to Tony, she'd cheated on him, she hadn't been the good wife she'd made out to be, and she was genuinely sorry for that. Sorry that she couldn't be what he wanted. But she also knew Tony well enough to know that he'd be riddled with guilt and shame.

Sighing, she straightened up her clothes. She looked business-like, which was exactly the look she was after. Yesterday, rather than going back to the house in London, she'd booked into an Airbnb, but not before she'd bought herself a change of clothes.

Luckily, although she'd left her bag behind when she fled the house, she still had her phone on her so it was just a matter of using her digital wallet. She breathed a sigh of relief that Ben had taken the gun out of her bag. God knows what Tony would've thought if he'd found it.

She took a deep breath, pushed Tony out of her mind, and walked out of the bathroom. She was meeting one of her old colleagues in ten minutes, so she needed to pull herself together.

She headed out of McDonald's onto the busy high street. It was a typical commuter town, forty minutes' drive from London, a bland sprawl of identical new-build houses and boxy apartment blocks lining wide, featureless streets, the monotony broken only by the occasional chain store or coffee shop. She entered the nondescript shopping precinct and hurried through to the large car park behind it.

'Ava! Hey, Ava, how are you doing? Oh my God, what happened to you?' Sarah Crawford, a short blonde in her forties, came to a sudden stop as she looked at Ava's face.

Ava smiled at her. It had been over three years since they'd seen each other, and a good few years before that since they'd worked together. 'One of my clients decided that he didn't like the look of me.' She shrugged casually, knowing it would ring true with Sarah because it was one of the hazards of the job. When they'd worked together in a maximum-security psychiatric hospital, attacks on staff had been a common event. The truth would have been a lot harder for her to believe; Sarah knew Tony and it would never occur to her that he could raise a hand to anyone, let alone his wife.

'I thought you went into private practice to avoid that.' Sarah linked arms with her as they made their way across the car park towards the main wing of Rafley prison.

'I did and, let's be fair, having only one disgruntled patient in all this time isn't bad going.' She rested her head on Sarah's shoulder as they walked. Until that moment, she hadn't realized how much she'd missed her. They had their weekly chat on the phone, but that wasn't the same as hanging out together. Back when they'd worked in the security unit, the two of them had been inseparable.

'How's Tony? Gorgeous as ever, no doubt? I've said it before, but when you get tired of him, send him my way, won't you?' Sarah laughed as they headed down a flight of stone steps to the prison entrance.

'He's fine, more than fine.' Ava glanced at Sarah as they headed into the waiting area. The air was thick with a sterile, almost clinical smell which mingled with a strong stench of bleach and sweat. The walls were painted in a drab grey while a harsh fluorescent light buzzed overhead, casting a harsh glare on the lino floor. 'It's all good,' she added, and held her smile. 'Anyway, I need to hear more about this guy you were telling me about last night. He sounds perfect.'

Sarah raised her pencilled-in eyebrows. 'When have I ever met perfect? I think you got the last of the good guys.'

Ava nodded. 'Lucky me.' Even to her, it sounded false, and she picked up on the glance Sarah gave her, although she didn't say anything. 'So, thanks for doing this, and driving up to meet me. I owe you big time.'

'Not a problem, just count your blessings that the governor and I are, or were' – she licked her lips suggestively – 'very well acquainted at one time.'

Ava laughed. 'So, what happened to this *acquaintance*?'

'What always happens . . . He turned out to be married.' She wrinkled her nose. 'I didn't mind though, I'd already got bored of him – not that he knows that. He felt bad, probably worried

I'd tell his wife . . . which suited me, because it allows me to pull in the favours.'

Ava shook her head and spoke warmly. 'Has anyone ever told you, Dr Crawford, that you're very manipulative?'

'Perks of the job.' She pursed her lips. 'I learned from the best: you don't work with sociopaths and not pick up tips.' Sarah giggled as they approached the reception, which was manned by a disgruntled-looking prison officer.

'Hi, I'm Dr Crawford, and this is Dr Barclay. Governor Philips is expecting us.'

The officer nodded, then picked up the phone. 'Take a seat, I'll let his assistant know.'

They sat down on the scratched orange plastic chairs which were screwed to the concrete floor. Sarah turned her head to look at Ava. 'So, how about while we wait, you tell me what's really going on with you and Tony.'

'We're fine, I told you. Actually, we're more than fine. Can you believe we've been married ten years?'

Sarah tucked her hair behind her ears. Her piercing blue eyes met Ava's. 'That's another tip of the trade: when you spend as much time as I do with sociopaths, you get a gut instinct for when someone's lying to you.'

Forty-five minutes later, Governor Philips finally made an appearance. It couldn't have come too soon for Ava. Sarah had quizzed her relentlessly until she'd finally conceded that all wasn't well in paradise. A ten-year lull, she'd said. A case of them both working too hard and not spending enough time together.

Sarah had seemed to accept this explanation. She'd given Ava a hug and let her know she was there for them both, if support was needed.

It just went to prove, Ava supposed, that two could play that game. Years as a psychologist had taught her everything she needed to knowing about conning people . . . Touché.

'Sarah.' The governor strode into reception and Ava was surprised to see he wasn't Sarah's usual type. She normally went for younger men, but the man smiling broadly in front of them looked to be in his mid-sixties, with a thick head of silver hair, tall and well built. He had an air of confidence about him that put her in mind of Ben.

'Lovely to see you, and thanks for this,' Sarah trilled. 'This is Dr Barclay, who I was telling you about.'

The governor reached out to shake Ava's hand. She saw him do a double take at her bruises, but he didn't comment. 'It's good to meet you, Dr Barclay. Sarah spoke very highly of you.'

Ava gave a quick smile to Sarah. 'Please, call me Ava. I'm really grateful to you for agreeing to this. I realize it's not through the proper channels.'

He waved Ava's expression of gratitude away. 'Just call it fast-tracking,' he said with a grin, and Ava could see why Sarah had liked him. There was a genuine warmth to him. 'Come this way.'

The governor began to walk towards the double doors of the corridor, which swung open as the face-recognition sensor activated. He talked as he nodded to a passing prison officer. 'So, Sarah tells me you're doing some research?'

'That's right, I've been asked to contribute to an academic paper, and one of the people I was supposed to speak to let me down at the last minute – or rather, he got himself put in solitary. Hence me begging a favour from Sarah, which is basically a roundabout way of begging a favour from you,' Ava said. She could already hear the noise of the main prison, and the smell of bleach and cabbage filled the air.

'Oh, don't worry about it.' Sarah brought down her voice as

she spoke to them both. 'He owes me a favour, don't you, Governor?'

The governor flushed but didn't reply. Instead, he addressed Ava. 'As you can imagine – and I'm sure I don't have to tell you – he's both a manipulator and a narcissist. That's probably why he agreed to see you.'

'A case of pathological vanity,' Sarah agreed.

'How long has he been here? I know he was transferred from the Isle of Wight prison some time ago.'

'I think I'm right in saying he's been here for around twelve years.' He slowed his pace and looked thoughtful. 'And he still makes my skin crawl every time I set eyes on him.'

They went through another set of double doors into an airy room with a few tables and chairs set out in a straight line.

'If you wait here,' the governor told Ava, 'an officer will bring him through. They'll let me know when you're finished.'

'Thank you.' Ava turned to Sarah. 'Would you mind if I spoke to him by myself?'

Sarah shook her head. 'I was hoping you'd say that. The last thing on this earth I want to do is be in the same room as Ash Barker.'

40

'You all right?' Joe came to sit down next to Tony in the staff canteen.

'Yeah, I'm fine. Just life.' He wasn't about to tell Joe what had happened last night. He found it hard to comprehend what he'd done. Even harder to comprehend was the fact he didn't feel in the least remorseful.

He knew exactly what he was supposed to feel like, but he didn't. He was still angry, and Ava's refusal to take his calls had stoked his anger. It didn't surprise him that she didn't want to talk, but it frustrated the hell out of him.

She might be a well-respected doctor of psychology, but she was terrible at self-help. She'd always avoided tricky conversations, always tried to make things better by opening a nice bottle of red. Why hadn't he seen it sooner? But then, maybe they were more alike than he'd realized. He wasn't one for confrontation either, which why last night had caught him by surprise.

What he'd done hadn't been planned. He'd seen red. Ever since Danny had put those images in his head – Ava fucking other men – the rage had been building. She was *his* wife, no one else's. He'd never been the possessive type, he'd always supported her, *allowed* her to do what she liked. He knew for a fact that most of the coppers who worked in this station would have denied their wives the kind of independence he'd given Ava. But he'd always been supportive of equality, of live and let live. God, more fool him.

Oddly enough, the guilt and remorse he'd felt over Danny's murder seemed to have disappeared overnight. It was as if what had happened with Ava had somehow distanced him emotionally from what he'd done to Danny. The guy had got what he deserved. So had Ava.

'Did you manage to find Ava?' Joe asked as he bit into a sticky iced bun.

'No.' Tony shook his head. 'I've spoken to her on the phone though.'

'That's good.' Joe sounded distracted. 'Look, have you got a minute?'

'Sure.'

'Come with me, I've got something to show you.' Joe took his iced bun with him and set off across the open-plan office, followed closely by Tony.

'Is this about Danny?' Tony kept his voice low.

'No – and what did I tell you? You need to forget about what happened.'

When they got to his desk, he sat down and turned his computer on.

Tony pulled up a seat alongside him.

'Remember that name you gave me – Claudia Davies? Well, I've found some stuff – not that it was hard to find, given what happened.'

'Go on.' Tony frowned.

'What with one thing and another, I didn't have time to look her up until yesterday, and when I did – boom! She was right there. Or rather, a person by the same name was right there. A Claudia Davies was found shot in London the other day.'

'What?' The news took Tony by surprise, although, like Joe had said, it might not be the right Claudia Davies.

'Anyhow, I did some discreet asking around.' He looked over

his shoulder to make sure no one was eavesdropping, then tapped a password into the computer. A woman's face appeared on screen. 'This is her: Claudia Davies.'

Tony stared at the crime-scene photos. As a gunshot wound went, it wasn't too messy. Unlike some victims, who'd end up with their face blown off, Claudia's features were unscathed. He stared at the image but couldn't see any resemblance to Ava, not in the eyes, not in the shape of the face, or the lips.

'Here's the thing,' Joe continued. 'Claudia is, or rather was, a hooker. But she's had no convictions, no arrests since she was in her twenties. However, a few years ago she was a passenger in a car that was pulled over. The driver was Felix Connor, a well-known gangster – or he used to be. He died of a heart attack a couple of years ago. Anyway, Connor had links with two known criminals named Terry Oldham and John Gibbons.' A photograph of three men appeared on screen. 'Now we're going back years, but all three men served time for perverting the course of justice in connection with a robbery in London. From what I gather, the CPS wanted to pin the actual heist on them, but there wasn't enough evidence, even though a man was shot.'

'So how long did they serve?' Tony asked.

'Between two and five years – out in half that time.' Joe shrugged. 'But there was one person who did serve time. He got life for the murder of a security guard who was shot down as they made their getaway. They never recovered the money. It was a couple of million, which back then was a huge deal. Anyway, this geezer served thirty-six years and kept his mouth shut the whole time.' Tony pressed a key on the computer, and another man appeared on screen. 'Anyway, he's out now. I reckon he must have come out to a nice earner. He's probably got all that money waiting for him.'

Tony pulled a face. 'I'm not sure it's worth thirty-six years inside.'

'I don't know.' Joe grinned. 'Thirty-six years of never having to pay the bills, never having to work, never having to have the missus nag you, and three meals a day, then at the end of it all, there's a wad of money waiting for you.'

Tony laughed, his eyes on the screen, studying the photo.

'Apparently, he's been spotted in Nottingham – picked up on CCTV. He hasn't done anything wrong, he's a free man now, but get this: he was seen with Billy Fields . . . or whoever Billy Fields actually is . . . Coincidence?' Joe bit into his iced bun again and, speaking with his mouth full, added, 'Not sure what it all means, but maybe Claudia is connected to Ava, because it's clear there's some sort of link.' He glanced at Tony, who was still staring at the screen.

'I've seen that man,' said Tony. 'I spoke to him when I was looking for Ava.'

'Are you sure?' Joe sounded doubtful. .

Tony stared hard, looking at the eyes, the shape of his face. It was an old photograph, but he hadn't changed that much. 'One hundred per cent sure. I'm not likely to forget that face.' He read the name under the photograph. 'It was definitely him. Definitely Ben Walters.'

41

'Hello, Harvey. Have you missed us?'

Harvey opened his eyes, and a sense of dread washed over him as he looked at the two men standing by his bed, but there was no way that he was going to let that show. No way at all. On top of which the hatred soared through him. The idea that they laid a hand, let alone a fist on Ava, made him want to do them some permanent injury.

He pushed himself up on his elbows and smirked. 'I wondered when you'd show. Have you come to finish off the job?' He glared at Jed and Dean. 'If you have, I'm not sure if I'd do it in here – there's always eyes watching.' He nodded in the direction of the nurse, who gave them a suspicious look before returning to her paperwork.

They pulled up a couple of chairs and Jed began playing with one of the drainage tubes that was still attached to Harvey. 'I was wondering if you'd thought any more about what we were discussing the last time we met.' He smiled and continued to twist the tube around his finger.

'You mean when you did this.' Harvey pointed to himself. 'When you fucking put me in here?' He lowered his voice, not wanting anyone to hear.

The comment caused Dean to laugh loudly, which resulted in the nurse giving an annoyed tut.

'Are you seriously going to cry into your tea?' He grinned.

'I don't care what you do to me,' Harvey hissed. 'You crossed the line with my daughter.'

Jed popped a piece of chewing gum into his mouth. 'She was collateral damage. Wrong place, wrong time . . . for now, that is.' He got up out of his chair and went to sit on Harvey's bed, leaning forward. 'You and I both know that we could have killed you if we wanted to, but what would be the point in that? You're no good to us dead. Your daughter, however . . .'

'You leave her alone, you hear me!'

Jed gave a look to Dean, who shrugged and smiled casually.

'If you don't want that to happen,' said Dean, 'all you have to do is tell us what you did with the money. Or rather, give us the money we're owed.'

Harvey stared at them. 'I already told you: I haven't got it. I never took it.'

'That's not what everyone else thinks.'

'If that's what they all think, why the fuck aren't they here saying the same thing? Why isn't Terry here, or John? Why ain't they giving me grief?'

Dean tilted his head. 'Because they ain't got the staying power. They're pussies. They've licked their wounds and moved on to other things. Let them crack on with it, but me and Jed, we're like fucking elephants. We don't forget.'

Harvey could see Dean's face turning red with anger.

'Then you fucking well need to forget, because there isn't anything to see here. I walked away with nothing. Whatever happened to that money, I didn't take it.'

Dean nodded, processing this bit of information. 'If that's the case, why does Ben think that you did?'

Harvey didn't give anything away as he looked at them evenly. 'He told you that, did he?' He watched them, then a smirk spread across his face. 'No, I didn't think so.' Harvey knew, no matter how angry and pissed off he might be, there was no way Ben would start talking, especially not to the likes of Dean and Jed.

There'd never been any love lost between Ben, Jed and Dean. It had been Ben and Harvey who'd been tight. Best mates, like Ben had said. But then the robbery happened, and everything had to change. As much as he'd loved Ben, his main focus back then had been Ash—Immediately, Harvey stopped that train of thought. This wasn't the moment to go there.

'He didn't need to say. Thirty-six years inside, then he lies low before he comes to see you. Don't you think that's strange, that he tracks you down?'

'We're mates, that's what mates do.' Harvey clenched his jaw. He had a sneaking suspicion that Ben had inadvertently led Jed and Dean to him. After all this time, his past had finally caught up with him.

'Mates?' Jed regarded him. 'From what I hear, you never visited him once. Not once in all that time, not even a postcard.'

'That's bullshit,' Harvey protested, although it was true, he hadn't.

Jed and Dean exchanged looks, but it was Jed who spoke. 'You're lying. You think we haven't been keeping an eye on him all these years? People inside the prison have kept us informed, so we know you *haven't* seen him . . . Now, if that was me, if I were Ben, if someone hadn't visited me in all that time, they wouldn't be the first person I'd want to see when I got out. Unless, of course, I wanted something from them.' He paused, and grabbed a plastic cup from the side, pouring himself some water from the jug. 'I reckon after thirty-six years sitting on his backside in a cell, Ben would want something from the man who stole from us all.'

'I never did anything with that money.'

'Then why disappear? Why go AWOL for all this time and

only resurface when Ben brings the cat to the mouse?' There was a threatening tone in the way he said it.

'I ran. That's all I did: run. A geezer got shot, remember. I wasn't about to go down for it, so I ducked out. I took my daughter, changed my name, and kept moving.'

'But why? Why duck out if the police weren't even looking for you?'

'I didn't know that, did I?' Harvey spoke roughly to them. 'Like I say, I had a daughter to look after, her mum was a useless cow who'd walked out on us a while before. So, what was I supposed to do? Wait around for the Old Bill and see if they wanted to nab me? They got Tel and John, didn't they? If they'd got me, who would've looked after Ava? They would've put her in care.' He shrugged. 'And I wasn't going to let that happen to her.'

Jed stood up, followed by Dean.

'If that's the best story you can come up with after thirty-six years in hiding, mate, you've wasted your time,' Jed sneered.

'Here's what's going to happen.' Dean threw Harvey a piece of paper with his number on it. 'I will give you a few more days to start remembering where that money went to, and then I'm going to pay your daughter a visit. After that, I'm going pay her assistant, Jude, a visit. And then Ben. They'll all start dropping like flies. So, if I were you, *Harve*, I'd put that thinking cap on. Call me when you remember, but do yourself a favour and don't leave it too late.'

They walked away and Harvey watched them go. Shaking, he reached across to the locker, and grabbed the phone he'd had delivered. He closed his eyes, trying to stop his heart from pounding to the point where it felt uncomfortable.

He pressed dial and within moments a familiar voice answered. '*Hello.*'

'Ben, listen to me, I've just had a visit from Jed and Dean. They want to know where the money is.'

'*Then that makes all of us.*' His voice was flat.

'Like I told you, I ain't got it . . . I never had it.'

'*Fuck off, Harvey, I've already told you I'm not buying your bullshit. And it looks like Jed and Dean aren't buying it either. That's one thing we've got in common. I don't care what you tell them, all I want is what's owed to me.*'

'Ben—'

'*I've heard enough of your crap. Now it looks to me like the walls are closing in on you. With Jed and Dean on your tail, you—*'

'Thanks to you. They must have followed you, and you fucking led them to me.'

'*That's not my problem. They would've found you eventually. It only took me thirty-six years to do it.*' The bitterness came hard and heavy from him. '*Now you need to get off this phone and bring me my money . . . I'm at your place. I'll be waiting.*'

'With Ava?' The panic in Harvey soared.

'*Just bring me my money.*' And with those words, Ben ended the call.

Seething, Harvey took a deep breath, keeping his emotions in check. He pressed the buzzer next to his bed. A moment later the nurse came in. 'Is everything all right, Mr Fields?'

He stared at the nurse. 'No, it fucking ain't . . . Get me my discharge papers.'

'Mr Fields, you aren't well enough to leave. The CT scan was normal, but that doesn't mean you'll be fine to be out and about. Besides, you've got plenty of bumps and bruises.'

'What am I? Fucking Humpty Dumpty? I'm not asking you, I'm *telling* you. Get me my discharge papers.'

42

Ava watched Ash Barker walk into the small room. The tense, expectant silence was broken only by the echoing clank of metal doors and the occasional muffled voice drifting from the corridors beyond, reminding Ava of the heavy, oppressive presence of the prison around her.

He looked different from his picture in the papers, but of course he would. The photo had been taken thirty-six years ago when he was in his early thirties. Although the picture she'd seen had been grainy, Ava had been able to make out his thick mane of jet-black hair, his youthful six-foot-plus build, strong and powerful. But this man, this man who stood before her, was almost unrecognizable.

Apart from a few tufts of grey hair, he was bald. His skin was sallow, and his face and body were ballooned, no doubt from medication. He shuffled in, his beady eyes pinned on her, shadowed by his long, wiry brows. Leering, he showed off his gums, now devoid of teeth. Everything about him was vile, and a stale smell of sweat hung around him as he came to sit down opposite.

He held his hand out to her, but she didn't shake it, she couldn't . . . wouldn't.

He shrugged and pulled his hand back at the same time as pushing his chair back to allow room for his bloated stomach. 'The governor told me I might be able to help you.' He sniffed, and held her gaze. His stare was intense and unnerving. 'An

216

academic paper. What's the subject?' He leaned forward. 'My crimes?' His eyes twinkled, and Ava saw his obvious delight at the thought of reliving his heinous offences. That was a common trait of men like Ash Barker. Most serial killers and stalkers revelled in their exploits.

'No, Mr Barker.' She spoke evenly. 'Not about your crimes.'

He narrowed his eyes, and Ava saw a darkness come into them. 'Call me Ash.'

'If you don't mind, I prefer to keep it on a professional level.'

He frowned and studied her face. 'Have we met before?'

'No.' She sounded sharper than she'd intended; she didn't want him to get up and shuffle back to his cell. This was her one chance, and she knew it, but to pander to him would be a betrayal of his victims, and there were many, ranging from children too young to walk through to teenagers.

He nodded and let out a small chuckle but didn't say anything.

Ava gave a quick glance to the officer standing by the door, who was busy playing on his phone. She looked back at Ash. 'I'm here to ask you about Harvey Fletcher.'

The surprise which crossed his face was genuine. He placed his hands on the table, looping his fingers between each other. 'Now here's me thinking I was going to be part of a useful project.' He began to get up to go.

'Just a couple of questions . . . *please.*'

He smiled at her, sitting back down. 'That wasn't too hard, was it? Manners go a long way with me, Dr Barclay.' Then, as he had done since he walked into the room, he continued to stare at her, blinking slowly. 'You're going about this all the wrong way, you do know that, don't you? You're not supposed to alienate me then expect me to answer your questions. Don't they teach you anything these days?'

Ava could tell he was mocking her. Letting the way she felt about him show was completely unprofessional.

'Separate the crime from the person, Dr Barclay. Hate the offence not the offender.' He let out a loud phlegm-filled laugh, spitting out a mouthful of mucus in the tissue he dragged out of his pocket. 'That's what my shrink used to say they were doing with me.'

'Mr Barker—'

'It's fine,' he cut in. 'I don't care what you think. Not you, not the world out there.' He stopped to regard her. 'That's because I don't feel anything, Dr Barclay. Did you know that? I feel nothing when it comes to hurt, to pain. I've been like that since I was a child, which made what I did very easy, as you can imagine.'

'I'd rather not,' she answered flatly.

'Are you married, Doctor?'

'I don't talk about my private life.'

Barker nodded. 'Yet you're wanting to probe into mine.' He paused. 'But I'm going to let that go. I'll answer your questions, Dr Barclay . . . if you answer mine.'

'That's not how this works.' Ava tried to keep the scorn out of her tone.

'Then I'll go back to my cell. It's been good meeting you.' He stood up, and Ava watched him begin to walk away. Everything in her told her not to react, to let him go, because this was what people like Ash Barker did. People like him were driven by power. And although she knew that, she knew it would thrill him, she found herself saying, '*Wait.*'

He turned around, and as Ava thought, he had a smile on his face: cruel and malicious. It crossed her mind that this look would have been the one his victims saw. She swallowed hard and emptied her head of that image. 'OK.' She took a deep breath. 'OK,

I'll do it.' Which she knew went against every professional boundary. 'What do you want to know?'

He strolled back across to the table where Ava sat motionless. Making her wait on him, he sat down slowly.

'You've got five questions, Mr Barker, and that's it. That's my deal, only five.'

'You're not in a position to make deals. However, I'm in a position to accept.' He smiled, clearly enjoying himself. 'So all right, five questions. I take it that the governor doesn't know you want to ask about Harvey.'

'No. That's one question.'

He laughed. 'I'm getting to like you.'

'I'd rather you didn't.'

He laughed again.

'So, now it's my turn . . .' Ava chose her words carefully. 'How do you know Harvey Fletcher? I take it you do?'

'That sounds like two questions, Dr Barclay.'

'Fine, I'll rephrase: how do you know him?'

Barker crossed his arms, resting them on his huge stomach. 'I'm going to enjoy this, it gets rather boring watching TV and playing video games all day . . .' He paused. 'Harvey Fletcher, I haven't thought about him for a very, very long time. We had a mutual friend.' He frowned. 'Robert. Anyway, Rob thought he was a bit of a gangster, dabbled in selling gear, but he also was a small-time pimp. If I remember rightly, he crossed some people he shouldn't have done – another pimp. Can't recall the ins or outs, but he ended up needing some protection, and that's where Harvey came in. He hired Harvey. And that's how I got to know him. Robert seemed to trust him, so why wouldn't I.' He leaned back in his chair. 'OK, my turn.'

Ava's mind was racing, though right now she didn't have time to process everything. She felt uncomfortable that this man was about to put the spotlight on her. She could get up and walk away, never look back, but she was so close to finding out. It made her sick to think Ash was the one who might hold the key.

A smirk appeared on his face. 'I'll start off with an easy one. Are you married?'

'Yes.' Even that tiny bit of information felt like she'd been violated.

'That wasn't hard, was it?'

She took a deep breath, her hands fiddling nervously under the table. 'Was he . . . was he part of this club . . . what I read—'

'Don't believe all you read, Dr Barclay.' He yawned widely.

'What I read, is that there was some sort of club. A member's club.' She stopped, and tried not to let the wave of emotions she was feeling get in the way of what she needed to do. 'Was Harvey a part of that?'

'Yes . . . It turns out he had similar tastes.' Barker gave nothing else up, and Ava dug her nails in her palms to stop herself being sick. The room felt like it was spinning round, and she struggled to catch her breath.

'My turn again . . .' He stopped and stared at her face. 'That looks nasty, Dr Barclay. Whoever did it must've been angry with you.'

Instinctively, she touched her face. 'It was a patient.'

'Really.' A smirk played on his lips. 'Let me ask you this: have you always been faithful, have you always been the good wife or are you a bad girl?' He smiled nastily.

'Excuse me?'

'You heard, unless that's another of your questions.'

'Of course, I have.' She snapped at him. 'I'm happily married.'

He got up slowly and nodded to the prison officer. 'I'm ready to go back to my cell now.'

'Wait . . . Mr Barker, we haven't finished.'

He waddled towards the door. 'You might not have done, but I have . . . It's not fun playing this game with liars, Dr Barclay. If you're not going to play fair, then I'd rather not partake.'

'Just a few more minutes . . . Ask me anything.'

'Anything?'

'Yes, anything.' Ava spoke fast. 'Anything at all.'

'Who exactly is Harvey to you?'

She took a deep breath. 'He's my father.'

He held her stare. 'Goodbye, Dr Barclay.'

'Wait, no . . . wait . . . I thought . . .'

'You thought I was going to change my mind. Aren't I playing fair?' He laughed, but when he got to the door, he turned round. 'I remember you now. There's no getting away from those eyes.'

'I don't understand.'

'The last time I saw you, Dr Barclay . . . you were a little girl. That's right, everyone loved you. You were very special.' He leaned into her, and a cold chill washed over Ava. 'Harvey's little girl.' He roared with laughter and walked out of the room.

43

It was later the same day when Harvey, having discharged himself, took the small path that led to the red front door.

He took a deep breath, trying his best to ignore the pain, which felt like a tight electric band around his ribs. As he knocked on the door, his mind wandered to Ben. How the fuck was he going to sort it out? He remembered Jed and Dean from the old days. They'd been ruthless, brutal. And he doubted that the passage of time had softened them any. When they said they were going to start picking people off one by one, they meant it.

The door swung open.

'Hello, Billy.' Tony stood on the doorstep, holding a half-bottle of whisky. He was wearing a stained, creased grey tracksuit, and he reeked of alcohol. Harvey had never had him down as a drinker, and he was usually pristine. Far too strait-laced and uptight to be otherwise.

'Is Ava in?' Harvey had no time for his son-in-law, and it took all his willpower not to barge past him and walk into the house.

'No.' Tony kept his stare on Harvey, although Harvey could see how dilated his pupils were. He'd clearly been boozing for a while and seemed more than half-cut.

'Then when will she be in?'

'How the fuck should I know when your daughter is coming home? She does what she likes, when she likes, and I'm only the idiot who lives here.'

Harvey stepped towards him. He'd never seen him like this.

'You need to lay off the sauce, pal. What's your fucking problem? Has my daughter finally seen sense, is there trouble in paradise?'

Tony rested his body against the wall as Harvey stood in the open doorway.

'You'd like that wouldn't you? You've never wanted Ava and me to be together, have you?'

Harvey shrugged. 'No, so get over it.'

Tony seemed enraged, but he spoke in a low murmur. 'You've always been a cocky bastard, but let me tell you, soon that smile will be wiped off your face.'

Harvey was taken aback that Tony had the balls to speak out like this. 'What's that supposed to mean?'

Tony shook his head while Harvey looked at him with disdain. The last thing he needed was to be wound up by a mug like Tony. 'Then I'll wait for her.' He went to take a step forward, but Tony blocked his way.

'What the fuck are you doing?'

'As I say, Ava's not in, so there's no need to wait.'

'Jesus Christ, mate! The booze made you brave, has it?' He laughed. 'Right now, I haven't got time to deal with you, I need to see Ava and check she's all right.' He wasn't going to tell Tony why he wanted to see her, and he certainly wasn't going to breathe a word about Jed and Dean. He just needed to see her.

'Why wouldn't she be all right?' Tony frowned.

'When she left the hospital, she was upset. I thought I'd pay her a surprise visit.'

'Ava went to see you?'

Harvey narrowed his eyes. 'I take it she didn't tell you?'

'Nope. But then, your daughter seems to like keeping secrets.'

'If you reckon I'm going to stand here and let you dog out my daughter, you need to think twice, mate. I may have just got out of a fucking hospital bed, but that doesn't mean I'm not up for putting you back in your box. So I'd watch your mouth, if I were you,' Harvey raged.

He'd never had time for Tony, and that had caused a lot of tension between him and Ava over the years. Ava thought it was purely because Tony was Old Bill. While that hadn't sat well with Harvey, it was only part of the reason. What he despised was the fact that Tony played the nice guy, but he was sure there was something else under the surface, something darker. Ava had seemed oblivious to it, although he suspected that was a case of her not wanting to see the truth in front of her. She was always too busy running from herself, determined to create a happy family – something he'd clearly failed to do, even though that's what he'd hoped to achieve. As a result, she'd got together with Tony and ignored the fact that, deep down, he didn't make her happy.

Tony shook his head. 'You never change, do you? Do you get a kick out of trying to put me in my place? Is that what's going on here?' He slurred his words. 'Well, I've got news for you, that's over. It stops, right here.'

Harvey roared with laughter. 'Are you being serious, *mate*? You are, aren't you? Let me tell you something, you better hope that I put this down to you being pissed, and not you disrespecting me.' He glared at him.

'You know something, Billy? I couldn't care less what you think – I'm beyond caring. But if you want to talk about disrespect, you might want to have a word with your daughter.'

Harvey turned his head slightly to the side. 'What's that supposed to mean?'

Tony blinked and took a swig out of the half bottle of whisky. 'You know your daughter's a whore.'

Instinctively, Harvey went to leap at Tony, but the pain that shot through him with the sudden movement made him yell out in agony. He grabbed Tony's sweatshirt and hung on for support. His breath was staggered as he spoke. 'How fucking dare you.'

'Oh, I dare. And I told her as much last night, although she wasn't too keen to listen. But in the end, I think she did. Let's say I put her in her place.' The alcohol flowing through him had given Tony confidence.

'You best start talking sense, otherwise I won't be responsible for my actions.' Harvey pinned Tony against the wall. 'I am so tempted to put you through that wall, do you understand?'

Tony smiled nastily. 'Oh, I understand. But whatever you do to me, it won't change things . . . What I said about Ava was true. Every Friday night your precious daughter, my good wife, has been snorting cocaine like it's going out of fashion.' He shrugged. 'And by the sounds of it, she was sucking dicks like there was no tomorrow.'

Harvey kicked the door closed and began to lay his fists into Tony, ignoring his pain, ignoring the fact he could barely breathe. Because right then, in his mind's eye it wasn't Tony he was beating, but Ash Barker.

44

'Ava . . .' Ben opened the front door. It was late, gone midnight and he'd been waiting for her and had gone from pacing around the room, to trying to pretend he didn't care, to sitting by the window like some worried husband. 'Are you all right, darlin'? I didn't have your number so I couldn't call . . . What the fuck happened to your face?' As he stood on the step, he reached out and gently touched her cheek and eye.

'I . . .' She stopped and realized that she couldn't tell Ben it was a patient. He knew she wasn't working. 'I had a drink and I fell over.' She stared at him. 'A bit humiliating, really.' She shrugged and moved past him into the hallway.

'Ava.' He held onto her arm. 'You can talk to me, babe. I know . . .' He blew out a sigh. 'Well, I realize we ain't known each other that long, but . . .' He stopped. He wasn't one for sentiment, and his head was a bit of a mess – only a couple of hours ago he'd been shouting the odds at Harvey, baiting him about Ava – but he was relieved to see she was all right. That was fucked up, and he knew it.

'Where've you been?' Ben asked, closing the door.

'Did I forget the memo that says I have to answer to you? . . . Sorry, sorry, I didn't mean that.' She looked away, unable to hold his gaze. 'I just went to see a friend – Sarah. I needed to get away for a bit. As you said the other day, it's a lot.' She held back the tears.

Ben nodded, he wasn't going to mention his run-in with Harvey, nor the fact he knew that Ava had been to see him.

'Anyway.' Ava wasn't sure why she felt so awkward. 'How are you? Are you all right?'

He clenched his jaw. 'Apart from worrying about you?'

Ava took off her coat, throwing it down on the hall table. 'You didn't have to.'

He gave a crooked smile. 'Going on the state of your face, maybe I did.'

She walked into the kitchen. Every part of her wanted to go to the bar and have a drink, but she stopped herself. She didn't want to end up in a stranger's bedroom, which she knew she would once she began drinking. The idea of abusing herself because of the likes of Ash Barker made her sick to her stomach. But that didn't mean she didn't want to disappear into a bottle of whisky.

'What about you, have you heard anything else about your brother?' She turned to Ben, wanting to change her focus on to something else. 'I know you're worried about him.'

He shrugged. 'I'm sure Sam's all right. He's a grown man, he doesn't need a keeper.' He gave her a smile, but his heart felt heavy. This was so unlike Sam, and he only hoped he was being overly paranoid. 'Look, I was just thinking . . .' He paused, not quite knowing how to word it. 'I was wondering, maybe . . . maybe it might be better if you stayed in a hotel or something.'

'A hotel? Why?'

Ben struggled to come up with an explanation. Knowing Ava, whatever he said, she'd pick it apart.

'Is this to do with Sam?' Ava wondered.

'No . . . no, of course not.' Another lie. 'Well, the police aren't any further forward with finding out who attacked your dad . . . and you, so . . . I dunno, what with us asking questions and . . .' He trailed off. He wanted to say so much more. He wanted to tell her, or was that warn her, about Jed and Dean, but of course he couldn't.

'Ben, you don't just say that sort of thing for no reason. You're worrying me now.'

'I'm not trying to worry you – maybe I'm overthinking things – but—'

'You are overthinking things . . . But thank you. I appreciate you caring.' She let out a sigh, which came out louder than she'd intended. Ben looked at her and frowned.

His piercing green eyes locked on to her gaze. 'Talk to me. What's going on? I ain't saying I'm a psychologist.' He gave her a crooked grin. 'But I can listen.'

'Sorry to disappoint you, there's nothing to say.' She fiddled with her hands. 'I'm tired, that's all.'

'I think it's more than that.'

She shook her head. 'Nothing to see here.' She spoke quietly.

They were inches away from each other and for a few seconds neither of them said anything. Then he pushed her hair back behind her ears, and trailed his finger along her cheek, everything else fading out of his mind.

'Ben, we . . . I don't think this is a good idea.'

'I don't think it is either.' He whispered his agreement. But he reached up and gently touched her torn lip. 'Does it hurt?'

Staring at Ben, Ava placed her hand over his. She knew how complicated this would make everything, but she found herself locking her fingers between his. She held her breath and neither of them moved. In that instant, being here with Ben felt so right. 'A bit.' She smiled. 'A lot.'

He leaned forward and kissed her mouth gently, then kissed her eye, then he pulled away slowly. 'I've been trying to turn off my feelings,' he whispered gruffly, trying to pretend to himself that this was all part of him getting back at Harvey.

228

'Right now, it doesn't seem like you tried very hard.'

He kissed her neck, then grinned. 'I don't think I did. Note to self: must do better.' He took her hand and led her out of the kitchen, through the hallway, and up the stairs to his bedroom, leading her towards the bed.

Ava turned and looked at him, and as she did, he kissed her so gently on the lips, it felt electric. She found herself catching her breath.

Ben put his hand on her back, feeling her skin through the thin layer of fabric. 'Are you all right?' he murmured.

Ava just nodded as Ben bent over her and began to undress her, undoing the buttons on her shirt and trousers, slipping her out of her pale pink underwear.

Effortlessly, he scooped her naked body up in his arms and placed her on the bed. He smiled, and she smiled back as she leaned against the pillows.

'Ben.' She whispered his name.

'You want me to stop?'

She shook her head. 'No.'

He didn't reply, but he took off his own shirt and jeans, revealing his muscular body, which could've belonged to a man half his age.

He looked into her eyes. 'Are you sure this is all right with you? Because if you ain't—'

'I'm fine. More than fine.' She pushed herself up and looked down at him. 'I want to.'

He nodded and moved up the bed towards her, pressing his hard naked body against hers. He began to kiss her all over and she gasped, closing her eyes as he circled her nipples with his tongue. Slowly he moved further up the bed, kissing her passionately.

She felt his penis enter her and she bit down on her lip as he thrust harder, and deeper.

'*What the fuck! What the fuck do you think you're doing?*'

A loud bellow came from the doorway, and Ben rolled off Ava to see Harvey standing there . . .

45

'Get some fucking clothes on . . . Cover yourself up, for fuck's sake.' Harvey stared at Ava. '*Now.*' He yelled again, aware of a shooting pain rushing down the back of his head and behind his eyes. 'And *you*. You . . .' He pointed at Ben, but he was too enraged to finish his sentence.

'Harvey.' Ben sat up and stared at him. 'What the fuck are you doing here? I thought you were in hospital.'

'Don't say another word, otherwise I am going to blow your fucking head off. You hear me?' Harvey turned his attention to his daughter. 'Ava, listen to me, darlin'.' His voice was firm but loaded with warmth as he spoke to her. 'I want you to get your stuff on and go downstairs, because Ben and I need to have a word . . .' He stopped and blinked, taking in her face for the first time. Tony's words about putting her in her place suddenly came back to him. 'Did he do that to you? Did Tony hurt you?'

Ava wrapped herself up in the sheet. She saw Ben turn his head to stare at her.

'You told me you fell over, when you were half-cut . . . Ava?' The concern in Ben's voice showed on his face. 'Is it true?'

'Just shut the fuck up, Ben,' Harvey growled. 'This has nothing to do with you.' The tension between them was palpable and Ava looked between them.

'Sweetheart, look at me, did Tony do that?' Harvey spoke quietly. 'Because you know I'm going to kill him if he laid his hands on you.'

Ava didn't say anything. She couldn't. What Tony had done seemed to disappear into insignificance, compared to what she'd learned from Ash Barker about her father. It made her ill. It made her hate him; it also made her question if . . . if . . . if he'd let people do things to her when she was little, or . . . worse – she swallowed hard as she kept her gaze on her dad – had he done something to her himself?

The thought made her squeeze her eyes shut, not wanting to look at him. She could feel herself shuddering at the thought, and she breathed in deeply, fighting off a panic attack.

Was this the reason she was so messed up? Was that why she struggled in her private life? She'd thought it was to do with the fact her father had left her in the care of nannies or at boarding school, only ever spending short periods of time with her, time that she'd loved, like she'd loved him, then disappearing without warning, and she wouldn't see him again for months.

Growing up, she'd always tried to please him, desperate to be perfect so he'd want to stay and not leave her. By the time she'd realized that she was powerless over what he did and didn't do, the damage had been done. She'd sought out harmful relationships, harmful one-night stands, as if to prove to herself she wasn't good enough for anyone to *want* to stay with her. God, she was pathetic. A classic, textbook case.

And then Tony had come along. In a way, being with him was a form of self-harm, self-sabotage, because each time he'd looked at her, it had made her feel unworthy. It hammered home how much of a failure she was and what a mess she'd made of her life compared to her perfect husband, who never seemed to do anything wrong – until the other night, that was.

Suddenly it had all become clear to her. She'd been messed up by things that had happened deep in her past. Things that she couldn't remember. Things that were long forgotten, buried for self-protection. Trauma. How many clients had she dealt with over the years who had no clear recollection of what had happened to them in their childhood, only for the memories to resurface like a nightmare years later.

She opened her eyes again. Trembling, she took a step forward. 'Get out, Harvey. *Get out of this house.*'

A look of surprise crossed his face. 'Me? Sweetheart, what are you talking about? I ain't going anywhere, not until I have a word with Ben.'

Ava shook her head. She spoke through gritted teeth. 'I already told you: I don't want you here . . . I don't want you *anywhere* near me. Not now, not ever.'

Harvey tilted his head to look at her. 'What the fuck is wrong with you?'

She picked up her clothes and discreetly slipped her top and jeans on, throwing down the sheet she'd wrapped herself in. 'What's wrong is, I know . . . You sick, sick, fucking bastard.'

'Can someone tell me what's going on here?' Ben was clearly puzzled, but Ava ignored him. She lunged at her father, pushing him out of the room.

'Go!'

Harvey peered over Ava's shoulder. 'Is this something to do with you? Have you put her up to say this shit?'

'I haven't said anything.' Ben was hurriedly tugging on his jeans, not wanting to stand there naked.

'Then why's she saying this shit?' He turned to Ava. 'You do know this thing with you and Ben is all his way of getting at me, don't you?'

Ava was thrown. 'What?'

'I am so sorry, darlin'.' He sounded sincere. 'But Ben feels nothing for you. All this . . . him giving it the big 'un, playing fucking Casanova, is his way of getting at me. Ain't that right,

Ben.' He stared at Ben with so much disdain that Ava turned to look at him.

'Ben . . . Is this true?'

'Of course it ain't. He's pissed off because no father wants to see their daughter in bed with their mate.' Ben was tense.

'He's lying to you, Ava. It's all bullshit.' Harvey raised his voice.

She turned from Ben to her father, not knowing who to believe, furious with herself that she was feeling hurt by the possibility it might be true. She directed the anger at her father.

'Don't talk to me about people lying, when that's all you've done my whole life.' She pulled out her phone. 'You know what, it's over now, Harvey.' Ava had tears in her eyes, but she refused to let the way she felt, or rather used to feel, about her father get in the way of what was right. And this was right, wasn't it?

'What are you doing?' Harvey stepped forward.

'I'm doing what I should have done a long time ago . . . I'm calling the police.'

'Are you crazy?' Harvey went to grab the phone, but he flinched as the broken ribs he'd sustained sent a shock wave through him. 'Give me the phone.' He gestured to her. 'Ava, give me the fucking phone. Whatever is going on with you, this is not the way to handle it.'

'Oh, but it's all right to do what you did, is it? Tell me some-thing . . . how can you live with yourself?' She held the phone in one hand. '*How can you?*' she screamed.

'Babe, you need to help me out here. What am I supposed to have done that would make my own daughter pick up the phone and call the Old Bill?' He shook his head. 'How has it come to this?' He sounded genuinely pained.

'When are you going to give up the act, Dad? I know, because I went to see Ash Barker.'

Harvey visibly drained of colour, and he leaned against the

chest of drawers. He rubbed his chest, then slumped on the chair. 'When? When did you go and see him?' He was panting so hard it was a struggle to get the words out.

'What difference does it make when I saw him?' she snapped. 'But if you must know, that's where I've been today.'

'Jesus Christ!' This from Ben.

She turned to him. 'Are you part of this? Are you part of this club?'

Ben stepped towards her, but she moved back.

'No, I swear that piece of scum Barker has nothing to do with me.'

'Then why do I get the feeling there's something you're not telling me.'

Ben seemed uncomfortable. 'OK, I'll come clean . . . When I went back to Claudia that night, she told me about Ash, about the club down the docks that's been operating all these years. I didn't want to tell you because I didn't know the facts. I . . . I didn't know how to.' He shrugged.

Harvey, who'd been sitting with his head in his hands for the past few minutes, looked up. He got back to his feet, but he was pale. Ava suspected that had little to do with his injuries and everything to do with the fact that his past had finally caught up with him. 'You know me.' He spoke to Ben rather than Ava. 'You know I ain't like Ash. Tell her, Ben.'

'So now you want me to help you?' Ben snarled.

'Just *fucking* tell her.'

Ben stayed silent as Ava swung round to look at her dad. 'Then why did Ash Barker say you were? "Similar tastes" – those were his exact words. Why did he say he remembered me? That you used to take me there?'

'Fucking hell!' Ben sat down on the bed, stunned.

235

Harvey leapt towards him, grabbing his arm. 'Why the fuck aren't you telling her I ain't a nonce?'

Ben stood up, his face inches from Harvey. 'I can't.'

'You mean you won't . . . Ben, don't do this to me. Don't fucking destroy my life pretending you don't know that I ain't like that. I love my daughter, and I would never hurt her, *ever*. I would never hurt any kid.'

'Destroy your life? Yours?' Ben was incensed. 'Don't talk to me about destroying your life, not when you single-handedly destroyed mine. That day you left me, my life was over. I can never get that back.'

'What's he talking about? Left you? What do you mean, Ben?'

'He didn't mean anything, did you, Ben?'

Ben's eyes never left Ava. 'Nah, I didn't.'

Harvey nodded. 'Ben, you've known me for thirty, forty years.'

'You said you'd only known him ten years!' Ava turned on Ben. She was sick of the two of them keeping her in the dark. 'Oh my God, both of you, both of you are just lying to me.'

'I already told you, darlin', you can't trust him, all this is an act,' Harvey said firmly.

Ben stared at Harvey. 'You don't know that.'

'Didn't you tell me just this afternoon that you were going to mess with my daughter? Isn't that what you said? Come on, Ben, tell her the truth.'

Ava watched Ben tense, although he didn't say anything. 'Is that true, Ben . . . Did you say that?'

He clenched his jaw, glanced sidewards at Harvey, then faced Ava. 'It's not how it sounds.'

Harvey let out a loud, bitter laugh. 'Then tell us how it was, eh? Come on, Ben, tell us the other interpretation of it.'

'Fine, why don't I do that. You want her to know the whole story, Harvey?'

'Seriously.' Ava heard the hurt in her voice, and once again she was angry with herself for caring.

'Ava, I didn't mean it.' Ben looked her in the eye. 'A week ago, I might have done, I might have meant it, but even then, I wouldn't have done anything to you . . . not really.'

'Not really?' She raised her eyebrows.

'Look, I know it sounds shit, but things change. What I feel for you is real.'

'Yet you still said that. You know what, Ben, I don't care. It's fine, you don't owe me anything. Besides, in case you haven't noticed, I've got more pressing issues to deal with.' She turned back to her dad, but as she did, there was a loud hammering on the door downstairs.

'Stay here.' Harvey held up a hand to his daughter, and immediately pulled a handgun from his pocket with the other hand.

'Harvey, no, *wait*!' Ben moved across to where he was standing. 'It could be nothing.'

'What the hell is going on?' Ava's heart raced.

'Just stay here, darlin'.' Harvey lowered his voice, and nodded to Ben, who was grabbing his shirt from the floor. They moved towards the top landing, throwing glances to each other. The hammering stopped as suddenly as it had started.

Ben led the way downstairs, frowning when he saw an envelope lying on the floor. He hurried over and picked it up. His name was written on it. He tore it open.

'What is it?' Harvey came up behind him.

He stared down at the contents of the envelope. 'Photos.' He passed them to Harvey.

'Jesus Christ, that geezer's taken a battering.' He stared at the man tied to a chair, blood all over his face, his body covered in cuts and bruises. 'Have you any idea who he is?'

Ben nodded. 'Yeah . . . yeah, I do. He's my brother.'

46

'What the fuck are we going to do now?' Harvey spoke to Ben as they sat in the kitchen of the house in Meard Street.

'We? *We* aren't going to do anything. Nothing has changed. You owe me, Harvey. So don't start this shit like you and I are mates.' He hissed at Harvey through his teeth. Seeing Sam like that made him feel sick.

'Ben, I know how—'

'No, you don't. Don't even go there, because you have no idea how I feel. If you did, you would give me that money. I might sound like a broken record, but that's how I feel. I sat in that cell for thirty-six years, and the only reason Jed and Dean are doing this to Sam is because—'

'We don't know it's them,' Harvey cut him off. He took a sip of the coffee he'd made, wincing at the bitter taste.

'Who else would it be? I should never have trusted you. The whole set-up was flawed from the start. I didn't know Jed and Dean – you were the one who introduced me. You said everything was going to be fine – and I went along with it. And you know why I did that? Because I looked up to you. Fucking Harve, back then, you were like a brother to me. It never occurred to me that you would stitch me up.' He looked towards the door and lowered his voice. 'Jed and Dean mean business, Harvey. You know that as well as I do. They've been trying to find you for the past thirty-six years. Like me, they want to get their hands on that money. Unlike me, they don't care who gets hurt – they won't stop 'til they have it.'

Harvey rubbed his head. The day felt like it was catching up with him. Apart from his fists, still throbbing from where he'd battered Tony, his whole body was hurting, and his head felt like someone was stamping on it.

'OK, OK, so let's say it is them,' Harvey conceded. 'How can I give them something I haven't got?' Desperation gripped him. Ben didn't know the half of it, and he wasn't about to start telling him now. If he had his way, Ben would never know the truth.

Ben said nothing. The thought of his brother being tortured by Jed and Dean was doing his head in. If he had the money, he'd trade it for Sam in a heartbeat. But he couldn't think of a way to get his hands on it. He knew Harvey well enough to be certain that, even if he held a gun to his head, he wouldn't tell him where it was.

'Look, Ben, I know you're not my greatest fan. But we need to make a few phone calls and see if anyone knows where Jed and Dean are hanging out. Someone's sure to know, we just have to get them to talk, and then—'

'What is this *we*? I've just told you, there is no *we*, not anymore.'

Harvey fell into silence. He could think of one person who might know where Jed and Dean were holed up, but he wasn't sure he could go and ask, not after all this time. Then again, what choice did he have?

He took a deep breath, hoping to clear his head. He was finding it a struggle to concentrate. 'Ben, come on, think about your brother.'

'What the fuck do you think I'm doing!'

'You can't do this on your own. Apart from the fact I feel responsible, this isn't only about you and Sam, it's about Ava.

They'll be coming after her too, so we need to do this together. We need to stop them.'

Ben leapt out of his chair and shoved Harvey in the chest. 'Then give them what they want! Give them the fucking money. I swear to God, if they kill Sam, I will put a bullet in your head.'

Harvey closed his eyes for a moment, then opened them and held Ben's stare. 'If I had the money, I would . . . I would've given it to you first, though. You deserve it. Fucking hell, you've lived a nightmare. But I ain't got it. I never did have it. So the only way we can sort this out is if we work together. First, we need to find your brother, then we can deal with Jed and Dean . . . Ben, don't look at me like that. Do you think I'd put my daughter at risk just for money? You have no idea how much I love her.'

Ben sneered. 'How do you love her, Harvey? What kind of love are we talking here?'

'What?' Harvey's head jerked up.

'All this shit I'm hearing about you and Ash – is it true?'

Harvey leapt at Ben, catching him by surprise and knocking him to the ground. The pain that shot through Harvey's body was overshadowed by his anger, he crouched over Ben, bringing down his fist, wanting to pulverize him.

Ben took the punch, then he rolled over and grabbed Harvey, who was no match for him due to his injuries.

Scrambling up, Ben ran for his jacket and grabbed the gun. He pointed it at Harvey. 'Give me one good reason why I shouldn't pull the trigger.'

Harvey raised his hands. 'Because then you wouldn't get your brother back, and that's all that matters. Keeping him and Ava alive is the only thing we should focus on right now . . . Ben, I am so sorry. I am sorry what happened to you.'

Ben took a step closer. 'Not sorry enough.' He lifted his arm and placed the nozzle of the gun on Harvey's forehead.

'Ben, you don't want to do this, mate.'

'Oh, but I do. Have you any idea how often I thought about doing this?' His finger was on the trigger. 'Every night in my cell, I said my prayers, and this is what I prayed for.'

'Please, Ben, I'm begging you . . . is that what you want me to do? Beg? Because I will.'

Ben shook his head. 'What I want is my life back, and as you can't do that, what I want is the money, then I can take it to Jed and Dean, and get my brother back.'

'What can I do to prove to you, I ain't got it.' There was an edge of fear in Harvey's voice, the vein in his neck was pulsing as his heart raced.

'Get on your knees.' Ben pushed the nozzle harder into Harvey's forehead.

Harvey winced as he sank down; the agony from his fractured rib made him catch his breath.

'I'm going to count to five, and then your time's up.'

'Ava's in the house – Ben, don't do it, not here, not here.'

'One . . . Two . . . Three . . . Four . . .'

'OK, OK . . . I'll tell you.' Panic rushed through Harvey. 'I'll tell you . . . I had it. I had the money, but I haven't anymore. I didn't have it for long. If there'd been any other way, I wouldn't have taken it. You've got to believe me.'

'A minute ago, you wanted me to believe that you didn't ever have the money. Clearly that was a lie. You left me to take the fall . . . why, Harvey? We were mates. I would've done anything for you. After the robbery, I waited and waited. I thought you'd been caught inside the warehouse, when all the time you had fucked off with the money. I've replayed it in my head over and over, and I can't come up with a reason why you did that.'

'I'm sorry. Fucking hell, if I could change it, I would, but . . . Ben, mate, I didn't have any choice.'

Ben lowered the gun. He had to try to stay focused, but his mind was on his brother. 'Bullshit! You had a choice, and you chose to put it on me.' He turned away, slipping the gun back in his jacket. He spoke with his back to Harvey. 'After I get my brother back, you're a dead man.' He walked out and Harvey listened as Ben's footsteps faded down the hallway. He slammed the front door, and the house fell silent.

Harvey blew out his cheeks in a sigh of relief. But the relief was short-lived. The look on Ava's face as she came into the room told him she was going to give it him with both barrels.

'I called them. They'll be here soon.' Her eyes were ice-cold.

With some difficulty, Harvey stood. 'You're bluffing, tell me you're bluffing.' His voice cracked, not with anger but with disappointment and hurt.

'No, Dad, I'm not.'

Ava watched the desperation cross her father's face. 'Please, Ava, don't do this.'

'I already have. You can't do the things you have and get away with it.'

'You have no idea what you're talking about.'

She looked at him. 'Because you never told me, and you let me find out from Ash Barker . . . Ash Barker, Dad – a sadistic paedophile. And I had to learn who you were from him.'

He shook his head. 'Jesus Christ.' He was breathless. 'Is that what you really think? Do you seriously believe I'm capable of that? Most of your life, it was only me and you, and—'

'No, it was only me and a long line of short-term nannies,' Ava cut in.

'That's not true, babe. Everywhere I went, you came with me. Yes, sometimes I had to go away, you know that. But I only went away for work, and the minute I could, I came back. Ava, you were the only thing on my mind. Your welfare was all that mattered to me . . . That's why I never brought another woman into your life.'

'Oh please.' She rolled her eyes.

'OK, I had relationships, but they weren't anything serious. You were and have always been my priority.' He limped over to her, unable to hide the pain he was in. 'Did I ever hurt you in any way? And I'm not talking about my lack of parenting skills – I didn't know the first thing about being a dad, but I swear I tried my best, darlin'. It's just, there were things I couldn't tell you. Things I was trying to protect you from.'

'Like Ash Barker.'

'No . . . no.' He looked away and Ava felt the tears welling in her eyes. 'Can I ask you something, babe,' he pleaded. 'Did I ever give you any reason to feel uncomfortable around me? Did I ever make you feel unsafe?'

Ava shook her head. 'No.'

He took a step towards her. 'That's my point, darlin'. If all this bullshit you're saying was true, you wouldn't have felt safe with me.'

'That's not true, victims can forget. Trauma makes them forget.' Her voice edged on hysteria.

He slammed down his hand. 'Stop, just stop, all right! This is crap, sweetheart. It's all crap. All that psychobabble shit is keeping you from thinking straight. What does your heart say, babe? Does it say that I would be able to do what you're accusing me of?' He shook his head sadly. 'I don't know what's going on with you, but it's not normal. And neither is what Tony told me. He said he knocked you around because he found out you were out with other geezers. Not that I'd blame you, I never liked the geezer, never trusted him. Sounds like the whole marriage was a mess.'

Ava was taken aback, not to mention humiliated. 'My life isn't a mess because of Tony. It isn't a case of me not being a good wife because of him.' She raised her voice, but then lowered it again, afraid she'd lose control. 'Until now, he has been the most stable influence in my life, and I owe him for how he's cared for me all these years.'

'You don't owe him anything,' Harvey snapped.

'I do. It would be easy to blame you for everything, but the truth is, my life's a mess because of *me*. And things won't start to improve until I can fit all the pieces together. This is just the start.'

Harvey went to say something but there was a loud knock on the door.

'*Police, open up.*'

He stared at Ava. 'What have you done?'

'I told you, I wasn't bluffing. This is what should've happened a long time ago.'

'Babe.' He closed his eyes and took a deep breath. 'I love you so much, so I ain't angry with you, but I wish you hadn't done it, you have got it so wrong.'

She walked out into the hallway, fighting back the tears. 'Let's leave that for the police to decide, shall we?'

47

Tony sat in the police canteen eating a runny bacon and egg sandwich. The painkillers he'd swallowed before leaving home had taken the edge off his hangover, and he was reflecting on all that had happened. Once again, instead of feeling guilty or ashamed about the way he'd acted – this time towards Harvey – he told himself it was justified. Finally, he had seen the truth, and it felt liberating. Yes, that was definitely the word he'd use.

'Hey, Tone.' Joe hurried over to where Tony was sitting. 'Fucking hell, what happened to you?' He stopped and stared at Tony's face.

'I got jumped on last night.' It was a partial lie. Ava's father had laid into him like a thug, and if it wasn't for the fact the old man had just come out of hospital, Tony was certain his injuries would've been much worse. 'I went into town, had a few beers – drowning my sorrows a bit. Ava and I aren't in a great place, as you know, and I think it's finally starting to hit me.'

Joe raised his eyebrows. 'Well, something has. It looks nasty.'

'It's my own fault. I had my phone out, and I should've handed it over when the little bastards asked for it, but instead I decided to play the tough guy.'

'Did you report it?'

Tony shook his head. 'What's the point? Haven't you heard, the police are rubbish.'

Joe put his head back and roared with laughter, causing all the officers in the canteen to look their way.

He patted Tony on the back. 'I'm sure it'll work out between you and Ava, just give it time.' He shrugged and pinched a chip off Tony's plate. 'That's as far as my marriage advice goes.' He grinned. 'So, listen, I've got an update . . . It's about your father-in-law.'

'Billy. What about him?'

'Actually, Harvey. Turns out his name is Harvey Fletcher.'

Tony took a sip of his milky tea. 'How the fuck did you find out?'

'The unit here hadn't found anything yet. So far, they'd come up with nothing, but there was a tip-off. He's been picked up for questioning.'

'When?' Tony frowned.

'Last night, or rather in the early hours of this morning.'

'I thought he was in hospital.' He didn't add that he knew Billy, or rather Harvey was out, given that he'd been the one who'd battered him yesterday evening.

'He was, but for some reason he discharged himself. Like I say, someone called it in. I don't know all the ins and outs of it, but it was something to do with Ash Barker.'

'As in the . . .'

'Yeah, as in *the* Ash Barker, who got done for life.'

'Jesus Christ.' Tony didn't have to feign astonishment this time. He sat back in his chair. He'd only read in the paper about Ash. Like most people, the crimes Ash had committed made him sick to his stomach. 'Where is he now?'

Joe took another chip, causing Tony to push the whole plate towards him. 'London. That's where they picked him up. He was in his house in London.'

'Billy had a house there? I mean, Harvey . . . I had no idea. I wonder if Ava knew.'

'No, she would've told you,' Joe suggested.

'Yeah right.' Tony shook his head, not wanting to go there. 'Have you any idea who called it in?'

'It was anonymous, but I do know it was a woman. They swooped in because of the investigation we're conducting . . . I'm not sure how long they can keep him in for. Not without any evidence. After all, it's not a crime to change your name. I don't think they arrested him, just suggested he come and speak to them at the station. But it's fucked up if he did have any links with Ash.'

Tony absorbed everything that Joe had said. 'Can you find out where this place was? The place in London?'

'Yeah, sure – but you didn't hear it from me, all right? I don't want this coming back on me.' He paused. 'And you know, I'm not one to judge, but people have been talking.'

'About what?'

Joe took a deep breath. 'About you. They've noticed you're not yourself.'

Tony bristled. 'Well, who the fuck am I, then?'

Joe pulled a chair up to Tony. He sat down. 'It's not an insult. They're worried about you.'

'Who's *they*? And if it's not an insult, I'm not sure what the fuck it is. And whoever is talking, tell them not to . . .' He stood and glared at Joe. 'Tell them I'm fine.'

'OK, but perhaps if you don't come to work smelling of booze, they might believe me. Not only that, the drink makes you a bit of a loose cannon.'

Tony worked hard not to lose his temper. 'I can't believe you just fucking said that.'

'Well believe it . . .' Joe sighed. 'Look, Tony, if you're struggling, then maybe you should take some time off.'

'You've changed your tune,' he hissed. '"Just act normal," that's what you said, and that's what I'm doing.'

'But you aren't, and the guys have been asking because they're concerned about you. They know what it's like when there's grief at home.'

Tony felt his face flush. 'You told them?'

Joe glanced around and lowered his voice. 'I had to. They wanted to know why you were acting so strangely. They wanted to know what the problem was – I had to come up with something.'

'Yeah, I suppose it's better to say that than to tell them we killed a man.' And with those words, Tony stormed off.

48

Ava was nodding in and out of sleep. She'd been trying to push away her feeling of guilt for calling the police on her father. Even though she knew it was the right thing to do in the circumstances, she couldn't help feeling like she'd betrayed him. Which was ridiculous, but that didn't make it any easier for her.

They'd spoken to him, and he'd gone with them quietly, agreeing to go down to the station. But on the way out, he'd looked at her, and the hurt and the sadness had shown in his eyes. That was what she couldn't get out of her head.

She'd had to fight the urge to go in search of a late-night bar – which, being in the heart of Soho, would've been easy. Booze might take the edge off but it wouldn't help her work out what she needed to do next. Maybe she'd already done all she needed to. Did she really want to uncover more of her father's secrets, learn more about him and Ash and their similar tastes? But then what of her mother . . . ? Ava had a feeling that the only thing she would achieve by searching for her would be more pain. But perhaps it would be worth it to find out the truth.

In the dark, she watched the headlights of passing traffic make their way across the ceiling. She sighed again and thought about Ben. She hadn't seen him, not since she'd heard him storm out the night before, slamming the door behind him. Not that she particularly wanted to see him – or at least, that was what she kept telling herself.

She'd been hurt when she found out Ben had been using her

to get at her father. It hurt because she cared. She'd cared much more than she'd thought, and that had surprised her.

Yawning, she tried not to wonder where he was, not to remember how it had felt when he'd kissed her. Jesus, what was she, a teenager? There were so many things going on right now, yet here she was, thinking about a man she didn't trust, she didn't know, who was the same age as her father. God, what did that say about her?

She stretched her legs out and tried to force herself to get some sleep. She needed to shut off her thoughts.

'Ava.'

The sound of the voice in the room made Ava's heart leap and she froze, terrified.

'I wanted to see this secret life that you had. It's a nice place you've got here.'

Ava leapt up out of bed.

'Where are you going? I want to talk to you.' .

It was too dark to see. Ava turned in the direction of the voice while reaching for the light switch. She found it, flicked it on, and the room lit up. She stared at Tony. He looked back at her, wild-eyed. His face was almost as bruised and battered as hers.

'What are you doing here?' The way he was looking at her sent a shiver of fear down her spine.

'I've already told you, I wanted to see this secret life of yours. I thought it be a nice surprise for you. Especially after you ran off without telling me where you were going. Call me old-fashioned, but I think a wife belongs at home with her husband, don't you?'

He took a step towards her and Ava darted for the door, but Tony immediately grabbed her and pulled her towards him.

Ava hit out, trying to push him away, but she stumbled. Tony picked her up and threw her onto the bed. She kicked out furiously with her legs, but he was stronger and was able to strad-dle her and restrain her flailing limbs. He gave her a hard backhand. 'Calm the fuck down, I'm not here to hurt you, I'm here to take you home.'

'I'm not going anywhere with you.'

'Yes, you are. You can't seriously think I'm going to let you stay here. I was going to say, on your own, but you're not on your own, are you?' He stared down into Ava's face.

'I am.'

'Liar.'

'I'm not lying. I came to stay with my father and his friend. I needed to get away. You hurt me, Tony – you couldn't expect me to come home after that. We need to have a break, and maybe then we can somehow get back on track and start to heal.'

The laugh which escaped Tony's mouth was loud and bitter. 'I'm not one of your clients. You don't have to talk to me in bumper stickers.' He trailed his finger down Ava's face. 'You're going to come home with me tonight, and you're going to become the wife I deserve. A good wife. Do you understand me?' He slapped her face again and she squealed in pain. 'From now on, I'm not going to put up with your shit.'

'Tony, don't do this . . . You need to go.'

'You heard her, mate.'

Ava looked up to see Ben standing in the doorway.

Tony glared at Ben, then he looked back at Ava. 'Oh my God, don't tell me, she's been fucking you as well? You need to be care-ful, mate; you might catch something nasty from her. And in case it's escaped your notice, she's my wife, not yours, so I suggest you turn around and close the door behind you.' He threw a look at Ava. 'Get your stuff, the car's parked outside.'

Ben scowled. He was sick with worry about Sam, and the last thing he needed was this prick giving it the large one. 'That's not going to happen. I'm giving you a choice. You either get up and go now without another word, or I will do you some damage – and you wouldn't want that, not the way I'm feeling right now.' Ben's eyes pierced into Tony.

'You do know she's second-hand goods, don't you? You're just one of many. She's been passed around the whole of Derby, so don't kid yourself you're anything special.'

'I warned you not to say anything, didn't I?' Ben launched himself at Tony.

'No . . . wait. Don't!' Ava stopped Ben with her words. 'Leave it. I don't want this. Ben, *please*.'

He nodded and dropped his fists, but the moment he did, Tony leapt at him, shoving him off his feet. As soon as he was down, Tony threw a punch, but Ben blocked it and struck Tony hard across the face, breaking his nose.

Roaring in anger, blood spurting from his injured nose, Tony leapt on top of Ben, preventing him from getting to his feet. He wrapped one arm around Ben's neck and pulled it tight with his other hand, squeezing as hard as he could to choke the life out of him.

'Stop, for God's sake, Tony – *stop!*' Ava ran over and tried to pull him off. 'Tony, stop, you'll kill him.' Ben's face was beginning to turn blue; his eyes were red and bloodshot. Unable to break the stranglehold Tony had on him, she looked around her for a weapon. There was a foot stool in front of the armchair. She picked it up and swung it at Tony.

There was a loud crunch and Tony fell forward. Ben began to cough, turning on to his side and rubbing his neck.

'Ben, are you OK?'

He could barely speak; instead he nodded his head.

Ava looked back at Tony and saw blood trickling from his head. 'Oh Jesus.' A cold chill washed over her, and she scrambled across to where he was lying. She tried to feel for a pulse, but she was shaking too much. 'Is he dead? Oh my God, what have I done?' Ava stared at Ben, panic-stricken. All she could do was babble: 'I think he's dead. He's dead . . .'

Ben sat up and crawled over to Tony. His throat felt like it was on fire. He put his fingers on Tony's wrist and neck, then looked at Ava. 'He ain't dead.' His voice was a croak.

Ava let out a huge sigh of relief. 'Thank God. But we need to get him to a doctor.' She took a deep gulp of air to try to steady herself.

'I'll take him. I'll drop him at the hospital. You stay here, I'll be back soon.'

'Wait, let me get his keys, I'll move his car. I'll park it away from the house.' She hurriedly pulled the keys from Tony's pocket.

'OK, I better go,' Ben said firmly.

'Are you sure?'

'Yeah, course I am. I think you've had quite enough shit for one night.' He spat out a mouthful of blood and kissed her on her head. 'And look, Ava, what your dad said wasn't true. I do care.'

'It's fine, like I said before, it's no big deal.'

He stroked her face. 'That's just it – it isn't fine. I didn't want to feel anything about you, cos, let's face it, you're what I'd call *complicated*, not to mention you're the daughter of someone I know. But there it is, shit happens, right? I can't help the way I feel about you.' He stared at her for a moment then turned to pick Tony up. The years he'd spent working out in the prison gym meant he could throw Tony over his shoulder without much effort.

'I'll take him out to my car, but I'd appreciate it if you could make sure the coast is clear. I don't fancy having to explain what I'm doing. My keys are on the table in the hallway.' He attempted a smile, and Ava nodded and rushed down the stairs.

She opened the front door and peered out into the dimly lit street, then used the remote to unlock Ben's Range Rover before rushing over and opening the back door. 'Coast is clear,' she called softly.

Ben immediately hurried across, and dumped Tony on the back seat.

Closing the door, he looked at her. 'I don't know how long I'll be, but I'll see you later. Once you've moved Tony's car, get yourself back inside. It might be a good idea to clean up. Then, if you can, get some sleep.'

Ava nodded. She stood on tiptoes and kissed him gently on the lips. 'Thank you. Thank you for everything.'

Ben watched her walk away, then he clambered into the driver's seat. He turned to look at Tony. There was no point taking him to hospital. He knew a dead man when he saw one. The only question now was, what the fuck was he going to do with him . . .

49

It was the next morning and Harvey hadn't bothered going home. He hadn't wanted to see Ava. It wasn't that he was angry with her for calling the Old Bill. The damage had been done, so what was the point?

They'd released him last night after only a few hours of questioning. Most of their questions had been about Ash. His answering 'no comment' had clearly frustrated them, but there was nothing they could do about it. They had nothing on Harvey Fletcher, or Billy Fields for that matter. He'd spent the past thirty-odd years making sure no one would be able to point a finger at him. He'd also spent the past thirty-odd years running, but now that had caught up with him. The past always did.

Yawning, he turned to Ben. 'Thank you.'

Ben nodded as he sat in his car. They'd been up all night, sorting out the *problem*. 'I did it for Ava, not you.'

Harvey stared out at the forest. They'd made sure the grave was good and deep before chucking Tony's body in there and filling it in, then covering the freshly dug soil with branches and dead leaves. 'You're sure Ava hasn't any idea?' Harvey asked.

'She was in too much of a state last night. When I took him out of the house, she didn't even realize he was dead.'

Harvey nodded. 'We need to keep it like that. She can never find out.'

Ben rubbed his face. His thoughts filled with Sam. 'I agree, but has it ever occurred to you that her whole life is just full of secrets?'

Harvey watched Ben as he reversed the car and pulled out on to the road. There was no way anyone would find Tony's body. It was just one of many nameless bodies buried in Epping Forest over the years.

'Let me worry about that,' he said. 'I've always tried to do my best by Ava, no matter what you think.'

At the junction, Ben indicated right. 'I don't think anything. Except, all roads seem to lead back to you and bloody Ash . . . Anyway, I'd better call her. She'll be worried. Punch her number into my phone, will you?'

Harvey did as he was told and pressed dial on Ben's phone.

'Now don't say a fucking word, I don't want her to know I'm with you,' Ben snapped.

'Do I look stupid?'

Ben didn't answer. A moment later the call connected.

'Hey Ava, it's Ben.'

'*Oh my God, I was so worried, and when you drove off, I remembered you didn't have my number so you couldn't call.*'

'Yeah, I got your number from your dad. I asked him for it when we were in the kitchen last night. It's a good job I did.'

There was a slight pause. '*I'm surprised he gave it you.*' Ben thought she sounded sceptical.

He glanced at Harvey. 'Yeah well, lucky for me he did . . .' He trailed off and there was a moment of silence.

'*So, how's Tony? What did they say?*' Her words rushed out.

'They didn't say anything because he didn't go.'

There was another pause from Ava. '*I don't understand.*'

'I was taking him to UCL, but the traffic was so bad, I did a U-turn, thinking I'd head over to Guy's, but then . . . he woke up. He started to get lairy again, giving it the big one. I tried to

256

explain I was taking him to hospital, but he was carrying on about how he didn't want me near him . . . then he jumped out at the lights.'

'*And you let him?*'

'Ava, come on, what was I supposed to do? Run after him and force him back in the car?'

'*No, of course not . . . I'm sorry.*'

'The geezer reeked of booze. No doubt he's gone to lick his wounds in a bar somewhere . . . And look, I'm sorry I didn't call earlier, I had to go and talk to a couple of guys, just business, but the signal was shit.'

'*OK, well, thanks for calling.*' Ben picked up on the disappointment in her voice.

'Ava.' He didn't want her to put the phone down. 'What I said last night? I meant it. I've got a lot going on right now, though.' The photo of Sam, bloody and beaten, flashed into his mind. 'Don't think I didn't mean it, OK.'

A pause.

'*I'm glad. I feel the same.*'

'I'll phone you later.'

Ben ended the call and stared at Harvey. 'Don't say a fucking word. What we do is our business – we're consenting adults, and unlike you, I ain't going to hurt her.'

Harvey glared back at him. It fucked with his head that Ben was screwing Ava. 'Sure you won't, that's why you've just lied to her.'

They drove in silence for the next hour or so, with Harvey deep in thought. There was so much he felt about Ben being with his daughter, but even he knew it wasn't the right time to be focusing on that. His mind was full of other stuff. Ava's childhood, her life, the person she'd grown into, for a start.

There'd been times in the past when he'd wanted to confess,

to tell Ava everything. But how could he? His fear was that she'd hate him if she knew the truth. And now she knew part of the truth and she already hated him, so what chance would he have once he told her the whole truth and nothing but?

Turning into a car park, Ben came to a stop by a large tree. He flicked on the window wipers as a light hail began to fall.

'I'll wait for you,' he muttered gruffly.

'I don't know how long I'll be,' Harvey replied as he stepped out of the car. He felt the cold, icy wind whip around him.

'Yeah well, I'm relying on you,' Ben told him. 'At least get this one thing right.'

Harvey gave him a nod, closed the door, and headed for the prison.

In the kitchen of the house in Meard Street, Ava sat and stared at her phone, mulling over what Ben had said, but also the way he had said it. After a lifetime of dealing with her father, she knew enough to recognize when she wasn't being told the whole story.

Well, two could play that game . . .

50

Harvey sat in the cold visiting room waiting to face his past. There were other visitors occupying seats in front of the long row of tables, keeping up a quiet hum of chatter. A few children were playing in the corner by a tatty old toy box. It wasn't a place he'd have wanted to bring Ava when she was that age, but then, hadn't she been in worse places? Much worse.

He blew out a long sigh at the thought of it all, and as usual he struggled to come to terms with the past.

'Harvey.'

Harvey looked up and swallowed hard as Ash Barker waddled towards him. He was surprised by Ash's appearance; the bald head and bloated body bore no resemblance to the Ash he remembered. But then it had been years since he'd seen him. Thirty-six years, to be precise.

'When they said you were coming to visit, I thought they were taking the piss, but here you are, handsome as ever, apart from those bruises. Have you been fighting again, Harve? Some things never change.' He grinned and sat down, his beady eyes examining Harvey's face. 'Fucking hell, mate, it's good to see you. I thought I'd never see your mug again.' He leaned back on his chair and began to cough, then wiped his mouth on his sleeve. 'You'll have to excuse me staring, but I'm in shock,' Ash went on. 'Though not as shocking as it was to see your daughter. What a turn-up for the books that was, to see little Sophia, although I understand her name is Ava now.'

Harvey shuffled in his chair.

'I never recognized her at first, but then she said who she was and it all came flooding back. Who could forget those big eyes, the way they used to look up at you.' He stopped to laugh, then leaned forward, his eyes twinkling. 'She was a special little girl, but I don't have to tell you that, do I?'

Harvey clutched his chair. He didn't say anything, only nodded as Ash grinned.

'Shame they have to grow up, ain't it?' Ash leered.

Again, Harvey didn't answer. He needed to keep calm. He was only here for one reason.

'So, what's with all the visits. What's going on?' Ash sounded eager. His eyes lit up in excitement. 'She wanted to know all about you. I thought it was strange – what's the deal?'

Harvey rubbed his chin. 'No deal, you know kids, they want to know stuff.' He shrugged.

Ash pulled a face. 'It seems a lot of trouble to go to when she could've asked you.' He looked at Harvey suspiciously.

'Well, I guess what I've told her hasn't been enough. There are some things you don't want to tell them.' Harvey pictured Ava. 'Things that are best left in the past.'

'Oh, I don't know, I enjoy thinking about those times. It's a funny thing, Harvey, sometimes, if I think really hard about it, I feel like I'm back there in my little club by the docks, having fun.' He closed his eyes and smiled, letting out a groan. 'Little Sophia.'

Harvey breathed deeply, once, twice. He wouldn't, he couldn't allow himself to say anything. Again he reminded himself that he was here for one reason only. To get information about Jed and Dean.

Ash opened his eyes and stared straight at Harvey. 'But maybe it would've been good for her to know everything. Perhaps she'd enjoy remembering.' His laugh was coarse and nasty. 'She's clearly forgotten.' He grinned again.

Harvey rubbed his chest. 'What did you tell her?'

'Why, are you worried?'

'No.' Harvey hoped that he sounded convincing.

'I just told her that you shared my tastes.'

Harvey looked down.

'Well, it's true, isn't it? You were the most eager one, especially when it came to Sophia.'

'Yeah . . . yeah.' He gave Ash a tight smile. 'Anyway, thanks for seeing me. I appreciate it.'

'I'd say the pleasure was all mine.' He sniffed and looked thoughtful. 'When I heard you'd gone on the run, I wished you nothing but luck. I was pleased for you, Harve . . . It was only you, Jed and Dean that managed to get away. Fucking police swooped down like vultures. And just like that, the good times were over – for me, anyway.' He sounded wistful. 'They're still operating down the docks – on a much smaller scale, of course. And very much underground now. You should get yourself down there. Lorni will be pleased to see you.'

Harvey could only nod, and it took him a beat to say, 'It's actually Jed and Dean I'm here to see you about, Harve.'

'And there's me thinking it's all about me.' He winked at Harvey, and his pudgy fingers brushed against Harvey's hand. 'I hear they're not well pleased with you. They think you've got their money.' He locked eyes with Harvey. 'I never told them, you know.'

'Told them what?'

Ash grinned and leaned so far towards Harvey, that he could smell the man's rancid breath. 'Come on, Harvey, you didn't just pull all that money out of your arsehole. We both know where you got it – and where it went.'

Harvey shook his head. 'I don't know what you're talking about.'

Ash spread open his arms. 'Harve . . . Harvey, it's me you're talking to. How do you expect me to help you, if you don't trust me?'

'The money came from other sources. I did other jobs, jobs you didn't know about. Same goes for Jed and Dean, they didn't know.'

'You want to know what I think?' Ash smiled, and Harvey noticed the pieces of food dried in the corners of his mouth. 'I think you were running more from them than the Old Bill, because you knew they wouldn't be very happy with what you did . . . I actually admired you for that.'

'Ash—'

'Don't insult my intelligence. They thought they were the brains behind the robbery, and they brought you in thinking you would be the brawn. The meathead. When all along you were one step ahead of them. You took the money right from under their noses . . .' He stopped and sniffed again. 'Harvey, you know my loyalty lies with you and not them. They were acquaintances and you were my friend . . . So tell me, what is it you want to know.'

'I need to find them . . . They threatened Ava.'

Ash gave an exaggerated gasp. 'Not little Sophia! Oh, that will never do, especially as I know you've got no money to give.' He tutted playfully.

'So will you help me?'

'What's it worth for me? How about you bring me something I might like.'

Harvey stared at him; he knew exactly what he was talking about. 'I can't, Ash, you know I can't. They're hardly going to let me, are they?'

Ash turned to look at the officers in the corner. He nodded slowly. 'That's true . . . Shame really.'

'So will you help me or not?'

Ash turned back to look at Harvey. He was silent for what felt like a good few minutes, then a smile spread across his face. 'All right, as it's you . . . I don't know much. I haven't had any contact with them in years, but I heard through the grapevine that they were looking for payback from you . . . People know them still. Word gets round, and you reappearing was the talk of the town.' He shrugged. 'But as you can imagine, a lot of people want to keep their distance from me.'

Harvey thought Ash sounded disappointed.

'I suppose that's the downside in getting a life sentence, you're not on the top of people's Christmas card list.' He chuckled, but Harvey caught the darkness in his eyes. 'All I know, Harvey – and this might be old news, cos we're going back some years now – is that Jed and Dean had a place in Kent, an old farmhouse near Eynsford. There's a bridge on the way out of the village, and from there, it's set right back from the road.' He stopped and tilted his head. 'But if you're thinking of paying them a surprise visit, I'd think again.' Ash got up. 'From what I gather, they won't be giving you the warmest welcome.'

Harvey stood as well, watching him head back to his cell. Suddenly he called across the room. 'It was me, Ash.'

Ash turned around. 'What was?'

'I was the one who called the police that day. I was the one who told them where to find you.'

The puzzlement on Ash's face turned to a bemusement. 'What did you say?'

'You heard.'

He snorted. 'You're joking?' His eyes were wide open. 'Tell me you're joking,' he snarled. '*Tell me!*' he screamed, causing the prison officers to rush over to him and grab his arms, dragging him out of the visiting room.

Harvey shook his head. 'You and I were never the same, Ash. *Never*. And for your information, we were never friends.'

And with that, Harvey turned around and walked out. Somehow he made it outside before having to lean against the wall while vomiting up the contents of his stomach.

Ash Barker stomped into his cell, fuming as he stared at the young lad who was stretched out naked on his bed. 'Get out . . . Go back to your fucking cell. *Now!*' he raged, watching him pick up his prison uniform and hurriedly get dressed. As soon as he was gone, he kicked the cell door shut and went across to his mattress, where he hid the mobile phone he'd had smuggled in.

He clumsily scrolled through the contacts with his large fingers, then pressed dial. 'Jed, it's me,' he growled into the mouthpiece. 'Guess who just came to see me . . .'

51

Ava had been in deep thought as she walked out of the deli shop and pulled her collar up to stop the flakes of snow trickling down her collar. Even though she hadn't done much today, she felt exhausted. She'd tried to sleep, but she hadn't been able to. In fact, it had only made her thoughts race even more. All she was able to think about was Tony and Ben, not to mention her dad, of course, but that wasn't anything new. Her dad had always been on her mind, whether she wanted him to be or not.

It was ridiculous, she was a grown woman – a trained psychologist – yet she still didn't know how to cut him off, to wash her hands of him. Yes, she'd told him what she thought of him; yes, she'd called the police on him. She'd done what needed to be done, but even so, she couldn't stop thinking of him.

What did that say about her? What did it say when she couldn't cut out of her life a man who had the same *tastes* as Ash Barker? Ava took a deep breath. She felt sick at the idea of that. Of course, she understood that people had unhealthy attachments, and in extreme forms, like Stockholm syndrome, victims developed feelings for their captors or abusers. She understood it, she'd studied it, she'd helped people through it, but never had it occurred to her she was one of those victims. Never.

She took a sip of cappuccino and walked to Tony's car, which was parked down a side road off Peter Street. She'd parked well away from the house, but she needed to move it. Perhaps she'd drive it back to Nottingham, later today or tomorrow, but for now, if she didn't want to run up hundreds of pounds in parking fines, she'd have to move it to the long-term car park in Euston.

She got in the car, and immediately she picked up the scent of Tony's aftershave. For a moment, it took her breath away. So much had happened, so much had gone on. She leaned her head on the steering wheel, trying to stop herself from trembling, and before she knew it Ava found herself weeping for what had once been.

It was at least five minutes before she had the strength to sit up and pull herself together. She wiped the last of her tears on her sleeve and reached to turn on the ignition, but then froze. Ducking down slightly in her seat, she stared ahead of her. Not more than a hundred feet away, where the side street she was parked in met the main road, was Ben's Range Rover. And in the passenger seat next to Ben was her father.

What the hell was going on? Last time she saw her dad he was being carted away by the police. She'd assumed he was still being questioned. As for Ben being with him, it made no sense. How could the fight they'd had yesterday have been resolved so quickly?

She continued to watch them, trying to understand how Ben could be with her dad. He had heard the allegations thrown around yesterday, yet here he was, looking almost relaxed as they chatted away.

Her heart racing, she got out her phone and pressed dial.

'*Hey, Ava, how are you doing?*' Ben sounded cheerful – a little too cheerful, a little too forced.

'I was wondering where you are. I'm at a bit of a loose end, and I thought maybe we could finish what we started.'

'*Yeah . . . I mean, yeah, that would be great, but I'm a bit tied up right now.*'

'OK.' She was cool with him.

'*Look, it's not that I don't want to – I can't think of anything I'd rather do right now – but I have a bit of business I've got to attend to. Soon as that's taken care of, I'm all yours.*'

'Have you heard from my dad?'

'*No . . . no, not at all, have you?*' Ben's voice was firm.

He sounded so convincing. If she wasn't watching him right this minute, sitting in a car with Harvey, she might have believed him.

'Well, if you hear anything, will you let me know.'

'*Sure, no problem . . . listen, babe, I have to love you and leave you . . . I'll catch you soon.*'

The call ended. As Ava started the engine, she stared ahead of her, watching Ben and her dad set off. 'Not if I catch you first,' she said out loud as she put the car into drive.

She set off, eyes firmly on Ben's Range Rover as it turned left into St Peter's Street. She was careful to keep her distance as they headed towards the Thames, driving along the Embankment, past the Tower of London and Tower Bridge. Luckily for her, the traffic was slow, giving her an advantage. Eventually, they hit the East End before driving through the Blackwall tunnel and on to the A2. Ava pressed her foot on the accelerator, determined not to lose sight of them, pushing Tony's car to the limit as she sped along, weaving between cars to keep up. She doubted Ben would remember Tony's car from the other night – if he'd even caught a glimpse of it – so as long as she kept a few cars between them. Same went for her father; he knew her car well, but not Tony's.

For the next hour, she drove, not taking much notice of her surroundings as she kept Ben's Range Rover in sight. The weather took a turn for the worse as they headed deeper into Kent, and Ava struggled to keep up as rain and hail battered against the window. She was relieved when they left the dual carriageway and slowed down to negotiate the narrower roads through the picturesque villages of Kent.

Ava had no idea where she was; she hadn't spotted any signposts for a while. Suddenly she saw the brake lights glow red as they slowed down ahead of a small stone bridge. Ava pulled over beside a large oak tree, hurriedly turning off her headlights.

The rain was pelting down now, and she could just make out Ben and her father stepping out of the car. Where the hell were they going? She squinted through the windscreen, but it was no use, she was going to lose sight of them any minute.

Ava got out of the car and hurried after them, forcing her way through the wind and sleet. The Range Rover was parked next to a gravelled driveway lined with hedges and trees, but she couldn't see where it led to.

Picking up her pace, Ava pulled up the hood on her jacket and tried to catch up.

Panting, her face numb from the icy rain, Ava turned a bend and immediately ducked behind a wooden fence as she saw Ben only a few metres ahead, speaking to her dad. She couldn't hear what they were saying, but a few moments later, she watched as they set off across a field. Ava began to follow, crouching low in case they looked behind them.

With darkness drawing in, she forced her way through the long grass, making her way towards the woods where her dad and Ben seemed to be heading. Part of her wanted to turn back and wait by their car to confront them; no doubt that would be the safer option, but chances were they'd only lie to her again. If she wanted to find out why they were skulking about out here, her only option was to keep them in her sights.

Although she knew that, if she screamed, Ben and her dad would hear her, that didn't stop a cold chill of fear rushing through her as the wind howled through the trees. She had no idea what she was walking into. She didn't even know whether her dad – and Ben, for that matter – was friend or foe.

A couple of minutes later, Ava clambered over a broken-down wall and felt a sharp pain as a strand of barbed wire snatched at her trousers and dug into her flesh. She swallowed hard to stop herself crying out as she pulled herself free. Ignoring the warm trickle of blood running down her leg, she set off again. From where she was, she could just make out the silhouettes of her dad and Ben dashing up the hill towards an imposing building. It was only partly lit, but she could make out arched windows and ivy-covered walls. The windows would offer a clear view of anyone coming up the driveway, which explained why they'd taken this route.

Leaning against a tree, Ava paused to catch her breath. Gritting her teeth against the pain in her leg, she was about to set off again when a sudden loud noise caused her to throw herself to the ground. When she raised her head to see where the noise had come from, she saw four men come out of the house. Something told her that this wasn't good news.

Her heart was pounding as she scanned the darkness by the garden wall for a sight of Ben and her dad. Where were they? Perhaps they'd taken a right turn by the trees, and she'd missed them. But then from the corner of her eye she saw something moving. Suddenly there was shouting, beams of light shining, followed by a loud bang. Ava knew exactly what that noise was. A gun shot.

Ducking as low as she could behind some bushes, she watched as her father and Ben were dragged inside the house . . .

52

Ava pulled out her phone to call for help, but when she stared at the screen, she saw there was no signal. *Damn it.* For a moment, it crossed her mind to run back to the car to raise the alarm, but aside from the fact she wasn't sure of the way, she couldn't be sure all four men had gone back inside the house.

Think, she told herself. Despite their stealthy approach, Harvey and Ben had been spotted before they could get to the house. It was as if the occupants knew they were coming and had been looking out for them.

Ava followed the old garden wall to a line of the trees which would take her to the side of the house. Unlike the rest of the building, it was mainly in darkness apart from a small nightlight over the back door. She scanned the windows for watchers and saw no one, but she noticed that one of the ground-floor windows was ajar. Straining her ears for the sound of anyone approaching, she decided to take her chances and race across to the window. She peeked in to make sure the room was empty, then tried to push the window open but it was jammed. Part of her was relieved; it was stupid to think that she could just barge in and save the day like some superhero. What chance would she stand against four armed men? She checked her phone again, wiping droplets of rain from the screen, but there was still no signal.

With the pain in her leg getting worse, Ava looked around once more. Over to her left was a row of outbuildings. Perhaps she'd be able to pick up a signal over there. Or maybe there'd be something she could use as a weapon.

She'd barely taken a step when she caught her breath and pressed her body tight against the wall. A man was stalking towards the outbuildings with a gun in his hand.

Horrified, Ava began to shake. She was out of her depth, but what was she supposed to do? Turn and run? She couldn't. Regardless how she felt about her dad and Ben, she couldn't just leave them here.

She heard a voice, then the sound of a door closing. She needed to find cover, fast. Hoping the wind and rain would drown out the sound of her footsteps, she ran to the end of the building and flattened herself against the wall, then peeked around the corner to see if the coast was clear.

A few feet away was a broken window with a bush in front of it that would provide some cover. Ava crept towards it and glanced in. Her breath caught in her throat. There was someone sitting in a chair, their arms and legs bound with rope, their head hanging low, covered with a sack. They weren't moving.

There was another sudden noise, and Ava squashed herself into the bush as a stocky man stalked past. Not daring to breathe, she stayed hidden until she heard the door of the outbuilding creak open. She took another peek in the window and saw the newcomer remove the sack from the prisoner's head before un-tying the ropes binding them to the chair.

'*So, we're going to have some fun now, aren't we?*' The stocky man laughed as he grabbed a clump of hair to pull the defenceless man's head back, exposing his swollen, bloody face. Then he drove his fist into the man's nose.

Ava stifled a scream, ducking below the ledge. She could still hear what was going on, though she couldn't see.

'Oh, come on, Sam, I've got some news that'll cheer you up – your big brother has finally decided to come and look for you.'

Sam. This must be Ben's brother. So that was why he had come here. What the hell had Sam done that they would torture him? Or was this all about Ben. Ben and her dad?

She heard a grunt and the impact of fist on flesh as the man struck Sam again. There was no way Sam could fight back, even with the ropes untied – he'd looked in a bad way, barely conscious. Ben had been trying to reach him for days – had Sam been here all this time?

Worried about being seen, Ava moved deeper into the shadows. As she did, her foot banged into something. She looked down, and saw it was a length of timber with rusty nails sticking out.

Quickly, before she had time to change her mind, she scooped up the makeshift club and made her way along the outbuilding wall. The door was wide open, Ava peered through the crack between the jamb and the door, watching as the man took a run up to Sam. Seizing the opportunity, she slipped inside.

The man started to turn, a look of surprise on his face. Ava didn't hesitate to bring the piece of timber down on him with all the force she could muster. There was a blood-curdling crunch as it smashed into the man's skull. He fell to the floor, convulsing, then lay motionless.

'Sam?' she whispered, rushing over to him. 'Sam? Sam . . . can you hear me?'

He let out a groan, then lift his head slightly. She could see his eyes, struggling to focus on her.

'Sam?' she whispered again, looking over her shoulder as she did so. If someone came along now, it would all be over for her. 'Sam, I'm a friend of your brother.'

He nodded, and she could see the effort even that small movement cost him. She couldn't leave him here, she needed to get him somewhere safe, but there was no way he could walk far in that state.

'Where is he?' Sam spoke through clenched teeth, the pain etched on his face.

Ava hesitated to tell him the truth, but decided it was probably for the best. 'They took him into the house.'

'Who did?'

'I don't know, but they didn't exactly look friendly . . . Sam, we need to get out of here – someone could come along any minute. Let me help you up. You can lean on me, and I'll take you into the woods. You can rest there – it's not ideal, but it'll keep you hidden.'

He stood with difficulty and rested his arm across Ava's shoulders. They headed for the door with her stumbling under his weight, praying that luck would be on their side.

Outside, the sleet had turned to snow. The combination of the pain in her leg and Sam's weight made it slow going; she could only hope the snow would cover their tracks before anyone noticed Sam was missing.

'Why don't you rest here?' Ava whispered once they'd reached the shelter of an overgrown thicket. 'Hopefully, you'll be safe here.'

Sam tilted his head. 'Hopefully.' And he gave her the tiniest of smiles, before pushing himself up against the trunk of a broken tree.

Even in the dark, Ava could see how unwell he looked. The whites of his eyes were blood red, and his face looked like he'd been in a car accident. But she could also see how much he resembled Ben. Ava took off her jacket and draped it over him.

'Here take this.'

He managed the slightest nod in return. 'Thank you.'

'Have you been inside the house?' Ava asked.

'Yeah . . . on the first day. They took me inside. It was only today that they put me into that outbuilding.' His words came in fits and starts as he struggled to speak through torn lips. 'Jed said we were expecting visitors.'

'Who's Jed?'

He looked at her. 'The guy you just knocked out. They're not going to be happy.'

'How do you know him?' Ava turned to stare at the house as she spoke.

'I don't. They came to my place, wanting to know where Ben was . . .' He trailed off, gulping for air.

'Can you remember what the set-up of the house is? Do you know where they might have taken them?' Ava's words rushed out. She had a feeling they'd soon be wondering where Jed had got to.

'I don't know. I was taken through the back . . . there's a hall-way with some stairs down to a basement. That's where I was taken.'

Ava stood.

'Be careful.' Sam's voice was barely a whisper. 'These guys aren't playing.'

Ava didn't reply, she was already running towards the house. Jed had come through the back door to get to the outbuilding, and she doubted he'd locked it behind him. She daren't give her-self time to think about what she was doing, because if she did, Ava knew she couldn't go through with it.

When she got to the door, she took a deep breath, listening for movement or voices. Then she gripped the door handle, and began to open it . . .

53

As she crept through the hallway, Ava began to panic. What was she doing? It didn't bear thinking about what they would do to her if they found her in here. The sensible thing would be to turn back, head through the woods to the road, get in her car. Help would then be a phone call or a short drive away.

She was turning to retrace her steps when she heard voices. Which way? Panicked, she darted into the hallway with a grand staircase leading up. As she passed the foot of the stairs, Ava heard a woman's voice, followed by laughter. The panelled walls offered no hiding places, her only possible escape route was a door at the end of the corridor. She made a dash for it, only to find herself looking into a small cloakroom. *Shit.*

'*Where are they then?*' She heard the woman's voice again, louder this time.

Ava looked frantically around her, but there were no coats to hide behind.

'*OK, give me a moment.*'

Brisk footsteps sounded in the hall, advancing towards her.

She braced herself.

As the door swung open, she let out a gasp. Standing in front of her was the woman from the docks. Panic overwhelmed her; she began shaking uncontrollably. The woman smiled. 'Well, well, well. If it isn't little Sophia.'

Ava didn't know what she was talking about, and she was too terrified to ask.

'I think you'd better come with us, don't you? *Move it.*'

It was then Ava saw the woman was accompanied by the same tall, olive-skinned man who'd waylaid her and Ben at the dock. She could only nod and walk on in silence as they escorted her along the polished hallway.

'See if there's anyone else about,' the woman instructed the man, who hurried off. Then the woman opened a door that led into a drawing room. It was barely furnished, apart from a grand piano in the corner. Ava's father and Ben were standing against the wall; a third man was pointing a gun at them.

'Ava . . . Ava, what the fuck are you doing here?' Fear sounded in Harvey's voice. He tried to step forward, but he was pushed back by the gunman, although that didn't stop him talking. 'Let her go. She has nothing to do with this.'

The woman laughed, and casually took a packet of cigarettes from the side. 'Harve, come on, I'm hardly going to do that, am I?' She let out a trill of laughter and took a long drag. 'Besides, you and I both know that Sophia has everything to do with it.'

Ava looked between the two of them. and even though she was truly terrified, she couldn't help asking, 'Why do you keep calling me Sophia?'

Her words caused the woman to roar with laughter. Harvey, on the other hand, looked positively ill, even paler than when Ava had walked in.

'You haven't told her? Oh, Harvey, I'm disappointed in you. Would you like me to do the honours?'

'Don't . . . Don't you dare, I'm warning you.'

Cigarette in hand, the woman strolled over to Harvey. 'You're warning *me*? Tell me, how's that supposed to work.' She gestured towards the man holding the gun, and laughed, then turned back to Ava.

'You don't remember me, Sophia?'

'I said *don't . . . please.*' Harvey sounded desperate. He turned to Ava. 'Listen to me, darlin', anything that you're going to hear, it ain't true. I love you, I always have, and that's all that matters.'

The woman ignored Harvey and took hold of a strand of Ava's hair. 'I should be hurt that you don't remember. You were such a special little girl.'

'What the hell are you talking about?' Ava snapped. Her heart was pounding and it was hard to breathe. 'Why do you keep calling me Sophia?'

'Because that's your name.'

'Stop!' Harvey yelled out, and it was at this point the woman stormed over and slapped him hard across the face.

'Shut the fuck up, Harvey! I didn't say you could talk, but if you insist on interrupting' – her voice grew low and menacing – 'I'll get Matty here to dish out the punishment to Sophia rather than you. How would you like that?' She smiled as Harvey backed off. Whatever he'd intended to say, Ava knew from the look on his face, the threat had silenced him.

'Your dad and I were friends.'

'I was never friends with them, Ava . . . *never.*' Harvey couldn't resist shouting out.

'I said, *shut up,*' the woman raged, before turning back to Ava. 'There was a group of us, I'm surprised you don't remember . . . Ash, myself, Jed and Dean – we were all tighter than tight.'

'What's that got to do with me?' Ava's fear was overridden by her determination to hear the answer.

The woman didn't answer straight away, instead she stared at Ava through the smoke. 'As I say, you were very special, Sophia. Ash often talked about how you were his favourite. In fact, you were so special that a lot of people wanted to get to know you.' She paused again, and a nasty sneer spread across her face. 'So special that Harvey kept coming to see you – didn't you, Harve.'

Ava gulped down air. 'What is she talking about?' She couldn't remember anything, but this woman was insinuating . . . 'Dad?'

Harvey looked away.

'Fucking hell.' This from Ben. He shook his head. He'd had no idea that Jed and Dean had been involved with Ash Barker. Jesus Christ, no idea at all. Yes, he'd known they put the money up and supplied the weapons to carry out the robbery, and that their cut was going to be larger because of that. He'd always known that if they caught up with Harvey, they'd want their money, just like he did. But this stuff about them being part of the same set-up as Ash made him sick to his stomach. If he'd had the slightest idea they were nonces, he wouldn't have gone anywhere near them, let alone got mixed up in the robbery they were planning.

The woman cackled again. 'You were so special' – she turned to look at Harvey, who stood with his eyes closed – 'that Harvey decided to buy you.'

Ava couldn't breathe. Her eyes darted between her dad, who stood motionless with his eyes squeezed shut, and the woman.

'You're lying. YOU'RE LYING!' Ava shouted.

'No, Sophia, I'm not.'

'My name's Ava.'

The woman grinned. 'Not then, it wasn't. It seems the person who's been lying to you is Harvey . . . Or does he prefer to call himself *daddy*.'

'You fucking—' Harvey leapt forward but before he could finish his sentence, the man struck Harvey across the head with the end of the gun, causing him to stagger back and lose his footing.

Ava stared at her dad, watching a trickle of blood roll down the side of his head. 'Is it true . . . *is it true*?' She wasn't even sure if she'd spoken the words out loud, the noise in her head was so deafening.

'Go on, Harvey, tell her it isn't true. Lie to her again.' The woman grinned as she looked down at him. 'You can't, can you?'

'Ava . . . sweetheart.'

Ava backed away, shaking her head. 'No . . . no . . .' She turned to the woman, and as she had done when she'd seen her at the docks that day, she stared into her eyes. The familiarity was a faraway memory. The memory of a child, scared and alone.

She swallowed hard; the room felt like it was swimming. Through tears, she looked at Harvey. 'Dad . . . Dad . . .' She could hardly speak. She stared at Ben, who had a look of shock on his face.

'It's not how it sounds, darlin'.' Tears rolled from Harvey's eyes.

'Then if it's not how it sounds, tell me how it is . . . *Tell me.*' Ava's scream filled the air. 'Did you buy me?'

'Baby,' he appealed to her.

'Did you buy me?'

'Avie, *please* . . .'

'Did you – yes or no!'

'Avie.'

'I said, yes or no.'

'Yes . . . yes . . . yes.' Harvey buried his face in his hands and began to weep.

'Oh my God . . . Oh my God . . . Oh my God.' Ava held onto the piano to keep herself from falling. The more she stared at the woman, the more it was coming back to her. The room. The people . . . The men. Without warning, Ava began to vomit. She felt someone rub her back, and turned to see the woman was now standing next to her.

'Let it all out, Sophia.'

Ava shook the woman's hand off her. She remembered her clearly now, how she'd acted as a pimp – a violent, brutal pimp. 'Get off me.'

'Sophia, don't be—'

'. . . *It's Jed.*' The olive-skinned man burst into the room, interrupting the woman. 'It's Jed – he's dead.'

There was a sudden loud bang and the sound of shattering glass, then the woman's eyes rolled back and a gurgling noise escaped her mouth as a bullet hole appeared in her forehead. She fell forward, her body crashing to the ground.

Ava blinked away the blood which had splattered all over her. Then there was another bang, as the top of the olive-skinned man's head was blown off. Ava screamed and looked up. Just outside the window, she saw Sam holding a gun.

'*Sam!*' Ben yelled, leaping into action. Before anyone else could react, he dived forward, knocking the man with the gun to the floor and causing him to let go of the weapon. Harvey seized the opportunity to grab it.

Ben regained his balance and brought back his fist, crashing it into the man's face. He collapsed in a heap, and lay motionless.

The room was silent. Ava stared at the men, then spoke in a whisper to her dad.

'You bought me.'

'Babe, we need to get out of here, we ain't got time for this.'

'I'm not going anywhere, not unless you start telling me the truth.'

Her dad went to grab her, but she pulled back, wiping away her tears.

'Ava, come on, your dad's right, we need to get out of here. However fucked up this is, it can wait,' Ben spoke to her gently.

Traumatized, her mind racing, Ava nodded and followed Ben, with Harvey a few steps behind. They charged out into the night, and ran round the house to join Sam.

She watched as Ben threw his arms around his brother, but she could also see in the light that streamed through the window the expression of anger and concern as he stared at Sam's battered face.

'Come on, we'd better take the track through the woods – Dean's still about, so we need to be careful.'

They'd only gone a short distance, Harvey in the lead, Ava following, with Ben half-carrying Sam at the rear, when flashlights appeared up ahead of them.

'Fuck, we'll have to head around the side,' said Harvey.

The snow was heavy, and Ava could clearly see their tracks and the bloody trail Sam had left in the snow. Their pursuers would have no difficulty following them.

'Leave me here,' Sam cried out. 'I'll only slow you down, I can't run.' He was breathless and his head lolled to one side.

'I ain't doing that, mate,' said Ben, adamant. He turned to Harvey. 'Listen, why don't you and Ava make your way back to the car – I'll find somewhere to rest with Sam, then we'll make our way to the drive. You can pick us up from there.'

Harvey looked doubtful. 'I think we should stick together.'

'Look, mate.' Ben's tone was aggressive. 'Just do it, you want to get Ava out of here, don't you?'

Harvey nodded and glanced at Ava. 'Let's go . . . and Ben, thank you.'

Ava couldn't think straight. She wanted to stay with Ben, but Harvey was pulling her towards the trees. They plunged into a muddy ditch and then set off up a hill, but as Ava was nearing the summit, she started to slip back down.

'Ava, come on,' she heard her dad whispering her name, but startled by a noise behind her, she set off running in a different direction, tripping over the gnarled roots of trees.

She tried to ignore the pain in her leg, but it was making it hard to run. She slipped on the snow, trying desperately to get her bearings. There was another noise to the side of her which made her freeze, and she began to creep backwards, but almost immediately, she banged into something and a hand reached out and grabbed her.

Ava tried to call out, but her breath was taken away. Whoever was holding her had a tight grip across her throat.

'Let her go.' Her dad's voice boomed through the trees. '*Dean*, let her go, it's me you want, not her.' Without warning, Harvey appeared, with his hands raised in surrender. 'Do what you want with me, mate, but let her walk away. It won't make any difference, though: I ain't got your money.'

Dean's face was a picture of hate as he stared at Harvey. 'You turned me over, and there's only one thing that happens when people do that.' He let go of Ava and pointed the gun at Harvey, pulling back the trigger.

'*No!*' Ava dived in front of Dean, and she felt a thud in her back, then a warmth before everything began to spin, and she dropped to the ground, cushioned by the snow as the blood poured out. There was another shot, and somewhere in her mind, she was aware of Dean falling to the ground, his dead eyes looking at her as she lay in the snow.

'Ava!' She heard her father shout her name, then she felt her head being lifted.

'Ava, baby . . . I'm going to get help. You understand . . . hang on, darlin', I'm going to get help.'

'I'm so cold,' Ava whispered.

Harvey whipped off his coat, covering her. 'Don't you leave me, you hear . . . don't you dare leave me.'

He held her hand, and she tried to pull it away, but she was too weak. 'You hurt me.' Tears rolled down her cheeks. 'You hurt me.'

'No, baby, I never hurt you. I would never hurt you.'

The snow fell on her face. 'But what she said . . .'

'What she said wasn't true – not like that, anyway. I love you, and I always have.'

'*Oh my God.*'

Ava heard Ben's voice, but she couldn't focus on him as she drifted in and out of consciousness.

'Ava, listen to me.' Her father's voice again. 'I met Ash through work, I didn't know what he was, I swear, I fucking swear to you, but then he told me, he showed me his club . . . That's when I met you, baby. You were three years old. The first day I saw what they were doing, what the set-up was, I tried to report them, but nothing was done. Some of the club members were Old Bill. I didn't know who to trust, and I couldn't risk them making you disappear, taking you God knows where. I came to see you every day – that's why they thought—'

'You're lying.' Ava's voice was faint.

'I'm not, I swear I'm not. I pretended that's what I wanted. It made me sick . . . but I needed them to think I was like them, I needed them to believe it, but I wasn't, never, ever. I needed to get you out of harm's way, Avie, before . . . well, before anyone did anything to you.' He squeezed his eyes shut. 'I had to make sure that no one touched you. I had to make sure that they knew I was serious, so I came every day, and I offered them big money, even though I didn't have it.'

He stroked her hair again. 'I needed to keep you safe, Avie. Those bastards dealt in human trafficking, sex trafficking from Eastern European countries. They targeted orphanages. I knew I had to protect you, but I didn't have the kind of money they wanted: they kept putting the amount up, because they knew I wanted you. There were others but they were older, and most of the time they kept them elsewhere. There were so many people coming and going . . .' He paused, struggling to keep his emotions in check. 'When the job came up with Dean and Jed, I jumped at it. I made a plan: I'd do the robbery and get you.'

Harvey glanced at Ben, who was staring at him in shock. 'I never meant to leave you, mate. I was taking the money to Ash to buy Ava because he warned me that if I didn't hand over the money by a certain time, the deal was off. That's where the money went . . . By the time I came to get you, it was too late. The Old Bill was swarming all over the place after Jed shot the guard, and the alarm went off.'

'So what, that was it?' Ben stared at him.

'I didn't know what to do. Maybe I should have taken Ava to the police station, but I didn't trust them. So I called the police on Ash, I told them there'd been a shooting, and that's why they swooped in.'

'That's how they got Ash?' Ben continued to stare.

'Yeah.' Harvey nodded as he cradled Ava. 'But the others got away . . . and I ran, I took Ava and ran . . .' He shrugged, all the memories coming back thick and fast. 'I made a new life.' He looked down at Ava then. 'I made up a new history for you, baby . . . Cos I figured you were so little you wouldn't remember . . . I thought I was doing what was right. I loved you like a dad, I always wanted the best for you, I wanted to protect you, but I guess I fucked up. I fucked up badly.' He looked up at Ben. 'And you, mate, you spent your life in prison . . . I'm so sorry.' He glanced back down to his daughter. 'I'm so sorry, Ava . . . Ava? . . . Ava? Oh fuck, stay with me . . . *Ava!*'

There was the sound of sirens and Ava opened her eyes. 'Go, just go.'

'I ain't going to leave you, baby.'

She looked at Ben and her dad, and although it was an effort to talk, she urged him again. '*Please*, just go . . . they'll arrest you and Ben . . . so take Sam and go, get out of here . . . Do this for me . . . *Run now.'*

The blue lights were coming nearer, and Ava felt her dad kiss her. She saw Ben and Harvey take hold of Sam and set off running. The moment they did, Ava blacked out.

54

THREE MONTHS LATER

Ava smiled as she stared at Ben, who was still fast asleep. She crept out of the bedroom and headed along the hallway and down the stairs. The past few months had been the most peaceful she'd ever known. She felt something like happiness. What she'd found out had brought a sense of acceptance, and with it came a renewed understanding and love for her dad. What he'd done had been unconventional, to say the least. She was sure a lot of people would've seen it as wrong. But his desperation to save her had pushed him to take extreme measures. He'd spent a lifetime looking over his shoulder, sacrificing any hope of a normal life for her. And in doing so, he'd sacrificed Ben, who'd served a life sentence for her freedom.

She was certain that there were still unresolved issues between her dad and Ben, but they were working it out and trying to re-establish some sort of friendship – perhaps for her sake, perhaps because they'd genuinely cared for each other.

She was under no illusion how much of a tough call it was for Ben to put it all behind him. Thirty-six years was a hell of a long time. It was for ever. He'd been robbed of his life by circumstances beyond his control, and she had nothing but admiration for the fact he felt no bitterness towards her.

'Hi, darlin', you want me to make you a coffee?' Her dad smiled as she walked into the kitchen. They'd all decided to make a fresh start in the house in London. It was big enough to accommodate them all without anyone getting on top of one another. It was perfect. She'd decided not to bother moving her practice; instead, she'd cut down her hours and now worked three days rather than five, travelling up to Nottingham each week.

It suited her – not to mention it suited Jude, who was on part-time hours and full-time wages. Most weeks, Ben kept her company, travelling up with her.

'That would be lovely, thank you.' She kissed her dad on the cheek. She'd missed this, missed him being in her life, and she hadn't realized how much until now.

'Are you OK, babe?' Her dad grabbed her hand.

'I'm good. I really am.'

'And you're sure you're happy? I mean, is there anything else I can do for you?'

Ava grinned. 'Like I said yesterday, and the day before, and . . .' Teasing him, she stopped and laughed.

'OK, I get it. But you would tell me, wouldn't you . . . ? I mean, you do seem happy. Here with me, and Ben.' He shrugged.

For the most part, her dad avoided discussing her relationship with Ben, but that was understandable. She got it. He'd always been overly protective of her, and seeing her with Ben had taken some getting used to.

She nodded. 'I wouldn't want it to be any different.'

Harvey pressed the button on the coffee machine. 'What about Tony? You sure you're OK about him taking off like that?'

Ava shrugged. 'I've done all I could. I know you weren't happy about me filing a missing persons report, but one of his colleagues, Joe, came to see me afterwards. Apparently, Tony hadn't been himself for a while. He'd show up at work smelling of booze, and when they asked if he was all right, he'd fly off the handle. Joe reckoned he was heading for a breakdown, told him to take some time off. That was when Tony lost it big time, in front of the whole canteen. Stormed off and never came back. It must have hurt his pride, his colleagues seeing him in that state. Knowing Tony, he'd have found it very hard to face them after that.'

Harvey grunted. 'Him being in digital forensics or whatever it's called, I suppose he'd be an expert in making sure they couldn't track him down if he didn't want to be traced. I could have done with someone like him back when I did a runner.' He started to laugh, then looked at her apologetically. 'Still, it's one thing him walking out on the job, but walking out on your marriage . . .'

'Tony and I were broken a long time before he left, I just didn't see it.'

Harvey handed her a cup of coffee and she took a sip. 'You know I'm here, doll, if you ever need to talk. If it's ever doing your head in.'

'I know, and thank you.' She fiddled with her fingers and took a deep breath. 'I'm not saying it's easy with Tony gone, but with you and Ben here, I think I'll be all right.'

Right then, Ben walked in.

'Hey sleepy head.' Ava gave a genuine smile.

'Hey babe.' He walked over and kissed her on the top of her head, then he turned to Harvey. 'I was wondering if you fancied playing a game of pool later. This could be the day I'll finally beat you. What do you think?'

Harvey laughed, and took a drag on the cigarette he'd just lit. 'I think hell will freeze over first, but let's give it a shot. Why don't you invite Sam around, then I can beat two Walter men at the same time.'

Ava watched them. It was good to see, and she'd been telling the truth when she said she was happy. She was. Not that she didn't know there were still secrets between them. There were. She knew what they'd done. She'd known that Tony was dead that night when Ben loaded him into the car. There hadn't been a pulse. Not even a faint one.

She'd grieve in her own way about Tony, and she knew that it would take time. But she owed her dad, and she owed Ben to keep their secrets. *Especially* Ben. Did that make her bad? Or did that make her someone who was just trying to right a wrong?

'You OK, Ava?' Ben asked. 'You sure? You know you can tell me anything.'

Nodding, she smiled again. 'I know, but there's nothing to tell.'

She knew how to play the game. After all, she'd been doing it her whole life, hadn't she. So all she needed to do was go along with it, show the world, she was the good daughter . . . the good wife.

ACKNOWLEDGEMENTS

A huge thank you to all at Pan Macmillan for being so supportive of my ideas and my writing. I also want to say a huge thank you to Darley Andersen, my wonderful agent who I adore, as well as all the other wonderful people at Darley Andersen literary agency, who are real champions. Then a big, massive thank you to all my family and friends, who support me throughout this wonderful journey I'm on, I'm truly grateful. And last but not ever least, the biggest thank you to all the readers, without which none of this would be possible.

THE STREETS
JACQUI ROSE

She thought her secret was safe . . .

Ten years ago, Jo Martin was released from prison after serving twelve years of a life sentence. She is now out on license – and she isn't Jo anymore. Given a new identity by the courts, and with a different appearance, a ready-made history and even a change of age, Jo can pretend to be anyone . . .

Cookie Mackenzie is not only Ned Reid's lover – but she also works for him. She supplies the girls – and boys – for Ned's clients. There's always some runaway kid who needs shelter.

Natalie Ellis works at Barney's bar. A fierce and loyal friend, she's a shoulder to cry on, a listening ear – but should everyone really trust her to keep their secrets?

Lorni Duncan needs to keep running, always looking over her shoulder, especially with a young child in tow. But how will she survive? The refuges are full, and the last thing Lorni needs is the authorities getting involved. Who is she trying to escape from?

Everyone has something to hide and a lot to lose, but which of them did Jo become?

The streets of London's Soho hide a multitude of secrets in this hard-hitting gangland thriller from bestselling author Jacqui Rose.

THE WOMEN
JACQUI ROSE

The sentence is just the beginning.

Within these walls, friendships are forged that will last beyond a sentence. But some inmates can turn in the blink of an eye, because that's all part of being locked up. In here you are kept from your loved ones and forced into a surrogate family with women you wouldn't even look at on the outside, let alone call friends. But at Ashcroft, alliances can mean everything.

Each one of these women has their own story to tell and their own penance to deal with. But whilst they fight for their rights on the inside, who is looking after their family, their friends and children on the outside? Whilst they battle to survive in a closed off world what's happening in the real world?

At Ashcroft there's always a price to be paid, and for some it's high, but these women are prepared to pay any way they can . . .

A women's prison cages in much corruption in this gripping street crime thriller from bestselling author Jacqui Rose.